CW01279773

LATE IN THE DAY

LATE IN THE DAY

Geraldine Kaye

*To Sarah
With best wishes
from
Geraldine Kaye*

HEADLINE
REVIEW

Copyright © 1997 Geraldine Kaye

The right of Geraldine Kaye to be identified as the Author of the Work has been asserted by her in accordance with the Copyright, Designs and Patents Act 1988.

First published in 1997
by HEADLINE BOOK PUBLISHING

A HEADLINE REVIEW hardback

Pages 145-147 first published as extract in 'How Maxine learned to love her legs and other tales of growing up' *Aurora Metro*, 1995

10 9 8 7 6 5 4 3 2 1

All rights reserved. No part of this publication may be reproduced, stored in a retrieval system, or transmitted, in any form or by any means without the prior written permission of the publisher, nor be otherwise circulated in any form of binding or cover other than that in which it is published and without a similar condition being imposed on the subsequent purchaser.

All characters in this publication are fictitious and any resemblance to real persons, living or dead, is purely coincidental.

British Library Cataloguing in Publication Data
Kaye, Geraldine, 1925–
Late in the day
1.English fiction - 20th century
I.Title
823.9'14[F]
ISBN 0 7472 1908 7

Typeset at The Spartan Press Ltd
Lymington, Hampshire

Printed in England by
Clays Ltd, St Ives plc

HEADLINE BOOK PUBLISHING
A division of Hodder Headline PLC
338 Euston Road
London NW1 3BH

LATE
IN THE DAY

PART ONE
A Cold Day in February

Chapter One

Early one morning a plane flying over Bristol woke three women, Anna, Patsy and Francesca, who had been friends for a long time.

Anna Bolt woke with words from her dream still sounding in her head. Was it 'Flying free' or 'Falling free' she had heard? And who had spoken, Icarus perhaps? It was cold but the sky was so blue and brilliant she got up to look at the tiny silver speck. A fly on the ceiling of the world.

It was her new idea to intensify the passing moment, make it her own. It was all there was in the long run, myriad passing moments. She knew she needed to change her life but she edged away from deciding what and how, since she lacked the energy to initiate it. The plane was a symbol of freedom, autonomy, suggesting something was going to happen anyway and raising her spirits.

It could well be Mark's plane, she thought; Patsy had said on the phone he was due back from somewhere, her tearful voice precluding questions for fear of precipitating a deluge which would do no good.

A moment later *The Times* dropped through the front door of the Cliftonwood house where Anna now occupied two rooms, advertised as a *flat* inaccurately since landlord and tenants shared bathroom and kitchen. Miss Baker from above being already in noisy and highly perfumed occupation of the bathroom, Anna dragged a comb through her hair and ran downstairs. Delivery of *The Times* was a ritual preserved from her former life, which had ended abruptly when she and Rupert were divorced four years previously. Actually she would have preferred the *Guardian*, but *The Times* seemed so fragile, symbol of another way of life, that withdrawing her support had been impossible.

Geraldine Kaye

Upstairs her telephone began to ring.

At this hour it was almost certain to be Francesca wanting to kill her with kindness, offer a silk scarf bought in error, a coat hardly worn or a pub lunch. And Francesca was relentless. 'Why on earth did you let Rupert get away?' she had scolded loudly in Park Street the day of the court hearing, when the pavement was already undulating like jelly under Anna's feet. When Freddy left home three months later, it seemed like poetic justice. Not that Fran appeared grief-stricken or even put out; she thrived on vicissitude, she always had.

The phone stopped as Anna regained the flat.

She really wasn't equal to Francesca so early in the morning but she would have answered in case it was Oliver. It was on her son's account that she had invested in a mobile phone. It was also a way of reminding herself that in theory she was free to go anywhere. But where, and what would Cathy her daughter say, and what about Mother, not to mention Mr Brewster who depended on her, and poor Mr Phillips? In practice she was roped to the ground as firmly as Gulliver by other people's expectations and her own need to fulfil them.

Anna had lived in the same unsatisfactory flat since her divorce, at first with Olly sharing in the school holidays. It was then he had painted the wings of her cream-coloured 2CV emerald green. 'So you can spot it anywhere,' he said and so she could. Now Olly was driving a van for a wine merchant in London and unlikely to phone so early. But Olly was often unlikely. Not that his calls were particularly welcome. The rush of maternal warmth was soon swallowed up by her enforced acquaintance with what he presented as his lifestyle, 'E' and 'speed' deliberately slid into the grid of their conversation. It was showing off, she hoped. She tried to be optimistic about Olly, tried to avoid loading him with her anxieties.

Before her divorce she would have expressed her disapproval of drugs, but the loss of husband, home and status as 'doctor's wife' had undermined her firmness of character, revealed her fragile sense of self. Besides, she had plenty to sort in her own life without tangling with Olly's. He was twenty-two now and parents' plans for young adults were invariably counterproductive. When the children were small 'nurture' was in fashion, but now the pendulum had swung back to 'nature'. It was all predeter-

Late in the Day

mined by the *genes*, parents of grown-up children told each other with relief.

Overhead Miss Baker emerged tumultuously from the bathroom. Anna grabbed her spongebag and hurried up.

Half an hour later Anna laid *The Times* across the table as she ate her muesli, a mainly aesthetic gesture as she rarely read more than a line or two. All the furniture in the flat was pink. It was the pleasure of Mr Phillips, the landlord, to buy job lots at auction sales and respray them into uniformity of colour. The streaked-chilblain effect which resulted from pink over dark brown contrasted starkly with the carefully selected pieces which had furnished her former home, Rose Lodge at Stratton. 'From Rose Lodge to pink flat,' Olly had remarked jokily. His sense of humour was the most attractive thing about him but actually Anna had never cared for pink. The garden of Rose Lodge was all cream-petalled Peace, white Iceberg and crimson Fragrant Cloud. Like the bathroom shared with five strangers who were strangers no longer, the pink flat had hastened the weaning process.

It was a new life she had started and neither happier nor unhappier than the previous one. And there were good sides to the flat, the moulded ceiling with its patterns of vine leaves, the lacy wrought-iron balcony, the floating harbour below, at night lights bobbing on tar-black water.

The notice of Miss Snape's death in the personal column was a relief. She had intended for months to visit the nursing home where her old headmistress had ended up but never got there. Now she need no longer feel guilty about her defection, her several defections. But after the relief there was something else, not sadness but hollowness, opportunity finally lost.

Did she still draw succour from Miss Snape's high regard for her ability? How ridiculous, how vulnerable to opinion those years had made her. A fee-paying boarding school conditioned its pupils to work for a future goal, a millennium which never arrived. It was little better than a cargo cult. For all her 'early promise' Anna had ended up at forty divorced and barely qualified to earn her living. Whose fault was that, as her daughter, Cathy, would say, and frequently did.

The telephone rang again and this time she was sure it was Francesca. But it could be Patsy and she felt even less equal to

Geraldine Kaye

Patsy. Sad because the three of them had been close friends once, 'The Three Graces' Miss Snape had called them as they pirouetted on the lawn at Avon Towers one summer evening. Friends just happened, in school days and apparently all through life. Friends were people who needed you, so you gave them the office telephone number and the Mercury one too because you needed them to need you. What a cross to carry, Anna thought, slipping on her anorak and starting downstairs for the office.

She would phone Patsy tonight.

Ten miles away in Stratton Patsy Simpson had been woken by the same plane. It was Mark's plane, she decided, staring at the bedroom ceiling, since he was due to return from a fortnight in Majorca with some girl, knowing she knew he knew she knew. What part should she play? Her happyface was a work of art. Or there was deeply felt hurt, sophisticated recognition of the male menopause, martyrdom and several others. She used them all but found it difficult to stick to any attitude for long.

The bitter residue of sleeping pills still flavoured her mouth but she swallowed a Valium. One, Dr Walters had said, two for a difficult day, and all days were difficult.

'Basket,' she scolded, pushing Rex, the old Newfoundland, off her feet. Mark was fastidious, couldn't stand dogs upstairs. Could stand even less the half-inch of grey visible in the roots of her still luxuriant and mostly chestnut hair. An appointment at Orlando's salon; eleven o'clock, wasn't it?

Rex whined at the bedroom door and Patsy slid out of bed.

Mark would never actually leave her, she told herself, descending through the house to the back door. He loved OldPlace, one of the few moated farmhouses left in Somerset, loved it as much as she did. For years he had worked at it every weekend, discovering with cries of rapture a sixteenth-century fireplace behind the eighteenth-century panelling.

Besides, there were the girls. He would never leave Harriet and Briony, Patsy decided, ignoring for the sake of argument the fact that both girls had already left home. Harriet, their first-born, had always been his favourite and hers, though why she had to hide herself in that seedy flat when they had offered her the OldPlace cottage next door was beyond Patsy's understanding. She had made it clear she expected and would welcome Patrick. A young woman Harriet's age should have a boyfriend. She and Mark could not be described as old-fashioned parents in that respect. 'Oh, Mother,' Harriet had protested, accenting the second syllable, when she'd attempted to explain this.

Patsy switched on the kettle for coffee, opened the back door, picked the *Daily Telegraph* off the mat, turned to the deaths column and groaned aloud. Miss Snape was dead. 'I can see such a lot in this little girl.' No doubt what she had seen was a potential fee-paying pupil in a dwindling supply, but nobody had even pretended to see anything in Patsy before. In appointing her head girl, Miss Snape had made her an acolyte for ever.

Today was the saddest day of her life. Patsy abandoned the idea of coffee, moved to the sitting-room and poured herself a sherry. A morning sherry was a comfort. Two even better. A sherry party, why not? An anniversary party. She and Mark had been married twenty-six years more or less and after all not many people reached such a score nowadays. She might invite Anna though extra women made the numbers difficult. Patsy began to jot names of couples from the older Bristol families on her telephone pad. Blunts, Drurys, Clarks, Robertsons – not the jam Robertsons of course – Harriet...

Anna closed and locked her flat door, though no doubt Mr Phillips had his own key.

'I thought I heard your telephone.' Mr Phillips's face loomed in the darkness of the basement where he lived and observed the comings and goings of his tenants. 'Isn't that your cellular telephone, Mrs Bolt, still going now?'

'Yes,' said Anna coolly as the telephone stopped. 'Thank you.'

'Miss Baker and her young man,' he gripped the banisters and hurried on, 'young *men*, I should say, car doors slamming all hours, waking the street. Still, she doesn't try to bring them into the house.' His eyes gleamed, catlike. 'No permissive society, not in my home. I told her straight, this isn't the sixties, miss.'

'Perhaps if she did bring her young men in, we'd all get some sleep,' Anna remarked crisply, stepping out into the winter sunshine.

'I didn't hear that,' Mr Phillips said as the front door slammed.

Anna sprinted across the road, exhilarated by the exchange, but her left foot twinged punishingly. Rupert had fancied her in heels and for years she had worn them. She had given her two good feet to Rupert whatever else she had withheld. But really it was hardly fair to treat pathetic Mr Phillips to her spleen. When exactly did nosiness, a recognised human failing, become voyeurism, a recognised human aberration?

Every social change had its victims. Nowadays lots of marriages failed; her situation was too commonplace to be interesting. She really had no right to be rancorous. By now she should be used to an urban environment, the begging homeless, the vandalism. As she walked to work she often passed a body stretched out in an alley, sleeping rough. Sometimes she offered a packet of sandwiches or a carton of milk, but was this just encouraging dependence?

She shivered in the biting cold and switched her thoughts to the Gambia. Sunshine and white teeth, market women draped in brilliant cloths chattering like magpies, a baby on each back. Terracotta-coloured huts built of swish, no homeless here, the extended family took care of its own. Had it really been like that, or was she reconstructing a fantasy paradise with little bits of memory and a lot of imagination?

She had a lot to be thankful for, Anna thought, silently reciting the familiar litany: a job even if it was boring, fortunately she had had the prescience to take a secretarial course before her marriage broke up; her children, Cathy and Olly, were more or less *all right*; three bonny grandchildren; good health except for the rash on her wrists; a roof over her head even if it was Mr Phillips's roof; a car even if her old Citroen 2CV was likely to fail its next MOT; and a network of welfare services to catch her should she fall. There was Mother, but then most women her age had to cope with a difficult elderly relative.

She was babysitting that evening, as she did every Thursday, and happy to do it. Though Cathy always seemed to imply that her having three children under six at the age of twenty-five was her mother's fault. Tiresome since nobody could have been more conscientious about sensible talks and visits to the contraceptive clinic *beforehand*.

Anna sighed and scratched her itching wrists. One started with such high hopes for one's children and ended relieved if they stayed at school for the statutory time and avoided AIDS. Marital ideals were even more flexible.

Late in the Day

'Fight the Blood-Lusting Demons of Vivisection' had been sprayed inexpertly across a shopfront in Queens Road, and still dripped scarlet on to the pavement. Anna's heart gave a sudden leap and her footsteps faltered. She did hope it was nothing to do with Briony, her god-daughter, who went about with a spray can in her jeans. Surely even Briony didn't have the energy for anti-vivisection as well as minke whales, Amnesty, gay rights, Bosnian refugees and approaching finals.

Three shops further down a woman in a green coat was standing on the pavement shouting furiously with her eyes closed. Anna could not hear the words above the traffic, or even be certain that there were words. Was the woman married or single, she wondered. According to a report in *The Times* a higher percentage of married women broke down. Had there always been women who shouted in the streets, or had unemployment and homelessness finally destroyed traditional British phlegm?

Despite Mr Brewster's absence in Manchester, she was only two minutes later than usual this morning. Had he been there he might well have congratulated her, Anna smiled to herself.

She unlocked the office door as the phone began to ring.

Chapter Two

'Why don't you do something about your hair?' Francesca Smith said as she and Anna settled in a corner of the crowded bar of the White Hart in Park Row. She always chose to eat where the university students ate and had already given the young men along the bar an appraising look.

Francesca's hair was gold, just a shade brighter than it had been originally. She looked elegant and expensive in a long oatmeal skirt, short jacket and daffodil silk blouse. She was a pretty woman; as a girl she had been beautiful, and her eyes were still an innocent blue and almost unlined. There was something childlike too in the way she lived so eagerly. Even her son, Hereward, disappearing overseas had not diminished her.

'Do what exactly?' Anna asked. Francesca always made her feel dingy and inadequate. She knew she looked a mess in her much-washed green jersey and unfashionable skirt, neither short nor long, which she had failed to hang up overnight. Besides, she had forgotten how to feel at ease in a public place. Late in the day she had realised that if you didn't go out anywhere your social skills atrophied. She no longer knew how to slide remarks like 'How was your holiday?' 'You're looking great!' across the table like playing cards. She had slipped out of the moving stream of life. She preferred to eat her sandwiches in the office and cosset her geraniums, pleased when Mr Brewster commented kindly on the way she kept the salmon-pink flowering through the winter.

'You mean dye my hair?' Anna added.

'Highlights. The hint of a tint and a new you,' Francesca said brightly. 'Are you still living in that grotty flat, because something woke me at dawn and I rang you *frantically* early but nobody answered?'

Late in the Day

'Some of us have to get to work on time,' Anna said.

Stories of Francesca's bosses eating out of her hand by the end of a week and getting in her bed soon after were probably apocryphal. But she did seem to flourish wherever she went. Her job as part-time teacher of French at Brandon Lodge had expanded into personal assistant to the principal, just as the college itself had expanded from a small adult education institute to a further education college offering A-levels, GNVQs and B.Tecs. The changes had stressed Mr Austin, the principal, until he discovered Francesca's ability to deal with his paperwork. He preferred a quiet life and let her get on with it.

'Get real, get yourself another man and make Rupert pay up,' Francesca said. 'He's had the best years of your life.'

'He didn't buy them,' Anna said, deciding to look at the skirts in Marks on Saturday before visiting her mother. Francesca saw every woman as a commodity which deteriorated rapidly following the sell-by date. It was a view of personal relations Anna disliked, one of the reasons she didn't push Rupert on the sale of the house.

'Didn't he?' Francesca queried.

'Anyway he sends me something most months,' Anna added, crossing two fingers under the table.

'I should think so too. Get yourself a life, a little flat in Canynge Square say,' Francesca said, reaching for her lager. She did her best to make Anna assert herself. 'Doesn't it make you sick to think of *them* living in *your* house, that scrubby little Deirdre? I mean all that furniture you chose and your roses, that Albertine by the lawn . . .'

'Actually I don't think about it,' Anna said truthfully.

In the early days of being on her own, the last scenes between herself and Rupert had played themselves continuously in her head. 'What happens to you now just depends on what *she* wants,' Rupert had said. How could he say things like that after twenty-two years of marriage? She had turned to the church, fleeing as it were to her father, a gentle clergyman long dead. Outwardly she had been controlled but at the Wednesday evening 'healing surgery' it all came tumbling out, the tears, the rage, the broken promises still stuck inside her like shards of glass.

'You forget you do have a choice,' the duty clergyman said, passing a weary hand across his face, eyes tortoise-coloured.

How many times had he heard it before. 'You can choose *not* to indulge such thoughts. Your mind is your own place.'

Anna had found this was true. From then on she put aside the years of her marriage, dismissed every thought of Rupert, fixed her mind on her job, read *The Times* from cover to cover and joined the Clifton library. Was it her reluctance to think about Rupert which made her such a wimp about the house?

The decision had effected a sea-change. At least she had been capable of change then, Anna thought. She had become obsessive about detail, some advantage in an office job, and Mr Brewster was entitled to reap the benefit. Hadn't he taken her on when her only experience was one previous job from which she had been dismissed?

'It's difficult for him at the moment. I mean all the staff at the health centre have got to be paid,' Anna went on. She had said this or something like it in a calm and reasonable tone so many times. Resentment of a new younger partner provoked only pity and contempt. Besides, she wasn't sure she felt it any more. There were definite advantages to living alone. 'Deirdre's only just qualified, housemen work all hours and get an absolute pittance...'

'Tough toenails,' Francesca interrupted, her attention half on a blond young man in a mohair sweater at the next table. His hair was like Hereward's. 'If Rupert decides to throw you on the scrap-heap after twenty years of faithful service the least he can do is buy you a house.'

'Twenty-two years,' Anna said. 'And it wasn't all Rupert's fault. Women are responsible for their own lives.'

'Feminist garbage,' Francesca exploded and the mohair jersey turned to stare. 'Look at that army officer getting thousands because she got pregnant and lost her job. Being Rupert's wife was *your job* and he fired you and you're damn well entitled to compensation. How many women remarry over forty? After Freddy's first fling I had the house put in my name while he was feeling guilty. Half his salary went into my account by direct debit and it still does.'

'Perhaps women over forty don't want to get married,' Anna said. 'Don't you think marriage is out of date? I mean it goes on so long and you do get sick of people.'

'What else is there?' Francesca said. 'Single motherhood, tell

Late in the Day

me about it. Honestly, I was the thickest of the three of us at school but I've come out top.' She laughed and jangled her bracelets. 'You two are enough to break Miss Snape's heart.'

Anna smiled wanly. It was typical Fran, the kind of remark that was hard to forgive and impossible to forget.

'Well you had a love life when all the rest of us had was prep and chilblains!' Anna said. 'I wonder if Patsy knows Miss Snape's dead,' she added with a frisson of anxiety. She and Patsy had been neighbours in the old days, driving children to school. She had been Patsy's confidante then and worrying about her had become a habit. The closeness had ended with Anna's divorce which Patsy regarded as a probably contagious affliction.

'Mark's carrying on with some girl in his office according to the grapevine,' Francesca said. 'But that's nothing new. Oh, hello, Owen...' A man had come into the bar, tall and handsome despite his unkempt beard. 'It's Owen Evans who works at our place,' she added in a loud whisper, waving to the empty chair between them. He acknowledged the wave with a nod, seemed momentarily to consider it but then mouthed an excuse over the heads which separated them, gestured gallant chagrin, and moved on down the bar.

'Well...' Francesca said, her colour rising at this unaccustomed rejection. 'No skin off my nose. He drinks like a fish and you know what they say.'

'What?' said Anna.

'Shrinks the whatsit... I read it in this magazine.'

'Really, Fran,' Anna said. It was ridiculous to let Francesca embarrass her. 'You do get around, don't you?'

'I have a good time. These HRT pills, they really turn you on, not that I was ever turned off. Course tampons for ever are a bore!' Francesca flicked back her hair, the mohair sweater was listening despite himself. 'I've never slept with Owen but he's had three wives at least and...'

'You said you wanted to talk about Miss Snape,' Anna interrupted.

'Yes, well I was thinking about a memorial. She *was* Avon Towers, and now the school's closed she ought to have a plaque, don't you think, like, er... Hannah More and Mary Carpenter?'

'Not really,' Anna said. She could see Owen Evans's grey head above the dark and fair heads of assorted students. He appeared to be on his own and he did have something about him.

'But she got you into Cambridge,' Francesca said, her eyes widened. 'Coaching in her study, Horlicks over the gas fire.'

'People get themselves into Cambridge actually,' Anna said, nettled. 'All that hothouse forcing did me no good. Cambridge was her idea, not mine.' Her hands shook, she had not realised she felt so strongly. 'She got me up but I got myself down.'

'Rupert's blue eyes got you down,' Francesca said. 'Girls gave up everything for love those days.' She glanced at a student in purple dungarees and hooped earrings who had joined the mohair jersey. 'So you don't like my memorial idea?'

'I think it's nonsense!' Anna said, surprising herself.

'I don't mean a marble statue on College Green,' Francesca went on, unperturbed. 'Just a plaque. A buffet lunch at my house for starters. Ask all the old girls we can think of and charge say five pounds a head and take it from there?'

'But whatever for?' Anna said, dabbing at drips of lager on her skirt. There was something particularly shaming about Francesca's generosity when Miss Snape had so disliked her. Surely she had realised, everybody else had. 'Let the past go, the present's what we're lumbered with,' Anna went on, not that Francesca seemed particularly lumbered. 'There was this woman shouting in Queens Road this morning. Just standing there and shouting.'

'Anyway I wanted to see you,' Francesca said carefully balancing mustard pickle on yellow cheese. 'About this job at Brandon Lodge. Secretary to the language department, it's called, but really it's just helping me.'

'I've got a job, thanks all the same,' Anna said.

'You'd have your own office and word processor and plenty of free time,' Francesca went on. 'Mrs Jacobs knitted a whole Aran sweater in the autumn term. Course working for the local authority, the money's not great.'

'Doesn't a job like that have to be advertised?' Anna said warily. Did she resent Francesca's kind offers because she was mean-spirited or because Fran being bountiful was so overwhelming? In the same way she had packed her children with high-class dairy produce until they gagged. It was no accident that on graduation Hereward had fled to India.

'Oh, the ad's just a formality,' Francesca said. 'You'd have to apply of course but Mr Austin and I...' She extended two fingers close together to illustrate. 'I'm thinking of having a summer school at Brandon Lodge this year, teaching English to foreigners. Would you like to have a go?'

'You know I'm not qualified,' Anna said.

'Your year at Newnham?' Francesca said. 'Anyway, what happened to your shouting woman?'

'An ambulance took her away,' Anna said. 'Did you know married women our age break down *more* than single women?'

'Who says I'm your age?' Francesca said plaintively.

'I remember your fourteenth birthday cake,' Anna said. The huge green cake had been delivered by special courier.

'Papa so loved to splash out,' Francesca said but the green cake had been a splash too far, provoking Miss Snape to say loudly that such vulgarity was only to be expected from a shopkeeper's daughter.

'Actually you're two years older than me, not that you look it,' Anna said. 'Any news from Hereward?'

'Not for ages,' Francesca said and for a moment her face was bleak. At first Hereward had joined the survivors of Bhagwan Shree Rajneesh, now he taught school in the hungry parts of the third world. Francesca studied blurred postmarks but Hereward never revealed an address. 'His last card said, "Listen to the fragrance of your heart."'

'Bhagwan?' Anna said.

'I guess so,' said Francesca. 'I dreamt about Hereward last night. Do you think that means he was dreaming about me?'

'Could be,' Anna said. 'And Hugo?'

'Threadbare,' said Francesca. Hugo, her younger son, was never her preferred subject of conversation. 'If only the boys had gone to decent schools. Say what you like, Avon Towers gave us, well... a certain éclat. Those little hats with the silk tassels which Miss Snape designed herself...' Suddenly tears filled Francesca's eyes. 'Silly, aren't I?'

'I'll get us some coffee,' Anna said. The bar was less crowded now but Owen Evans still brooded over his beer at the far end. If Francesca could forgive Miss Snape surely she, Anna, should be able to? Dropping out of Newnham at eighteen to marry Rupert aged twenty-two had masqueraded as grand passion but in reality had been as much a gesture of defiance. She was in love

Geraldine Kaye

with Rupert but six months later, working as a filing clerk and living in a communal flat for which she paid the rent, she already suspected she had made a mistake. When she came home from work with a headache and found him in bed with a girl from along the corridor, the suspicion became a certainty.

Theirs had to be an open marriage, Rupert said. If she tried to dominate him with archaic Christian shibboleths, she would destroy it. Anna, oppressed by her failure to hold him, found her own views permanently disenfranchised. What she had supposed was perfect love was something rather less compelling and they might have parted at that point except that during a tumultuous reconciliation Cathy had been conceived.

'A bottle of champagne, please.' A girl had come into the emptying bar. She was pretty, deeply tanned, long dark hair swinging down her back like a horse's tail.

'Cost you, Miss?' The barman eyed her doubtfully.

'Don't worry, I can pay.' Her smile showed even white teeth and Anna smiled too. There was something intriguing about the girl's air of suppressed excitement. She began to pile coins and notes from her red plastic handbag on to the counter, her glance including Anna in the conspiracy. 'What's money for?'

'All right for some.' The barman shook his head.

'Thanks,' Francesca said as Anna put down the coffee. The girl cradled her bottle tenderly, carrying it to a table at the far end.

'Anyway what's Olly up to?' Francesca was rarely offended by the churlishness of her friends.

'Driving a van and taking some more A-levels,' Anna said. 'Cathy told me, I'm not supposed to know.'

'You don't see him?'

'Not a lot,' Anna said. 'He phones nearly every week.'

'Ah,' Francesca said, imagining Hereward phoning, the noise of a bazaar ... 'Hi, Ma!' 'Cathy's the only one of our children, yours and mine and Patsy's, doing things properly,' Francesca went on, counting on her fingers. 'Olly and Cathy, Harriet and Briony, Hugo and Hereward. Cathy's the only one.'

'Is getting married with a mortgage and three children by the time you're twenty-five *doing things properly*? You sound like my mother,' Anna said, pleased none the less. 'Cathy's always either fed up or very fed up.'

Late in the Day

'Weren't we all, stuck all day with little kids?' Francesca said. 'How is your mother?'

'Don't ask,' Anna said. 'Hey, look at the time. I must go.'

'I thought your boss was away in Manchester?'

'He thinks I'm reliable,' Anna said, getting to her feet.

At the far end the girl craned her neck towards the glass panel in the door. She jumped up as it opened and a man came through, grinning widely, his tanned face flushed peony pink against his grey suit.

'I've done it,' he said. 'Phoned her.'

'You've done it!' the girl cried, exultant. 'Oh, you clever, clever boy.' She flung her arms out, spinning him round and round. 'You're free, you're free, you're born again.'

The man allowed himself to be swung, smiling down at the girl with mystifying sweetness. Beyond the couple Owen Evans watched from his stool, his own smile almost a replica.

'Wasn't that Mark?' Francesca said as she and Anna reached the pavement. 'Patsy's Mark?'

Chapter Three

In the staffroom of St Chad's Primary, Patsy's daughter Harriet sipped her coffee and tried to listen to Lynn's uncertainties about a jacket in Dingles sale. Her head was throbbing. Three hours ago she had been lying under Patrick, uncomfortable in the narrow bed, thinking she had to get to school. 'Did you come?' he had said, rolling off her. 'Almost,' she said after a pause. She had never been able to lie, a fatal disability both in teaching and loving, the two activities in which she principally engaged. 'Just my luck to get shacked up with a frigid bird,' Patrick said. If she was frigid it was rather a downer, Harriet thought. But probably she was because Patrick was beautiful as well as experienced. But his saying 'shacked up' was something else, because they weren't actually, only 'going out', though they didn't literally go out because Patrick was unemployed, just ate and made love at her flat three times a week but if he considered they were shacked up, that was an upper.

'It's blue, well mauvish really...' Lynn was saying.

Harriet tried not to think of the bruise on her shin, blue as a damson-plum where Darren had kicked her. Twenty-five children plus Darren was more than should be asked of anybody. 'But you're doing so well,' Mrs Gregory had said yesterday. 'Darren's a very disturbed eight-year-old and no wonder.' The head's widened eyes were intended to remind her of Darren's babyhood of violent abuse. But Harriet couldn't leave it there, couldn't forget the guinea pig's scream. 'But the rest of the class... I mean it takes everything I've got just to keep Darren sitting in his chair.' Mrs Gregory glanced at her watch. 'I hear you, Harriet, but one can get too involved. It's not a life sentence, you know, just your first job in an inner city school.' Her heels

Late in the Day

tip-tapping away along the corridor seemed to express satisfaction with this riposte.

'Isn't it awful when you can't decide?' Lynn said with a self-deprecating smile. 'Love the colour but . . .'

The buzzer went then. Harriet got to her feet.

The cathedral clock was striking three as Anna drove towards Cumberland Basin, negotiating her old 2CV through the traffic already building to the rush-hour, and on to the straight grey backbone of road which led out of town and across the flat green fields of north Somerset. She was on her way to Patsy in Stratton for the first time in four years. It was a change indeed but not the self-initiated one Anna would have preferred. There was something demeaning about the way a friend's calamity restored one's own vitality and confidence. Political commitment and love had the same exhilarating effect, and if Mark was going to leave Patsy it was quite fortunate he had done so when Mr Brewster was in Manchester.

'Can you come? Mother's freaked out, she's asking for you,' Briony had said, automatically phoning in time of crisis, not realising the habit was in abeyance. Briony swallowing a plum-stone at five, Harriet's premature loss of virginity and Mark's *other* sexual life had all required Anna's calm, non-judgmental presence. Patsy needed an audience, against which her emotions could be flung like pots of paint. It was a role her daughters tried to avoid.

The car chugged along the A370, behaving well despite the cold. But Anna was aware of a growing tightness in her chest as they got near the village. Such nonsense, she scolded herself, Stratton was just Stratton. It had nothing to do with her any more. 'You're free, you're free,' the girl in the White Hart had shouted, spinning him round. Anna would never forget the look on Mark's face, that lost smile. They had made love once, she and Mark, at a party years ago, struggling and breathless in the piles of visitors' coats. Mark had been fairly drunk and probably didn't remember. But it was her one infidelity, an occasion of guilt. Was that why she had responded at once to Patsy's need?

The main road ran under a line of familiar trees, black and leafless now. A moment later Anna turned off down the narrow lane that wound a mile between high hedges and then widened into Stratton High Street.

19

Geraldine Kaye

It was no good *not* looking at things. Anna turned her head left to right in a rhythmic pantomime. Like the Queen, she thought, bracing herself for a hundred tiny cuts. And there it all was, the yews by the churchyard gate, the cardboard lamb in the butcher's window, the greengrocer transformed into a supermarket. Orlando's hairdressing salon had always been gold and pink but now his wet-haired seraglio was discreetly veiled behind ruched nylon.

She took in the house in a single gulp. 'My house!' a voice whispered in her head. How could bricks and mortar mean so much? How politically incorrect could you get? Rose Lodge was a solid Victorian house, almost ugly. The Virginia creeper which would enfold it in green and later crimson leaves was a spidery filigree on the yellow brickwork now.

But what had become of the roses? Anna gaped at the spindly wilderness six feet high which looked as if it had not been touched since she left and felt her heartbeat quicken. And curtains she had never seen hung at the bedroom windows. What about the strawberry thief pattern, made to measure, almost the last thing she had bought in an attempt to steady things? If there was something wrong with them they ought to go back to the shop, she could probably still find the receipted bill. She could ask Cathy about the curtains but Cathy would only say, 'Forget it, Mum, it's none of your business.'

Cathy would be right, Cathy had a habit of being right. Anna breathed deeply, glad to have passed the house which was *not* her house. It had been an emancipation too, the violent wrenching of divorce, but an emancipation from what? She had lived there for fifteen years, useful as the doctor's wife until the health centre was set up. It was not the job she would have chosen, not the stuff of her youthful dreams, but then neither had Rupert expected to become a general practitioner in a country village after his years of research into anti-malarial drugs in West Africa. Not many people did get exactly what they wanted, she had pondered aloud to him once. Rupert had not felt the need to dispute it.

Nothing had prepared her for the night when he suddenly shouted that it was her fault he hadn't gone on in research. She had crushed his ideas, his capacity to innovate, he had been regarded as brilliant once. Deirdre still believed in him, by God!

Late in the Day

He had been teaching a course one day a week at the university medical school on the work of a general practitioner. A fortnight before he had brought a nineteen-year-old student, Deirdre, back to tea. He was shouting to stifle his doubts, Anna realised, but there was no mistaking the black rage inside him. It was real and terrible.

It was the end of her life in Stratton, hardly a catastrophe since Cathy was married and Olly in the sixth form of his boarding school. If Anna loved Rupert she had to admit she no longer admired him. Who did admire their husbands after twenty-two years? Rupert needed admiration, the salve applied just where he was weakest, perhaps most men did.

Anna had moved out of Rose Lodge two weeks later. Rupert made no attempt to dissuade her and Deirdre had soon moved in. Had she spun him round on the Persian rug in the hall shouting, 'You're free, you're free,' Anna wondered wryly. Rupert got giddy so easily.

Patsy's house, OldPlace, was on the other side of the village. It couldn't be right that a woman, having raised a family, could be dispossessed of home and lifestyle by a girl with swinging black hair.

'It isn't fair,' Anna murmured, negotiating the bridge which spanned the moat. If she had renounced indignation on her own behalf, she could still resent on behalf of Patsy.

Briony's motorbike was parked by the back door.

'I can't live by myself,' Patsy was saying. She had drunk a good deal, moving from sherry to whisky, and her speech was slurred. She lay dishevelled on the sofa, the undone buttons of her dress showing peach-lace petticoat, her eyes so swollen with crying that she hardly seemed to recognise Anna.

'Tough,' said Briony.

'I simply can not...' Patsy said, accenting each syllable. Rex whined his sympathy, his muzzle on her thigh.

'I'll make some coffee, shall I?' Anna said, piqued that nobody remarked on her quick response. Recently she and Patsy had occasionally talked on the phone.

'Suit yourself,' Briony said. She was slumped in the chair opposite the sofa with her long, jeaned legs extended. Her infant years had inured her to her mother's emotions. She regarded weeping as an affront to liberated womankind.

Geraldine Kaye

Briony was not behaving well, Anna thought, withdrawing to the kitchen. She looked out at the black and silver motorbike, incongruous against the old flint wall of the barn. But she always made allowances for Briony, the refugee child appearing on her doorstep begging to stay, eyes dark as olives, Patsy's eyes. There was an affinity between Briony and Anna lacking in her relationship with Cathy.

'I can't live at OldPlace by myself,' Patsy repeated. 'There's a ghost, Woodman, I see him.'

'First I heard of it,' Briony said. 'Sell it then.' Her helmet cradled in the crook of her arm emphasised that her presence was temporary.

'I shall never sell OldPlace,' Patsy declared in a quavery voice. 'As long as I live I shall never sell OldPlace.'

'Suit yourself,' Briony shrugged. 'But you don't need eleven rooms, it's mega-ridiculous. You could get three or four homeless families in a place like this. Is the cottage empty, by the way?' Briony had worked for the Self-Help Housing Association last summer vacation. 'I mean OldPlace would make a marvellous squat. Bit far to the shops, though.'

'Stop it, Briony!' Anna scolded in a whisper, sliding the coffee tray on to the table. But Patsy had closed her eyes against the unacceptable present. She was breathing heavily, apparently asleep, with her bare feet on the arm of the sofa.

'Have a heart, love,' Anna went on more gently. 'Your mother needs this house. People are fragile; too many changes and they break down. I mean you can't just go back to the life you left at nineteen, don't they teach you that in sociology?'

'Yeah-yeah,' said Briony, accepting her coffee. 'But it gets up my nose, I mean why doesn't she *do* something?'

'She brought up you two children,' Anna said. 'And her romantic novels paid your school fees, not to mention buying OldPlace. Don't you think she's entitled to a bit of support from her daughters now?'

'I'm here, aren't I?' Briony said. '*And* I've missed a seminar on Radical Alternatives in Local Government. Dad phones and says *your mother needs you*, so I go.' She seemed astonished at her filial obedience. 'He scrambles the fucking eggs and I clear up the mess.'

Late in the Day

'There isn't a right way to leave your wife,' Anna said.

'It's that bastard Orlando gets me,' Briony said. Her cap of sleek black hair was divided into segments by lines of hennaed red. Why was reddened hair *right on* but reddened lips not, Anna wondered.

'Chucking her out like that,' Briony went on. 'He'll get a brick through his plate glass one of these nights.'

'Stop showing off,' Anna said, glancing at Patsy who was snoring loudly now.

'She tried to kiss him, kiss Orlando,' Briony said giggling as she fitted her head into her helmet. 'Bit naff, I admit. It's her pills. What's the use of a sex discrimination act if women have the same slavish mentality?'

'Search me,' Anna said, following Briony to the back door and across the cobbled yard. 'Equality looks a bit different at forty-five, you know. Years looking after children cut no ice in the job market, even if there is a job market. Girls getting married now *know* it may not work out but twenty-five years ago they didn't. At least your mother's got OldPlace.'

'You've got a job and a flat, haven't you?' Briony said truculently. 'I mean political prisoners are being tortured right this minute all over the world.'

'Well . . .' Anna said.

'And I don't blame Dad for leaving her,' Briony said, spreading her legs either side of her bike. 'He's got a right to live with who he wants, anything else is pure hypocrisy.'

'Don't feel obliged to tell your mother that,' Anna said, wondering if the young had always been so self-righteous. 'She shouldn't be alone but I've got to get back . . .'

'Harriet'll be here in a minute. Can't stop, we're picketing newsagents all over Bristol tonight.'

'What for?' Anna said.

'The top shelf!' Briony said, kicking the starter indignantly. 'All that boobs and bum stuff . . .'

'What about your finals?' Anna shouted as the bike started up. 'Your degree has to last all your life.'

'Yeah-yeah,' Briony shouted back. 'Get a first and you *might* get a job. Anyway who says I want a job, perpetuating the rotten system?'

'And living off your social isn't perpetuating the rotten

system?' Anna shouted as Briony sputtered away down the drive.

Patsy was still fast asleep. Anna perched on the arm of the sofa and considered the pleasant, low-ceilinged room. In the old days she and Rupert had come to parties here. The white-painted panelling had turned a mellow cream with time and smoke. There was a rose-pink carpet and the old red-brick fireplace which Mark had discovered. Patsy had had a party to celebrate the fireplace. A single-barred electric fire stood there now and the room was chilly.

Anna put the bottle of whisky high up on the back shelf of the cupboard and then carried the coffee out to the kitchen. It couldn't be right to leave Patsy sleeping or to wake her. What time would Harriet arrive? Mr Brewster was away all day but suppose he phoned the office.

The early evening sun was already slanting in the windows as Anna wandered upstairs. OldPlace was a marvellous house; no wonder Patsy loved it. In the bedroom there were so many pills, legions of small brown bottles marching across the dressing-table, a further clutch on the bedside table.

Patsy might be better off without them but you couldn't throw out a support system at a time like this. Even tidying might lead to fatal confusion. A couple of shabby jackets swung disconsolate in the cupboard on Mark's side of the room. Mark had always been a trendy dresser. Had he taken his suits out, stuffed in his briefcase item by item?

'He'll come back, won't he?' Patsy said, waking. Her hair in flattened corkscrews on her forehead, her eyes dark specks in puffy pink. 'Won't he?'

'I dare say,' Anna said, trying to sound casual.

'Course he will,' Patsy said with dignity. She pulled herself upright, smoothing her dress across her plump legs. Her speech was still thick. 'Actually I wasn't expecting him back right away.' She glanced at Anna to gauge the effect. 'We're having a month or two away from each other. My idea really, you know how worried they get about little things ... well once or twice recently he couldn't ...'

'Mm,' said Anna, glancing at her watch. It was almost five o'clock. Surely Harriet would have left school soon after four.

Late in the Day

'You didn't really think that Mark had gone for ever, did you?' Patsy attempted an incredulous laugh. 'Besides, he loves this house too much. I put the film money from *Enchanted Love* down on OldPlace just *because* Mark loved it so.'

'Well, you've still got your house.' If Patsy's predicament opened old wounds, Anna could take cold comfort in having lost Rose Lodge and survived. Being on your own was the reality of the human condition after all. She wondered fleetingly if Owen Evans lived alone and wondered why she wondered.

'As for Signor Orlando, I shall never go there again,' Patsy said. 'Gays hate women, well they would, wouldn't they? I shall get that Sandra to come to the house to do my hair... or one of the other girls who have... married.' She stumbled on the word and tears sprang into her eyes. 'Where's Briony?'

'She had to get back,' Anna said. 'But I think Harriet's coming after school.'

'Why do my daughters devote their lives to the under-privileged?' Patsy's waspish tone seemed to restore her composure. 'It's so old-fashioned. Our grandmothers took soup to the poor.'

'You heard about Miss Snape?' Anna said and added quickly as Patsy's eyes filled, 'Fran wants to put a memorial plaque up, have a buffet lunch for Avon Towers old girls to discuss it and raise the cash.'

'But wasn't she expelled?' Patsy said, momentarily diverted. 'And I mean she isn't quite... well you know? Why don't I have the buffet lunch at OldPlace?'

'Perhaps...' Anna said since the idea seemed therapeutic. 'But there'll be other functions later. Life goes on...'

'What's that supposed to mean?' Patsy said. She had always felt herself to be different, more wicked than other little girls Nanny insisted. If Patsy had repudiated wicked she still considered her nature special, more passionate, her sufferings more deeply felt. 'You think Mark's left me, don't you?'

'I don't *think* anything,' Anna said. 'But there are other ways of living besides wedded bliss.'

'Not for me,' Patsy said. 'I'm not brave or resourceful, I couldn't type all day and live in a grotty bedsitter like you. Mark is my whole life and I *can't* live without him.'

Geraldine Kaye

'You may have to,' Anna said.

'So you *do* think he's left me for good?' Patsy flushed accusingly. She sat up then, spreading the knees of her mottled legs wide apart, careless of propriety. 'He can't leave me after all I've put up with. He can't bear suffering... sat up all night when Rex had distemper...'

'Well...' Anna said. Patsy's conviction seemed more encumbrance than support. 'Lots of people get divorced...'

'Divorced?' Patsy stuttered and tears rivered down her cheeks. 'But I can't live without Mark.'

'You can, love,' Anna said, folding Patsy's shaking body in her arms and rocking gently. Rogue tears filled her own eyes and trickled into Patsy's hair. 'You might get to like it. No more disgusting socks to wash, how does that grab you?'

A keening sound came from Patsy's throat and went on longer than seemed possible. Rex raised his nose to the ceiling and howled in unison.

'Stop that,' Anna said slapping Rex's nose, more disturbed by this primitive manifestation of grief than she cared to admit. 'Stop it, both of you. Isn't that Harriet?'

A white Mini had parked by the back door. Harriet, pretty and plump, got out and glanced apprehensively at the house.

'So you've come home, my darling?' Patsy wailed, flinging her arms round her daughter's shoulders.

'Just for a night or two, Mother,' Harriet said. Her eyes fastened on the window where the outside world was receding like a mirage. 'Just to the end of the week.'

Anna drove back along the High Street with a lightening heart. It was a relief to get away from poor Patsy even if she was driving against the evening traffic, business executives returning to their homes. A little way out of the village, a barn adjacent to the road had been sprayed with huge straggling white letters, 'Orlando is a Gay Pig.'

Anna swerved and stopped. Briony was really too much. She dabbed hopelessly at the tacky paint with a tissue but soon gave up. She abhorred vandalism but she had to admit to a sneaking and quite reprehensible excitement.

Going back to the office after six o'clock was overdoing it, even creepy, Anna realised, but there might be something on the answerphone and besides...

Late in the Day

She was astonished to find the door unlocked and Mr Brewster at his desk.

'Oh . . . I wasn't expecting you!' Anna said, startled.

'Evidently not,' said Mr Brewster.

Geraldine Kaye

Chapter Four

Half an hour later Anna pulled up outside the mid-Victorian terrace house which Cathy and Dennis had bought two years before. There was a ruby and green glass fanlight over the front door and just enough front garden to accommodate a single laurel. As she crossed the pavement the ground seemed to undulate just as it had the day of her divorce. She had half expected the sensation to be permanent then but it had subsided and not recurred until today.

'Oh, it's you,' Cathy said. Her dress was made of hand-woven material, dark blue with a broad rust stripe down the front. There was a gauntness about her face at twenty-five which had not been apparent at twenty. Student life had suited her; being on the union executive she came into her own. Anna had been so proud of her then. Had the pride been manipulative, she wondered, an attempt to expunge her own student career?

'Sorry I'm late,' she said, following Cathy down the narrow hall into the kitchen. At least the house was warm.

'Don't worry, I've only just got the kids stowed,' Cathy allowed with unusual generosity. 'Gilbert went out like a light. Anyway I'm not sure pottery's my thing.'

'I nearly cancelled.' Anna was suddenly breathless. 'Would you like a pink geranium? It's in the back of the car. I'd have brought it in only I thought you might say *not something else to be fed and watered*. I've just lost my job by the way.'

'Lost your job?' Cathy glanced at the kitchen clock as if she feared the inevitable discussion was going to delay her. The remains of family tea lay scattered across the table. 'Not again. You never learn, do you?'

'Whatever do you mean?' Anna said. 'I worked at Kellys for almost two years. And very boring it was too.'

Late in the Day

'And how long have you worked for Brewsters?' Cathy said.
'About twenty-two months.'
'Exactly,' said Cathy. 'And after twenty months employers start looking for an excuse to sack you, because after two years you're entitled to redundancy pay.'
'So you think...'
'I don't think, I *know*,' Cathy said, rolling her eyes skyward. 'And Dennis knows too and so do you because we *told* you, Dennis and me. What planet are you on, Mum?' The fact that she resented her mother's freedom to have a job did not lessen Cathy's irritation now she had lost it. 'You just don't live in the real world. Like all that stuff about going back to university when I started school... but did you hell?'
'That was twenty-something years ago, for God's sake. Your father getting a job in Gambia is why I didn't,' Anna said sharply.
Not that she regretted those years. Africa had illuminated her as nothing else had. Where else did you find such friendliness, such lightness of heart? But Cathy was right, Anna should know about redundancy payments after two years, she just didn't believe people were so mean. Especially not Mr Brewster.
'Oh well, you'll just have to sign on and live off the poor old taxpayer which is me and Dennis by the way,' Cathy said, popping the children's crusts into her mouth and clattering the plates into the sink. 'All part of life's rich pageant.'
'Mm.' Anna nodded guiltily. She decided not to mention the month's pay in her pocket in lieu of notice. It gave her a bit of respite. Signing on would mean Mr Phillips knowing she had lost her job and he didn't like unemployed tenants.
'You could go for wrongful dismissal,' Cathy suggested.
'Afraid not. Mr Brewster was away in Manchester and I left the office at three o'clock and didn't get back till after six,' Anna said, chastened. 'Mark has left Patsy.'
'A situation your presence could remedy?' Cathy asked sarcastically. 'How many jobs has Patsy lost for you?'
'Why do people always send for me?' Anna said.
'Search me. Because you're calm, I suppose, pseudo-calm anyway. The thing is you don't really care, do you, Mum?'
Was she being accused of coldness or dishonesty or both, Anna wondered.
'I could have got the invoices done first thing. It was just

unfortunate Mr Brewster got back from Manchester early,' she said. His eyes, clear brown like Amontillado, had had a certain triumphant brightness at having caught her out. 'He said he wanted somebody he could rely on.'

'Don't we all?' Cathy said, wiping the white formica table with an air of intensity. 'He has a point, mind you.'

'Funny really, because I think of myself as reliable,' Anna said, sitting on a kitchen chair. 'Perhaps it's an early menopause?'

'Please don't take to shoplifting.' Cathy allowed a smile.

'I don't *want* anything enough to steal it,' Anna said. She was tired now that her anger had died away. 'Children make you reliable, don't they?'

'Do they?' said Cathy, taking two bites from an abandoned apple. 'I didn't know anybody cared about *reliable* nowadays. What's happening to Grandma?'

'Nothing yet. I'm not talking her into anything. Old people have rights too,' Anna said, imagining a future time when Cathy might give her 'rights' short shrift.

'But Eventide Cottage won't hold the place for ever,' Cathy said. 'I took the children last week and the flat was filthy. Couldn't you get her a home help or something?'

'Home helps are a myth surviving from the sixties,' Anna said. 'Like the Beatles and James Dean.'

'She was on about the people upstairs,' Cathy said. 'Must go. Make yourself some tea, there's a corned beef salad in the fridge. I fed Gilbert but there's a bottle if he wakes.'

'Should you still be feeding him? You're awfully thin.'

'Course I should,' Cathy said, taking her coat from the hook in the hall. 'It's what I'm for! Katie and Edward are waiting to say goodnight, OK?'

'Is the lodger in or out?' Anna said, flustered by Cathy's immiment departure.

'Who cares? She won't bother you,' Cathy said, suddenly smiling. She stepped back to kiss Anna's cheek. 'Cheers, love, you'll get another job.'

'Have a nice class,' Anna called as the front door slammed.

For a second she stood there looking at the street light filtering through the coloured glass pattern, like Keats's St Agnes' Eve, she thought. Was that her O- or her A-level? At least she had completed them.

Late in the Day

'Is that you, Granny?' Katie called, knowing better than to call before her mother left. 'Aren't you coming up?'

'Here I come, darling,' Anna called. Five-year-old Katie and three-year-old Edward shared the back room overlooking the garden. Katie sat up in bed in a daisy-printed nightdress with an exercise book spread on the duvet. Edward, a large humorous child, lay with his eyes half closed. With his curved profile and downy yellow hair he looked like a fledgeling eagle.

'I didn't know if it was you downstairs or some imaginary person,' Katie said, green eyes under long black lashes.

'What would an imaginary person be doing in your kitchen?' Anna asked and wondered if this was a wise tack at bedtime.

'You can't really tell with imaginary persons, can you?' Katie said with a shrug which was a small version of Cathy's much-used mannerism.

'What are you writing?' Anna asked, sitting on the bed.

'A story, of course.'

'What's it about?'

'Don't know,' Katie said. 'I can't read yet.'

'I don't like Great-Granny,' Edward suddenly announced, opening his eyes. 'I hate Great-Granny a little bit.'

'That's an unkind thing to say.' Katie pursed her small, pink mouth. 'Because Great-Granny is a very old person.'

'I like being unkind.' Edward grinned wickedly, showing small separate teeth.

Anna finished the washing-up and carried her corned beef salad into the sitting-room. Dennis had recently put French windows in and the light, not-yet-painted wood framed the dark garden beyond. A bucket and spade lay on the scuffed lawn.

It was a nice little house, she thought, unpretentiously cosy, roomy too, despite the narrow frontage which was brilliant from the council tax point of view. If Cathy didn't seem particularly happy, who was, outside romantic fiction? She was lucky after all, Dennis a solicitor with a good firm, the children doing nicely, the house her own even if she had to have a lodger to pay the mortgage. *My married daughter*, it was a focal point in her own security. As Fran said, Cathy was 'doing things properly', and yet it was ridiculous to regard marriage as a safe option in this day and age and children were definitely hostages to fortune.

Anna had found Dennis unprepossessing at first, a shortish,

plain young man with pale freckled skin and gingery hair. She had been surprised and disappointed when Cathy announced after her finals that she was going to marry him. Cathy, who had been so sought after, so widely fancied, had gathered plenty of rosebuds. So why choose Dennis? A reaction to Rupert perhaps, but that was too simplistic, children had their own desires and disappointments to contend with, as well as their biological inheritance. There had always been an affinity between Cathy and her grandmother, as well as a marked physical resemblance. Married to a clergyman, Anna's mother had cultivated grievance all her life, especially after Bunny, her son, left for Australia at nineteen. Had Cathy adopted her grandmother's pattern?

Anna ate her supper and settled down in the big chair. Nobody could be as sorry for Patsy as she was for herself. Her histrionics were over the top but her distress was real. It was no good blaming *her* for the lost job. Besides, it wasn't so much the losing it that upset her as having so entirely misjudged her rating in Mr Brewster's esteem. That he was waiting for an excuse to sack her had never entered her head. As Cathy said, she lived on another planet and it must stop.

In a minute she would phone Patsy. Anna sighed and slept.

As Harriet clattered the plates back on the tray, she could hear her mother retching in the downstairs lavatory. Rex raised his head from his paws. The boiled egg and toast Harriet had prepared, the posy of snowdrops from the garden, were completely wasted. She carried the remnants to the kitchen as Patsy emerged, chalk-white and quivering.

'What shall I do?' she whispered, clutching the door jamb.

'Just lie down on the sofa,' Harriet said. Her lips felt hard and thin as bacon rind. 'You'll feel better in a minute.'

She washed the plates under the tap since the process took marginally longer than stacking the dishwasher. It was dark outside, country dark. Patrick would have found her note by now. Should she phone him as well? It was embarrassing to use the downstairs phone, and if she went upstairs her mother would listen and Patrick did so lack a romantic manner.

'What shall I do?' Patsy said, lying on the sofa as bidden. 'If Mark has left me, what am I going to do?'

'You could just go to bed,' Harriet suggested.

Late in the Day

'But it's only half past eight,' Patsy said, pouting.

'I'll come up in a minute and tuck you in,' Harriet said.

'I shan't sleep,' Patsy objected but she got up obediently.

'Take an extra pill,' Harriet suggested.

'Dr Walters says it's dangerous,' Patsy said, shuffling to the door, and conscious of a good exit line added, 'Don't mind dying, long as I can sleep.'

Napping on Cathy's sofa, Anna dreamed of a Hansel and Gretel cottage. He had bought it for her, Rupert whispered, their divorce was a mistake. Hadn't they always had their own little world together...

'Hello, Mother-in-law. Care for a cuppa?' Dennis flicked the spectacles up his nose in a characteristic gesture. 'I believe you were having a quick kip.'

'Believe I was,' Anna said. How her psyche betrayed her in her dreams. How infantile that losing her job should project her back to Rupert. 'Ought to be making tea for you, surely?'

'Don't see why in my house,' Dennis said.

'How was the Legal Aid Centre?' Anna asked as Dennis came back with the tray.

'Just a wife-battering or rather an ex-wife-battering. She's divorced him and he's threatening to kill her unless she goes back to him. I got her into a women's refuge.'

'What about the police?' Anna said.

'Can't be everywhere.' Dennis shrugged. 'To be fair something like a quarter of a million women get seriously assaulted by their partners every year... if the police offered protection the force would collapse.'

Anna sipped her tea. How could Dennis be so matter-of-fact about gratuitous violence inflicted on women? 'Do you sometimes feel we're on the brink, civilisation breaking up?'

'Only when I drink too much the night before,' Dennis said.

'I just lost my job.'

'Bad luck! Technology taking you over, Mother-in-law?' Dennis said. 'More tea?'

'No thanks.' A constraint fell on Anna then. Did Dennis feel it too, she wondered. He always treated her with the same schoolboy facetiousness. Was it his way of coping with repressed sexual attraction, she wondered, glancing at Dennis's white ears nestling in their frame of ginger hair. She could honestly say . . .

'Young Oliver rang this morning,' Dennis said suddenly.

'Olly? Did he sound all right?'

'Cathy spoke to him. Got a case of wine for that bloke who plays the guitar. Wish I'd kicked around, you're nowhere if you never dropped out.'

'Too late now,' Anna said, shocked to find that the freedom she allowed her children didn't extend to her son-in-law.

'Unless I spring the trap.' Dennis grinned and poured a second cup of tea. 'Another kid and I'm off.'

Anna did not want to hear this. 'Surely Cathy's not thinking . . .'

'No?' Dennis's glance was quizzical. 'Bit over the top, our Cathy, obsessed, getting and begetting we lay waste our powers. Want a cuppa, darling?' he called as a key turned in the front door. 'How was your class?'

'Middling,' Cathy said, bright-eyed and happy, raindrops in her hair. Could she be having an affair, Anna wondered?

'What about a pottery plaque?' she said. 'Did I tell you Miss Snape died? Francesca Smith wants a memorial put up.'

'Ridiculous!' Cathy said. 'Not Florence Nightingale, is she? What did she do except give a sense of superiority to some not-very-bright middle-class girls?'

'Thanks a bunch,' said Anna. She had said as much herself but she resented it from Cathy. Upstairs the baby began to wail.

'Not you, Mum,' Cathy said, patting her arm. 'Why do you take things so personally? She's lost her job,' she added to Dennis. 'Anything going at the Legal Aid Centre?'

'I'll ask round.' Dennis flicked his spectacles. 'Shall I fetch Gilbert?' He was tender about the children crying.

'I'm going, I'm going,' Cathy said, unbuttoning her dress.

'In Africa you never hear a baby cry,' Anna said. 'Maybe it's better for them living on their mothers' backs.'

'Honestly, Mum, you do talk crap!' Cathy said, making for the stairs. 'What about Rwanda . . . no babies crying there?'

'A mother's place is in the wrong,' Anna murmured.

'Join the club,' Dennis said and they exchanged guilty smiles. Dennis grows on you, she thought.

'Look at the time, I must go,' she said.

The car was still warm inside and started at once.

Late in the Day

Mr Phillips had been standing at the banisters for some time and the fetid smell of his basement had invaded the hall.

'Your phone was going earlier,' he said.

'Thanks,' said Anna, starting up the stairs with her arms full of geraniums.

'Plants, is it?' He craned his neck, watching her legs.

'That's right,' Anna called, opening and closing the door of the flat, putting the pots on the table next to the window, lighting the gas fire, switching on the electric blanket.

Did Cathy really want another baby, she wondered? Had Dennis told her because he thought she had some influence? Had love always been so confused and ambivalent? People needed closeness, the human spirit starved without it, but maybe friendship was more essential in the nineteen nineties than love. Anna closed her eyes; so many changes in one day. 'Falling free' were the words she had dreamt that morning, but where was she falling to?

It was too late now to phone Patsy.

PART TWO
Spring

Chapter Five

Spring came slowly. Anna, unemployed, made the best of the unremitting cold, taking what pleasure and encouragement she could from snowdrops pushing up in other people's front gardens on her route to the hospitable warmth offered by the public library. She had been deeply shocked by the chance events which had led to the loss of her job. She realised she needed to consider her life strategies but at the moment it was too cold.

At least her time and life were her own, no longer leased to Mr Brewster, Rupert or her more or less adult children. But what was she going to do with it? The short run was easy, she could and did list all the books she had intended to read for ages. Now she could do so, when she found them. The long run was the real problem. Some people managed, Francesca for instance, always so cheerful, so busy, so well turned-out and with an undiminished appetite for life that nothing seemed to quench. What was it about Francesca, Anna wondered?

Early one morning, Francesca's telephone rang. It was still dark and, waking, she stretched her arm to the white smoothness of the receiver.

'Hello?' It felt like ice, the heating did not come on till seven. 'Hello!' She could hear noises, a fragment of excited Spanish. 'Hello?'

'Ma?' Hereward's voice said suddenly. It was seven years since she had heard it. 'I got married yesterday.' The voice sounded bold like Papa's, Francesca thought. 'Just letting you know.' His voice falling away sounded more like himself.

'Married?' Francesca sat up, fully awake now. Seven years

melted away, this was not the time for recriminations. 'My darling, how wonderful. Who to?'

'Carmel,' said Hereward.

'A Catholic girl?' Just as well she was alone, Francesca thought; across thousands of miles Hereward, intuitive as she was herself, would have sensed somebody like say Jack, in bed beside her spoiling the moment. 'Where?'

'Bogota, of course.'

'Why didn't you tell me? I could have come out,' Francesca said. Her startled voice trilled archly. Hereward had come in from the cold. 'Why don't I come anyway, book a flight . . .'

'No fuss, Ma. Anyway we'll be in Peru.'

'Peru? For the honeymoon?' Francesca translated into her terms. She knew it was fatal to try to pin him down but she couldn't help it. 'You're going back to Bogota?'

'Course.'

'But I haven't even got your address . . .'

'Oh God! Do we have to have all this?' Hereward muttered, barely audible. Sounds like the sea, the line went dead.

'Hello, hello . . . Hereward . . .'

Francesca put down the phone and lay back in bed. Her excitement fluttered and faded in a void of disappointment. Hereward married, Hereward who had smiled right into her eyes moments after his birth. Had she loved him too much or not enough? 'Do we have to have all this?' After seven years. If only the boys had gone to decent schools instead of having to be sacrificed to Freddy's career. Though she did see that the head-teacher of a comprehensive packing his own boys off to Bryanston would not have looked good in the *Bristol Evening Post*. How she would have loved to fly to Bogota, she could picture it so well, a cathedral wedding, incense, Virgin and Child, the mantilla of black and silver lace she had bought on the Costa Blanca years ago and never taken from its fancy box.

Francesca sighed and switched on her tea-maker. She shook off disappointment as a dog shakes rain from its coat. Your children were *your* children but you couldn't be held responsible for the quality of the original material. The boys had never been promising, too much Smith and too little Alexander. Her cousin's children for instance, you could tell they were high-grade stock right from the start. Scholarships dropped on their heads like pennies from heaven.

Late in the Day

Francesca sipped her tea, and as it grew light her eyes circled the spacious master bedroom. When Freddy left she had sent the twenty years of accumulated furniture straight to the auction rooms and done the bedroom over in off-white picked out with pale green. The fuss and flurry of it all had taken over, not that she had seen Freddy's departure as a calamity, more an opportunity, since she supposed he would eventually come back. But for the moment the trap was sprung, and doors opened all round her even if she had to push a bit. Assistant to the principal of Brandon Lodge, couldn't be bad? She worked hard and was free to buy what she wanted and make love where she wanted and she did. Her love life with Freddy had always been restricted by their frequent quarrels.

Francesca smiled at the dressing-table copied from a glossy magazine by the woodwork apprentices at Brandon Lodge and the off-white sofa from Maples. Expensive but worth it. Freddy, reared in a northern mining village, had always been stingy. But Freddy gone was a new beginning. She missed him of course, would always miss him, but you had to get on with things. Friday was a busy day at Brandon Lodge and Jack was coming for supper. Could she give him lamb Sheringham again?

Hereward married needed some sort of gesture and out of consideration for her phone bill she phoned the Foreign Office from Brandon Lodge. 'My son is getting married and I've lost his address.' How many times would she have to say it? But neither the Foreign Office nor the Colombian Embassy seemed to know anything about *H. Smith*. Finally it was suggested he might be teaching at the new English Catholic High School in Bogota.

If Hereward was actually teaching he would not be pleased at the interruption and Francesca smiled a sweet, placatory smile into the phone as it rang on and on and nobody answered. What she needed was a new project, Francesca thought. She had always been prone to instant decisions. The summerhouse was really Jack's project, his thank-you-for-having-me present. But it wasn't too late to get the English as a Foreign Language summer school off the ground, and then there was the Snape memorial fund.

'Oh, it's you,' Anna said ungraciously when Francesca phoned her on Saturday morning. 'I was just going out actually.'

'Going out where?'

'To the library.' Anna spent most of her days there, working her way purposefully through her reading list, leaving every morning only a little later than when she worked at Brewsters. She had signed on now but the wheels of the DSS grind slowly and if Mr Phillips knew she was unemployed he didn't mention it. 'And Saturdays I do Mother's shopping.'

'Hereward phoned yesterday,' Francesca said. 'He's got married and he's working at a school in Bogota but I've rung and rung and nobody answers.'

'Probably the middle of the night there or else a saint's day,' Anna said. Pursuit of Hereward could only end in tears.

'Her name's Carmel.'

'Sounds like a good Catholic girl,' Anna said. Probably a convent-educated American Indian, she thought. Navaho. A nomadic heritage might suit Hereward and if not it would serve him right. How long was it since Olly phoned?

'You know how he is,' Francesca said. 'Anyway, how's the job situation? Offer still stands at Brandon Lodge, nowadays it's all *who you know*. I really want you to think about it.'

'I have thought,' Anna said. 'Thanks, but no thanks.'

'If you're unemployed too long you become unemployable,' Francesca said.

'Thanks a bunch.'

'Have you thought any more about the Snape memorial? How is your mother?'

'No. And so-so,' Anna said and rang off. If Fran had thoughts on the latter subject, she didn't want to hear them. Disconcerting that your friends saw you so differently. To Fran she was a helpless Orphan Annie incapable of managing her own life, to Patsy she was a rock conveniently cleft to accommodate her personal despair.

The question of her mother remained unresolved. She ought to make a decision but the loss of her job had increased her tendency to vacillate. Miss Miles had reminded her that the place could not be held indefinitely and suggested that *meaningful choice* no longer applied to somebody of her mother's age and situation.

That afternoon Anna, laden with plastic bags, rang the doorbell of her mother's flat. As usual there was a long wait and then a click as fingers fumbled at the letter slot.

Late in the Day

'It's all right, Mum. It's only me.'

'I don't open the door unless I've got my stick,' her mother said, brandishing the silver-knobbed cane and toppling with the effort. Her face was very white against the scarlet lipstick inaccurately applied. She wore a stained pink dressing-gown. She no longer got dressed, it was too much trouble, too soon followed by the worse trouble of getting undressed.

'Shall we put the shopping away?' Anna unloaded on to the kitchen table. Items were apt to get into the wrong tins, leading to querulous accusations of neglect.

'Oh, leave it, leave it, you're as bad as your father always fussing. You may as well talk to me now you *are* here.'

'I came last Saturday, dear, and popped in Wednesday night.' It seemed wisest to keep to the same routine. 'Have you thought any more about Eventide Cottage?' Anna tried to sound casual but her heart started to thud.

'Whatever would your father say, you trying to put me in that place?' Her mother's stick tapped along the passage.

'Hasn't Miss Miles been to see you?' Anna said.

'I don't go letting strangers in, old lady like me, not safe these days.' Her smile suggested triumph at this inspired ruse.

The small sitting-room was overcrowded with furniture but the old-lady smell was surely no worse than usual. The photo of Bunny in its silver frame stood on the mantelpiece, flanked by rows of schoolboys, the complement of Clifton College, and several tarnished cups. Anna had long ago accepted the limits of her feeling for her mother. Just as she had had to accept the limits of her mother's feeling for her compared with Bunny. If Rupert had convinced her of one thing it was the futility of mourning over the unsuitable state of one's feelings. Even so she did her best to be an affectionate and dutiful daughter. 'Must try harder,' as they put on her school report.

'You sit over there.' Her mother pointed to the sofa with her cane. A dark depression was visible; some incontinence was to be expected at her mother's age, Miss Miles said.

'Sit on the comfy sofa,' she insisted shrilly as Anna picked the wicker chair. 'I left it for you specially.'

'I like support for my back,' Anna said.

'No business getting *a back* at your age.' Fortunately a box of tissues caught her mother's attention. Scarlet-tipped nails struggled with the recalcitrant layers for a full minute and finally triumphed. She blew her nose and smiled in Anna's direction. 'How are the children getting on at school?'

'Cathy's grown up and married with three children now and Olly's living in London. He phones every week. I babysat for Cathy on Thursday and little Gilbert . . .'

Anna recited a partly imaginary rundown of her week. There was an element of hypocrisy in the treating-mother-as-a-person ritual, ignoring the wandering gaze, the movement of the pendulous scarlet lips. But the visit had to be got through, and as she droned on about Edward's new nursery her own preoccupations surfaced in a new guise.

Would she ever make love again, Anna found herself wondering. Did it matter, or more to the point did she mind?

Francesca tried the garden. It was too cold for any digging but her Saturday walkabout provided for her what church on Sunday provided for others, an opportunity for reflection and renewal. Besides, she had to decide where the new summerhouse should go.

The garden was about the size of a tennis court and sloped up from the house with a broad grass path down the middle and lines of currant bushes and raspberries either side and unusual vegetables, salsify, celeriac, each year something different.

Spring was the beginning of everything. Already the clematis Montana was trying to climb into the beech tree which grew in the public park beyond the fence. By May the whole tree would be a pink-white sheet now Freddy wasn't there to hack it back. Freddy, a Marxist but part of the establishment, had needed some outlet for revolutionary fervour. One day he would come back but for the moment the clematis could flaunt.

Hereward and Hugo apart, her life had never been so pleasant. 'Season of mists and mellow fruitfulness.' Miss Snape had read poetry to the senior girls on Sunday evenings. Her own 'mellow fruitfulness' was no longer reproductive, thank God. But last year Desmond had put up the greenhouse, just for the cost of the materials, and now Jack, who had only consented to leave this morning after a substantial breakfast and various extravagant promises, was building her a summerhouse to give the woodwork lads practical experience. 'I have never known anything like you,'

Late in the Day

he had whispered, his square torso gleaming in the moonlight. 'I have never been like this,' she whispered from politeness but her inventiveness in bed did surprise her.

She had to visit Hugo and the prospect was lowering. Francesca rinsed her hands at the kitchen tap and gathered redcurrant flan, iron-hard from the freezer, and the large portion of stew she had put up specially in her last 'cook-in'. Hugo was so touchy but after all they were *her* grandchildren and only the most mean-spirited person could object to gifts of home-cooked food. But Hugo would. Twenty-seven years ago the mewling baby, dotted with eczema, allergic to her milk, had scrambled from her lap and never scrambled back.

Francesca closed the freezer lid. She never brooded on what could not be remedied. She was happy to lack that particular compulsion. Scavenging clothes from charity shops to fit Felix or Carrie or little Femi or Hugo himself was fun but handing them over was difficult. 'Thank you kindly, God bless!' Hugo would say in a grotesque parody of grateful tramp. Really they might have stopped at two children, she thought as she backed the dark grey Volvo out; she felt it as tax-payer and grandmother.

'Anybody at home?' she called into the open front door. At least Hugo's house was his own even if it opened straight off the pavement of a mean street. She had been pleased to provide the deposit and fortunately had not expected to be thanked. 'I'm just dropping by with one or two things. Hereward phoned yesterday, he's got married, did you know?'

'Welcome,' said Lottie softly. 'Yes, he sent a postcard.'

The kitchen was dark and she sat at a table which had legs of different lengths propped with bricks. There was a smell of fish glue and drains. Lottie was winding raffia round a wire lamp-shade frame, a pale, sallow young woman with dark eyes which drooped at the corners, giving her face a sad look. The children's eyes had the same shape. Femi, the youngest, sat in a box at his mother's feet, Carrie was drawing at the table, Felix playing boats with saucepans in the sink. A half-eaten can of baked beans and two cold potatoes sat on the table surrounded by several unwashed plates and some dolls' clothes.

'Sorry, but Hugo's gone off somewhere. Would you like to sit down?' Lottie said, looking doubtfully round at the motley of chairs which had been retrieved from skips. Mending things was something Hugo did well but not often. Lately he had been too angry. 'Like some tea? I can easily make some,' Lottie added.

'That would be lovely,' Francesca said, relieved that Hugo was out. He was still represented in the children's affronted stares which made her feel brittle but she knew that Lottie liked her. 'Just brought one or two things for the children. I'll fetch them, shall I?' She hoped they would run out to the car excitedly as children should but they didn't move.

Carrie raised grey eyes as Francesca carried the box in. 'What things?'

'Things from the garden, things to eat,' Francesca said, clearing a space on the table. 'Cake.'

'Oh, what dear little baby lettuces!' Lottie said, her fingers touching the soft leaves.

'What's that blue bit?' Carrie said, picking out a pellet.

'Just something so the slugs don't come,' Francesca said, scooping it up in a tissue.

'Are they organically grown?' Felix said, turning from the sink. His name hardly suited such a solemn child.

'That's a big word for a little boy,' Francesca said, concealing her irritation with a roguish tone. 'I make my own compost, Felix, with leaves and vegetable bits from the house,' she added, forbearing to mention the activator she applied. It was ridiculous to justify yourself to a six-year-old child. If only they would let Felix go to school instead of teaching him at home, an insane decision when a primary school was prepared to mind your child free five days a week. Hugo had never explained his views on de-schooling.

'Are those free-range eggs?' Felix said.

'I'm afraid there isn't any milk,' Lottie said, pouring boiling water into a teapot. 'Can you wash us a cup, Felix?'

'Doesn't matter,' Francesca said, shocked. When she thought of all the Jersey milk and best butter which had gone into Hugo and Hereward. Dairy produce *was* motherhood, that and trying to be nicer than you really were. She had had to try so hard with Hugo. 'Don't the children like milk?'

'I don't,' said Carrie. Lottie looked paler than usual, dark under the eyes. At first Francesca had considered her 'not quite', but managing to live with Hugo in any degree of harmony was an achievement.

Late in the Day

'No job on the horizon?' Francesca asked as if Hugo's unemployment was a temporary blip. Hugo had lived and raised his children on social security for six years. After a turbulent student career, he had qualified as a teacher of art and craft. Francesca and Freddy had been delighted but Hugo had never worked since.

'Would you like some flan, children?' Francesca suggested, sipping the dark bitter tea which had a faint flavour of hay. 'I took it out of the freezer this morning and it's still a bit cold,' she added as the knife scraped redcurrants like glass beads. The children were crowding round her now. 'What about washing those hands?' she said but nobody took any notice.

'It's got little bits of lolly in it,' Carrie said, spitting out frozen redcurrants. 'Shall I show you what Hugo's doing?'

The upstairs room overlooked the garden. There was a large wooden rocking-horse in the middle, painted white and not quite finished, a splendid traditional nursery rocking-horse.

'Did Hugo make that?' Francesca said, setting it into motion and wishing for a second that Hereward had made it.

'Oh, it's you snooping about!' Hugo said, pounding suddenly up the stairs. He had been angry for weeks, angry at the children, angry at Lottie. His black moods frightened him.

'I just dropped in,' Francesca said. She gave him the warm smile she gave everybody but it was an effort with Hugo. 'The rocking-horse is beautiful, should fetch a good price.'

'I just *make* things,' Hugo said flatly.

'But if you put it on display somewhere,' Francesca said, trying to moderate her enthusiasm. 'Like in the foyer at Brandon Lodge.' Her excitement was gaining momentum. 'A beautiful, hand-crafted product, you'd get dozens of orders.'

'Like go into mass production?' Hugo said with distaste. 'I only want to make one. We're not into the market economy.'

'Just as well,' Francesca said, quivering with the effort to contain a rage which could so easily make an irrevocable breach. She turned to the window and the thicket of weeds below. 'Why don't you grow vegetables in the garden?'

'And let the children play in the street?' Hugo said. Somehow he always managed to misrepresent her. 'Vegetables grown within ten miles of the city centre are dangerously contaminated. Cadmium, acid rain, right to the Quantocks.'

'Nonsense!' said Francesca. 'My garden vegetables have such lovely green leaves.' Hugo smiled patronisingly and she added, 'I thought Lottie was looking a bit pale.'

'Not surprising, is it? Didn't she tell you?'

'Oh, no! Surely not,' Francesca said.

'Nine weeks pregnant,' Hugo said.

'You can still do something before twelve weeks,' she said, glacing at Carrie. The conversation was hardly appropriate for a four-year-old. Such a skinny ill-clad child.

'Like have an abortion?' Hugo said, his face hardened. 'We aren't into abortions, Ma. Abortion is killing.'

'I'm not "into abortion",' Francesca said. She had done it though with her own strong fingers before they changed the law. 'But isn't it the sensible course? I mean what about the children?'

'Killing this baby would be better for them?' Hugo said. His eyes were sharp and grey as knives. She had never realised how much he disliked her. 'We'll manage.'

'Manage?' Francesca cried. 'With your children looking like Oxfam posters? I'll pay for Lottie to jump the queue.'

'We want this baby,' Hugo said. He could feel his mood lightening, the great albatross which had hung from his neck for weeks. 'Please understand we *like* babies, Lottie and me.'

'You think I don't?' Francesca said. She took a deep breath. Things had to be said, better out than in. 'It isn't as if you even *tried* to hold down a job. You just *take* like a parasite and act superior. But who are you to judge anybody?'

'Go away,' Carrie said. Francesca was aware of the slice of cold redcurrant flan which landed by her foot. 'Make her go away, Hugo.'

Chapter Six

Patsy sat on the sofa and stared at the telephone. She had not let it out of her sight for more than a necessary minute since Mark had said he wasn't coming back. It was seven weeks now since his phone call but Patsy didn't know that, only that Easter had come and gone. She had loved Easter in the old days, cochineal-led eggs for everybody at breakfast, home-made cards from the children, soon whiny from a surfeit of chocolate.

The new term at St Chad's had started and Harriet left for work each morning. Today Patsy had promised she would go out in the garden and pick narcissi for the hall. Tuesdays and Fridays Mrs Bond came to clean the house. Was it one of those days, Patsy wondered. Her thoughts were sluggish, burping slowly up like bubbles in a mud spring, and she was putting on weight. What would Mark think when he came back and found a wife swaddled in fat. She had not forgotten his previous return from a Mediterranean trip. 'Kiss, kiss,' she had said, her whimsical routine. His head had dipped towards her like a heron forced to drink stale water.

Patsy did not doubt that he would come back. It was natural justice. She was not at fault, she had always loved him, always *said* she loved him, told everyone how much, holding his arm and stroking him at parties. His obvious annoyance had turned the impulse into a masochistic habit she could not control. She wanted everyone to be as well acquainted with her lovingness as they were with his infidelities. Their *knowing* was her insurance, she relied on getting what she deserved.

She had given up her writing for Mark, stopped because he resented the part of her it absorbed and perhaps her success, stopped right in the middle of a book for which she had already received a substantial advance. Her publishers had found it hard to forgive but that made the gesture more worthwhile.

She thought about Mark all the time. To let him out of her head could allow him to escape entirely. OldPlace, every nook and artefact within it, encapsulated a memory, a reference to their life together. Her hand reaching slowly for the address book reminded her of the tortoises Mark brought back from St Nicholas market one hot evening. Harriet's slow, Briony's as quick and restless as Briony herself. She followed such memories to the end, a private film show with frequent repeats.

Baby-time was best. She had been queen then with Mark still wanting her, assiduous and loving. How he had disliked nappies and chewed rusks everywhere, how ashamed he had been of his unfashionable fastidiousness. It was Mark who had put on a performance then. But for the moment she was alone. Shut in the dark cupboard, at least Nanny had listened to her sobs.

'You could break down, you know, if you go on like this, just sitting about and not doing anything,' Anna said, phoning every few days. How could her oldest friend so entirely fail to appreciate the cataclysmic nature of what had happened? Perhaps she would break down, go out of her mind. Mark might come home then, Mark would want to take charge of things.

'You're a talented woman, you can make a life for yourself. Hundreds of marriages fail, hundreds more middle-aged women hang on in degrading situations rather than face the necessity of earning their next crust,' Anna said. 'Patsy Simpson was a popular success once...' Such exhortation had nothing to do with Patsy; she shut her eyes and tried not to listen.

Gathering narcissi was out of the question, she was afraid to leave the house. She had already phoned everyone she could think of. 'Mark and I have split up, have you heard?' she would say quite calmly though sometimes a ripple of quavery laughter intruded. Today she would start again at the beginning of the address book and work her way right through, people she hadn't seen for fifteen years, the cousins in Scotland. 'Oh, Patsy, dear...', 'I'm so sorry to hear that, Mrs Simpson', 'I'm afraid I don't think I know who you...' She always put the phone down then. She wasn't interested in *their* words.

At eleven o'clock when she found they were out of instant coffee she phoned the corner shop. 'I can't keep sending like this,

Late in the Day

Mrs Simpson.' There was no mistaking the testiness in Joe Cleeve's voice. 'Haven't had a delivery service for years, just try to oblige when people are poorly...'

Patsy was dumb with affront. How could he speak to her like that when she called him Joe and always laughed at his jokes. Besides, she dare not go out since that day she put the dustbins out and the sky suddenly darkened and the drive was pitted with holes. She had fainted and would have lain there until Harriet came home if it hadn't been for Mrs Bond.

'Walk'll do you good!' Joe Cleeve went on cheerily. 'Get you out and about... and there's another thing.' He cleared his throat. 'I shall have to ask you to pay cash from now on, Mrs Simpson, with the bills for Feb and March still not paid.'

'I'll see to it at once,' Patsy said loftily.

But how could she when the account was overdrawn and the bank manager intransigent. Red-printed bills piled up, the disaster of electricity cut off only averted by Harriet's pay cheque. Mark, it transpired, had emptied their joint account before his holiday. It did not signify. She could always forgive his dirty tricks. What she couldn't do was walk to the corner shop with a hundred eyes staring from the hedge and the women from the council estate nodding, 'Lovely morning, Mrs Simpson,' with sly and knowing smiles. If Joe refused to send she would have to starve.

Patsy wept.

At half past twelve, Anna left the central library and started up Park Street, deciding on impulse to have a sandwich at the White Hart and join the stream of life.

She loved the library of course, its book-lined security, the warm and generous accommodation offered free to the unemployed, the vagrant, the insane. The same marble walls of subterranean green had been her refuge in her adolescent years, only then had been a heady scent of freedom ahead, the world wide open with possibilities. Now she had developed a sense of territory for a particular chair and was put out if somebody else took it. An old man with turkey feathers round his hat sat at the end of the row and giggled his way through volumes of the Encyclopaedia Britannica. His hilarity raised her spirits. In the afternoon she wandered the streets, exploring outlying districts where ornamental cherry trees dotted the pavements with pink or white petals. Department stores provided shelter and doubled as museums when you couldn't afford to buy. How long could she live in this limbo of fortnightly cheques from the DSS, babysitting for Cathy, visiting her mother twice a week?

She put postcards advertising her typing skills in newsagents' windows. Most days she lunched on bread and hot soup in the cathedral vestry. But today she had just been paid for typing a post-graduate history thesis. 'Don't you go declaring it,' Francesca said on the phone, 'you'll lose your benefit for weeks.' But Anna was uneasy; absolute honesty was vital to the poor milch cow of the welfare state. No doubt Briony and Olly would say she was being bourgeois and ridiculous. But Anna, daughter of the manse, was unable to exempt herself from her own exacting standards.

She paused at a public phone box. She had promised to phone Patsy at half past twelve and she must phone Miss Miles, a task she kept postponing. Both numbers were engaged.

The White Hart was crowded. Anna, in red and blue plaid trousers purchased from a charity shop the day before, took a deep breath and launched herself on to a vacant bar stool and tried to look as if she sat on bar stools every day of the week. She was ensconced before she noticed that Owen Evans was sitting huddled over a pint of beer on the next stool. She ordered a ploughman's and lager and waited till it came. She ought to speak to him surely and if she waited she never would. *Must try harder*. Anna took three quick swallows of lager.

'Mr Evans, I think we met a few weeks back?' she said breathily. 'Aren't you a friend of Francesca Smith's?'

'Wouldn't say that, ma'am.' He turned slowly to look at her, his light blue eyes glassy in his wide, prominently cheekboned face. He looked rather Slav, she thought, but his name was Welsh and his accent sounded American. 'I'm choosy about my friends. What's she been saying?' he added belligerently.

'Nothing,' said Anna. 'I just mean you know her.'

'Are we talking Bible-speak here?' he said. His eyes were livelier now and his loud speech invited an audience. 'Got to watch your words, ma'am, know what I mean? These radical feminists'll get you in court for rape, slander, damage to their reputation, never mind they've got three kids from different

Late in the Day

fathers back home.' His fingers engaged an imaginary forelock. '"Cross my heart I never knew her, m'lud, sir." Too much regard for my personal health to tango with whores. We just work at the same place.'

'Brandon Lodge?' Anna said, wondering if loyalty demanded she object to 'whores'.

'Do you work there too? Ought I to recognise you?' His hands clapped into an attitude of prayer. 'Mea culpa, mea culpa. My trouble is I'm only interested in me.'

'That's honest.' Anna was disconcerted. Did people usually talk like this nowadays? Except for her mother and Patsy she had hardly spoken to anyone for weeks. You had to go out, get yourself a life. Wasn't she always telling Patsy?

'Poor but honest, that's me, eh, Jed?' Owen said to the barman. 'Know something, this is one of the only pubs in Bristol where I'm still persona grata.'

'Why's that?' said Anna, who had never heard of pubs excluding potential customers. 'Do you get drunk?'

'Suppose I do?' His eyebrows disappeared into his hair. 'Shall I tell you about my thirty per cent liver function?'

'Well, if you like, but wait a minute,' Anna said, slipping down from her bar stool. 'I promised to phone a friend and, er... someone. Keep an eye on my ploughman's, will you?'

'Lucky old friend,' Owen said, subsiding into gloom. 'Lucky old someone.'

Patsy's number was engaged but Anna got through to Miss Miles's assistant. 'I'm ringing about my mother and Eventide Cottage. I'm afraid she's still reluctant...'

'Oh, Mrs Bolt, the Eventide bed has long gone,' the assistant interrupted impatiently. 'We can't keep beds on hold, Miss Miles did tell you, not with our waiting list...'

'It isn't easy...' Anna tried to explain. Afterwards she paused a moment and wondered what to say to Owen Evans. What would he like to talk about? But when she returned to the bar, he had gone and so had her ploughman's.

'Cleared it, didn't I?' the barman said. 'Sorry.'

At OldPlace somebody flitted past the window. Rex raised his head from his paws and growled. School was over and the children came to smoke in the moat and run all over the orchard.

They seemed to know Patsy couldn't stop them. Some days they even flattened noses and tongues against the glass.

The deathwatch beetle she had had treated at such great expense ten years before tapped in the beams over her head. The martins nesting under the barn roof dropped on her if she crossed the yard. The pond cracked across and drained dry, and yellow fungus erupted along the crack.

Patsy wept.

Mark was there, she knew, leaning from the pale ceiling like Christ Pantocrater, his eyes liquid with sympathy. Mark was the only person who had ever really loved her, the only person who would understand her feelings now. But they would not let her talk to Mark. A search through Harriet's handbag had revealed his new phone number. She tried it every day but after her first word it was always cut off and left off the hook.

Outside it began to get dark. Marauding children left the garden, called to tea. Harriet would be home soon. Then she could take her sleeping pills which Harriet forbade before seven o'clock and lower herself into oblivion.

The phone rang suddenly.

'Yes?' said Patsy, waiting as the call box chirped desperately and finally engaged. 'Yes?'

'I was thinking of you in black lace panties,' a voice whispered breathily. Patsy put the phone down without a word as Harriet said. He called every day at the same time, on his way home perhaps, only the colour of the panties changed.

'Yes? Who is it?' she said when the phone went again.

'We are thinking of you, Mrs Simpson, dear,' said an unfamiliar voice. 'We are praying for you in your trouble.'

'Who?' said Patsy on a rising note. 'Who is that?'

'Marjorie Woods, dear. You don't know me but I know you, Patsy. May I call you Patsy? We meet each week of an afternoon for a cup of tea, the Reverend comes when he can, and we pray for you and your poor dear husband. A sheep strayed from the fold.'

'How did you know?' Patsy whispered, trying to fix the voice. Which of the women who sent their children to pinch logs from the barn or daffodils from the garden was it?

'The grapevine, dear,' the voice tittered genteelly. 'People talk in a village, don't they? If you'd care to come yourself to 5, West Crescent, you'd be more than welcome.'

Late in the Day

'He will come back, won't he?' Patsy whispered but the phone was already dead. If she broke down completely Mark would have to come home, Patsy thought, because she might ... because of what she might do ... Mark couldn't bear suffering.

Late that evening Harriet sat on her bed and stared out of the window. A full white moon made a wide path across the garden illuminating even the recesses of the moat. There had been a couple there earlier. She had felt an irresistible urge to walk out across the garden and look. What would she have seen? Sex was the only skill you were expected to acquire without benefit of demonstration. But nobody dared to admit to bafflement, the failure of instinct.

The garden was silent now. Along the window sill a line of glass animals furred with dust, her childhood crystallised. She thought of Darren, imagined giving him the glass animals, a sort of restitution. But he would only break the legs off, poor little sod. She didn't mind the hitting and spitting if only he'd leave the guinea pig ...

A latch clicked and the passage floor creaked. Patsy was liable to sleepwalk when she was distressed. In their childhood it had been a regular phenomenon. Voices raised by day, Patsy walked by night, arms extended, eyes wide.

'Go back to bed, Mother,' Harriet called sharply. The footsteps paused. 'Go back to bed at once, you naughty, naughty girl,' Harriet shouted furiously. The creaking receded down the passage, the latch clicked again, bedsprings sighed.

'Why me?' Harriet whispered into the darkness. She loved her mother, admired a colour and vitality she felt herself to lack. But she could not bear the snivelling, shuffling creature she had become. 'Stuck in a fucking prison.'

Chapter Seven

The pillars of the gate of Brandon Lodge in Redland were embellished with stone lions which expressed the satisfaction of the Victorian entrepreneur who had built it. Francesca, later than usual, smiled up at them, experiencing a moment of pleasure as she drove in and parked the Volvo in the gravel car park, recently extended under her initiative to take in half the acre of lawn in front of the house.

Her particular knack was to fall on her feet, she realised. For instance her painful expulsion from Avon Towers, later commuted by Papa's timely donation to the library extension, had resulted in two years at a finishing school in the Swiss Alps which had done much for her culinary skills and even more for her French. As the boys grew older, she began to teach the language to adults and her attractive appearance and good humour made her classes popular. Students repeated year after year, especially when she took to ending the course with a long weekend in Paris.

Her success was not lost on the principal, Mr Austin, previously head of a 'difficult' school. His history of stress-related absences was solved by his appointment to a small adult education institute. But the rapid expansion of Brandon Lodge had triggered his anxiety symptoms. It was the Peter Principle, his student son informed him, people promoted up the ladder beyond their ability and left there miserable for ever.

Francesca had proved Mr Austin's salvation, her particular competence being to get instantly right to the heart of things. Soon she was dealing with all the correspondence, disciplining unruly students, counselling dismayed parents and disgruntled staff, and she actually enjoyed visiting the education authority. When she was appointed his assistant, Francesca was delighted,

Late in the Day

Mr Austin more so. Increasingly, after a glance at the morning's mail, he devoted his time to studying maps, selecting places he and his wife had not yet visited. If he could get twenty students to sign on the noticeboard for a trip, the travel agent awarded Mr Austin two free places. Still he brooded on the Peter Principle and now and then strove to assert his authority. Fortunately Francesca knew the signs and could handle them.

She got out of the car and smiled down at the off-white gravel which crunched under her feet and which she had persuaded the contractor to supply instead of regulation brown at no extra cost. She worked at improving the environment of Brandon Lodge just as she worked to improve her own environment, her house and garden. She greeted the secretary in the outer office and passed into her own. The pile of letters which usually awaited her was not there. She tapped on Mr Austin's door and found him already in possession, carefully tearing all foreign stamps from envelopes for his grandson's collection.

'Ah, good morning, Francesca.' His face had its pale worried look. 'About this summer school of yours... I've been thinking...'

'All under control,' Francesca said with a tranquillising smile. She had already despatched application forms to countries with sound economies all over the world and advertised in the *Times Education Supplement* and *The Teacher* for EFL specialists for August, a lucrative alternative to marking exam papers.

'You're sure it's a good idea?' Mr Austin said.

'Positive,' Francesca said positively. 'We've got twenty applications from students and three highly qualified teachers already. Shall I get on with these?' she added, gathering up the rest of the correspondence. 'Trust me.'

'Oh, I do,' Mr Austin said nervously. 'But the summer school will involve us both in a lot of extra work...'

Francesca paused at the door. 'I wonder if you could find the time to make one of your really eye-catching wall-charts for the main noticeboard. A wall-chart makes all the difference, you know?'

'Certainly I will,' Mr Austin said. 'Right away. Did I tell you my son-in-law's got a special offer on all new tyres this week?'

'Yes, I'm having a think,' Francesca said, bearing the letters away.

Two hours later she had been through the correspondence, discussed replies, dictated letters to the secretary and had them duly signed. The buzzer went at fifty-minute intervals, followed by the hubbub of chatter in the corridors. At half past eleven Owen Evans tapped on her door.

'Owen, what can I do for you? Coffee?' Francesca said.

'Thanks,' he said, swaying and sitting down suddenly in front of her desk. He could do with a bath, Francesca thought, passing him to organise coffee.

'Met a friend of yours in the White Hart the other day,' Owen offered.

'Who was that then?' Francesca said. 'Thank you, Jenny.'

'Didn't give her name. In her forties . . .' he said but suspecting this was tactless he subsided to sipping his coffee.

'Was there something you wanted?' Francesca's smile did not waver.

'About this summer school thing?'

'Yes?' Francesca said, deciding instantly that Owen would *not* be a suitable addition to the staff.

'Teaching English, EFL, for a month, any chance for me?'

'But you teach statistics, don't you? I hardly think . . .'

'Teach it in English, don't I?'

'Quite so,' Francesca smiled. 'Well, I'll put your name on the waiting list, Owen, if you like. But I advertised several weeks ago and I've got a full complement of TEFL people already . . . but of course one or two may drop out . . .'

'Waiting list?' He swung his ragged head like a tormented bear. 'For a teacher with thirty years' experience? I've got six children you know, six mouths . . .'

'I can see it's difficult.'

'Difficult . . . difficult . . .' he shouted on a rising note. Could he still be drunk from the previous night, she wondered? 'It's bloody impossible . . . that's what it is . . .'

'Yes but really, Owen, I don't see . . .'

'What's going on?' Jack stood in the doorway, his fists clenched at his sides, eager for action.

'Mr Evans had a query but I think we've sorted it out.' Francesca's smile was still composed.

'Humph,' Owen Evans said. Jack stood aside reluctantly to let him pass.

Late in the Day

'Trouble?' Jack murmured a moment later. 'He'd better watch himself...'

'Absolutely no trouble,' Francesca answered smoothly. 'Did you want something, Jack?'

Jack opened and closed his mouth. 'Would Tuesday be all right for the summerhouse?' he said huskily.

'Perfect.'

Francesca asked to take Tuesday off to Mr Austin's alarm. Sometimes he wondered if he pushed her too hard. Suppose she should take it into her head to leave? The idea turned him quivery.

'Nothing wrong, I hope?'

'Nothing at all.' Francesca smiled reassuringly. 'Er... just a family matter.'

'Ah!'

Francesca did not care for young fellows tramping about her garden, even if Jack was there to supervise. Besides, there was the redecoration of the kitchen to be considered. Magnolia or off-white, she couldn't decide.

'Good morning, all of you,' she called blithely as the van arrived on Tuesday morning. She opened the front door and unlocked the side gate. She was wearing violet leggings from John Lewis which clung to her rounded thighs, but the cyclamen tunic in knitted silk which anyone could see was expensive hung loose and made the ensemble casually *all right*.

'Morning, missus,' the woodwork students muttered with shy grins, the five of them already unloading, shouldering timber and carrying it through to the back. The black-haired one was rather good-looking, Francesca thought, and despite his Celtic colouring a bit like Hereward.

'Looks like we got a good day for it,' Jack said, gazing skywards. 'Shouldn't take more than the one day, lads?'

'Don't know about that,' somebody mumbled.

'Scam if you ask me,' muttered the Celt, blue eyes bold.

'Practice makes perfect, lads,' Jack said. 'Need a bit of practice on the job, don't we?'

'Speak for yourself, squire,' muttered the Celt and one or two sniggered.

'Shall we say lunch at twelve o'clock?' Francesca said. She did not care for Jack's proprietary air.

'Very good of you, I'm sure, Mrs Smith, eh, lads?' Jack said. 'Mrs Smith giving us lunch?'

'Smashing,' somebody muttered.

In the kitchen Francesca washed salad, examined the pink chunk of butcher's veal and ham pie in the fridge, proud of its generous size. Jack's apprentices would hardly appreciate her *haute cuisine* but she had made a chocolate cake for their tea. Feeding people was her indulgence, whoever they were, and hang the expense. She got out the picnic plates. Eating outdoors would save the kitchen floor from muddy boots but she needed to get one of them inside to discuss the redecoration, the Celt perhaps.

Up the garden she could see the frame of the summerhouse already taking shape. Sounds of hammering and shouts drifted in. Were they already up to the roof? A summerhouse for the cost of the materials was something else, but you couldn't call it a *scam* when she paid for the wood and Jack's lads needed the practice.

Two young men were coming down the garden.

'A cup of coffee?' she invited.

'Well I don't think . . .' one said shyly.

'Brilliant!' the Celt said, following her inside.

'Do you do decorating in your spare time?' she asked, pouring him a cup of coffee.

'Cash in hand?'

'Of course,' she said. Really he was quite handsome. 'On the nail.'

'Sometimes . . .' he said, studying her. 'What did you have in mind?'

'This kitchen. Magnolia, I thought?'

'Brilliant,' he said. His eyes roved across the walls and ceiling. 'Better get back or the gaffer'll be after me. Give you a bell, shall I?'

'Right,' Francesca said, knowing he would.

It was time to get the lunch. A new summerhouse, she thought, slicing tomatoes, breaking up lettuce leaves, dividing the veal and ham pie into man-size portions. But you couldn't call it a scam when she not only paid for the wood but also for the special-quality laminated windows and double doors, *and* provided lunch and tea for this happy horde. You could give five thousand pounds for a summerhouse at a garden centre. Francesca pushed the trolley up the path smiling.

You could sleep in the summerhouse even, Hereward and

Late in the Day

Carmel and the baby, if they ever had a baby... lovely fresh air... or Femi and Carrie and Felix could sleep out here.

'Come and get it!' Francesca called.

By five o'clock the summerhouse was finished. Young men trailed down the garden with tools and bits of wood, flushed and sagging with the day's exertion. She needed something else now, Francesca thought. A party in the garden to celebrate the new summerhouse and start off the Snape memorial fund.

'Thank you all so much,' she said. 'The summerhouse is just gorgeous.' The Celt was already back in the van.

'Shall I see you later?' Jack whispered and for a long moment Francesca did not answer.

As Anna parked the car against the kerb, lace curtains twitched. Lace curtains should be white not grey, she thought, promising herself she would get them round to the launderette.

Anna was chastened. She had gone to see Miss Miles, contrite about the option on Eventide Cottage, but determined all the same to explain her views on the rights of the elderly. Miss Miles had listened patiently but then suggested that the real problem was Anna's reluctance to *let go* which made Mother over-anxious. *Unfinished business* was a two-way process which was best recognised and worked through. After that there could possibly be a place at Bexley House for Mother. 'But surely she doesn't have to go if she doesn't want to?' Anna had said.

'Of course not.' Miss Miles gathered the file together, reluctant to embark on more fruitless paperwork. 'But who is to take the responsibility?'

Miss Miles was right, of course. Her mother might so easily fall in the night and lie there for hours getting hypothermia. Their plights were confusingly linked, both dispossessed of house and husband. Perhaps she did over-dramatise her mother's attachment to her independence and her ground-floor flat. People needed to see other people every day, a necessary if not a sufficient condition for staying sensible for both of them.

In West Africa they knew that. 'The forest withstands the storm but the single tree is soon blown down,' they said. The old stayed in the centre of the family, listened to and respected, greeted as they walked through the village escorted by a tumult of grandchildren. Not stuck alone in a flat like a doll in a cupboard.

Geraldine Kaye

Perhaps she should take the job at Brandon Lodge after all, Anna thought, 'get herself a life' as Francesca advised her and she in turn advised Patsy.

'What do you want to bring your car for?' her mother demanded, taut with fright. 'Wasting your petrol.'

'I have to give it a run once a week or the battery goes flat,' Anna said. 'And I thought you might like a little drive for a change. Let's get you dressed . . .'

'I'm not going anywhere,' her mother said, grabbing the door jamb as if she expected force, eyes wide and startled. 'I'm stopping here in my own home.'

'All right then,' Anna said, taking her arm and propelling her firmly towards the sitting-room. 'But the spring flowers are so pretty. You always loved daffs.'

'I know your sort, you and that Miss Miles, you'd have me into Eventide Cottage quick sting as a wapsy?'

'The place at Eventide Cottage has gone long since, Mother,' Anna said. Miss Miles's view of their hang-up being mutual might be right; she had the experience after all. 'But have you thought any more about Bexley House?'

'Bexley House?' Her mother flopped into the wicker chair. 'I like my own place, thank you very much.'

'I know you do,' Anna said, sitting on the other end of the sofa from the dark patch. 'But at Bexley House you'd have your own room. Mrs Dewar in charge is very nice.'

'Smarmy. I know her sort. Worked my fingers to the bone for you children,' her mother declared, a pink spot in each cheek.

'And now you deserve a rest,' Anna said, trying to sound positive. 'Let other people wait on you.' But she could not get the picture of Bexley House out of her head, every possible surface made cheerful with a bright pattern in washable plastic. Ten old ladies staring blankly at the television as it chattered its way through *Play Bus* and *Grange Hill*. But at least they were warm and clean.

'You're not putting me in one of those places,' her mother screeched suddenly. 'Your father would never allow it.' Her hand plucked at her pink dressing-gown. 'Your father and I were always so happy. I thought the world of your father.'

'I expect he knew that,' Anna said softly. It was natural that the past, the marriage, should be glossed now with a tenderness it had lacked at the time. Once she had asked her father why he had married her mother. 'She was so alive, lovely too,' he sighed. 'Selfish of me, I sometimes think. Not everybody's cut out to be a clergy wife.'

'He cared for me, I miss him so,' her mother muttered.

'I'm sure you do, darling,' Anna said. 'Of course you do.'

'Why can't I have a granny-flat like old Mrs Griffiths?' She began crying, dabbing her face with the edge of her dressing-gown, lipstick smeared. 'Heartless, you are, hard as nails. Bunny's going to get me a granny-flat.'

'But Bunny's in Australia, dear,' Anna said, taking her mother's hand.

'I know he's in Australia, do you think I'm getting silly? Had a postcard just the other day.' She brightened and fumbled in her handbag, finding long-lost cough sweets, library tickets, bills, examining each with little exclamations of surprise and finally holding up a postcard of yellow sand and blue sea which had arrived six months before. 'Here it is! Read it out.'

'"Greetings and love from Bunny and Melinda,"' Anna read. Bunny had a couple of garages in Melbourne now and was quite well heeled but he rarely wrote. There was nothing unusual in that, Anna reminded herself. It was always assumed that a daughter took care of an elderly parent, especially if that daughter was middle-aged and single.

'Do you think I'm going to like Australia?' Her mother's tone was sprightly as she took the postcard back. 'You'll have to take me shopping at the sales, nothing too expensive.'

'Mummy dear, I really do want you to think about Bexley House,' Anna said flatly. What was the use of tact and trying harder with her mother's precarious grasp of reality?

'My daughter, Anna, is married to a doctor,' her mother remarked conversationally after a pause. 'She lives in Stratton, she's the doctor's wife in Stratton.'

'Not any more,' Anna said. She could hear rustling.

'What? Have they moved? Why didn't they tell me?' Her voice rose querulously. 'They're making a flat for me, a mobile home. My daughter's good, clever too, got her own cap and gown. It was Bunny got those lovely cups though. Won everything, Bunny did.' She began levering herself on to her feet with her cane.

Geraldine Kaye

'I wish I *could* get you a mobile home in the garden, dear,' Anna said, blinking. 'But I haven't got a garden. My two-room flat is one room really, we put a sheet up if Olly comes.'

'Disgraceful!'

'Please, please do think about Bexley House.' A definite rustling was coming from the sofa. Mice, Anna thought uneasily, mice made nests in old sofas. 'We all think it would be the best thing for you.'

'But I'm going to Australia,' her mother said. She had reached the mantelpiece and was gathering the photos together. 'You'll have to help me pack.'

'Oh, God!' Anna said. Her fingers had sunk through the damp patch in the blue velvet, soft as rotten leaves. There was grey stuffing underneath and white maggots curling and crawling. 'Oh my God! You can't stop here.'

Now she *had* to change, had to make changes. No escape.

'Bunny has asked me to live with him and Melinda in Australia. I just told you.'

'Sweet Jesus!'

'Be quiet,' her mother said, strong and peremptory. 'You should be ashamed of yourself, blaspheming like that, and you a rector's daughter. Whatever would your father say?'

Chapter Eight

Friday morning, Harriet's Mini puttered away down the drive of OldPlace and over the bridge. Patsy was alone.

'Have a lovely weekend, darling,' she called, waving from the back door. Her voice rising brave but tremulous into the unknown blue sounded like a skylark, she thought, if only there was someone to hear.

'"God's in his heaven, All's right with the world,"' she recited bravely, turning back into the house, dark as a cave after the sunlight. Alone was alone. But she must be getting better, pretending to be better, *acting* better, was in itself a kind of getting better. But it was dangerous to pretend too well, Harriet might leave altogether. Last week she had suggested Patsy try to let the cottage, so 'somebody would always be around'.

'Good dog, good old friend,' Patsy said as Rex sniffed her nightdress and licked her feet, wet from the dewy grass. She scooped a generous portion of dog meat into his dish, though the vet had said being overweight was bad for his heart. Never mind, she would take him for a walk later, Patsy promised herself, forgetting for the moment she had not been outside OldPlace for four months.

Harriet was spending an experimental weekend back in her own flat. 'Of course, darling,' Patsy had agreed, not mentioning Patrick since Harriet hadn't. As a mother she hoped it would work this time and also hoped it wouldn't. One weekend shut up in OldPlace on her own could be contemplated, had to be since Briony, approaching her finals, refused point blank to come home and Anna was working again and besides that claimed to be installing her mother in an old people's home this weekend.

Nobody seemed to care what happened to *her* any more, Patsy thought. 'Take each day as it comes,' Dr Walters said, 'busy yourself with the immediate problem.' The immediate problem for Patsy was what she was going to do until Monday evening. She stared round the kitchen. She could clear out the big cupboard or paint the hall. Four whole days to be got through and three whole nights. Had she taken her Valium this morning, she wondered, shaking pills into her palm just in case. She had always been reckless, driven too fast, swum out too far.

Letters flopped on to the mat and Patsy carried them into the sitting-room. The long white envelope was from her solicitor and hot tears were streaming down her cheeks even before she opened it.

'He shan't have it,' she declared aloud, slowly digesting the first paragraph. Mark wanted a divorce. She already knew that since her solicitor had come to OldPlace and explained. No doubt she would be charged extra for the journey and his patience. He had explained too that ultimately Mark could get a divorce whether she consented or not. Let him wait for *ultimately*.

The second paragraph was so astonishing, so absolutely preposterous, that the print danced dizzily before her eyes. Mark was claiming half the value of OldPlace, on the grounds that he, a qualified architect, had worked on it every weekend for fifteen years, transforming it from a derelict wreck to a highly desirable residence. But Mark had always acknowledged that OldPlace was hers. She had bought it after all, made the down payment with the money from the film rights of *Enchanted Love* plus the money scrounged from her father, alive then and still susceptible to her tears, the only person who had ever really loved her. And when the building society got restive about the mortgage arrears, it was she who had worked far into the night to pay it off.

How could Mark possibly claim it was half his now? How dare he suggest, even through a solicitor, that she sell OldPlace and buy a smaller house, when he had already dealt her a mortal blow? Somehow they had got it wrong. People always said solicitors were the worst part of a divorce, slippery as eels and dead against reconciliation in case it jeopardised their accumulating fees.

Patsy dialled Mark's flat. It was something Harriet said she shouldn't do and her heart was thudding as the phone was lifted the other end.

Late in the Day

'Mark, we must talk,' she whispered but instantly the phone went down and when she dialled again she got the *engaged* tone.

Later she dialled the office. 'Can I speak to Mr Simpson, please?' she inquired in a businesslike voice which should dispel rumours of hysteria.

'I'm afraid he's in a meeting at the moment,' the secretary replied with practised diplomacy. 'Can I take a message?'

'Will you tell him ... tell him ...' The pause while she composed a suitable message lengthened. 'Tell him I *must* see him,' she said but the phone had already gone down the other end. 'Mark,' she whispered. 'How can you do this?'

There was dust like pollen on the walnut tallboy. Mrs Bond did not come on Fridays any more. Thursday was more convenient, she said, gave her a chance with her weekend shopping. She had not been paid for a month and anyway her Tuesday and Thursday mornings were taken up with cups of tea and her role as counsellor, listening and advising, at times with the help of the ouija board. Mrs Bond had worked for Anna years ago. 'Do you want every detail of your personal life all round the village?' Anna scolded and Patsy realised that she did. It was what kept her going, imagining her grief and pain whispering through the local network. Everybody listening.

Rex crept up on the sofa, his tail between his legs because *dogs on the sofa* was something Mark had never allowed.

'Oh, Rex, I sometimes think you're the only creature in the world really loves me,' Patsy whispered as he settled. His eyes circled upwards showing pink edges and his tail flapped twice. 'Friday and Saturday and Sunday and Monday.'

Somebody was standing by the window, a dark figure silhouetted against the sunlight. She knew it was Woodman. He had died in the Black Death and been buried under the barn for seven hundred years. Woodman appearing heralded disaster, they said in the village, but for Patsy disaster had already come.

'Woodman,' she said and she got up then. Woodman had come through the ouija board recently and she had gleaned the details of his stark and hungry life. She knew as much about him as she did about her friends. Woodman *was* her friend. Her only friend.

'Woodman, help me, you must help me. Please ...' Her legs were reluctant to support her and she clutched the back of a chair. 'I shall die if he takes my house. I shall die.'

Geraldine Kaye

The windows of OldPlace were set in the two-foot thickness of cob and stone with white-painted window seats. Outside the espalier pear tree stirred against the crumbling grey of the garden wall as if trying to escape. There was nothing else.

'Help me, Woodman.' Patsy clutched the curtains. 'Somebody help me. Mark is stealing my house.' Her shout rang through OldPlace dissolving into the rafters of the attic which had been a great barn once, wintering cattle. But Woodman did not return, he never came twice in one day. His habits were as familiar to her as the seasonal changes in the garden, apple blossom in April, red tulips guarding the front path in May ... Patsy drew the curtains close and switched on the lamp.

'I wish I was dead,' she confided to the shadowed room. 'I don't know how to live.' Black wings fluttered at the edges of her vision and if she did not take her pills there would soon be great black birds in the low-ceilinged room. She lurched to the little table where the bottles of pills were massed, shaking them turquoise and white and red into her hand and swallowing them down with a mouthful of whisky, stinging and clean. She stood the bottle on the carpet and threw back her head, watching the ceiling and waiting for the wings to clear. Long ago she had stared at the ceiling and listened for a crying child.

The hearth rug which had once been white was grey now, curly like an old sheep. A tractor rumbling down the lane might mean it was four o'clock but she could not be sure. It was easier to watch the ceiling in the curtained twilight from the sofa.

'He shall not take my home as well,' she said lying down and Rex insinuated himself into the softness between her splayed legs with a contented sigh. 'Never.'

The telephone woke her. Patsy sat up. There was a buzzing in her head, her lips felt stiff like thick rubber.

'Hello?' There was no sound but heavy regular breathing, like a husband sleeping in your bed at night. 'Hello.' Waves of nausea ebbed and flowed in her stomach like a hot metallic sea. 'Stratton 663.' The breathing seemed louder now, loud as the wind in the trees outside. Monstrous loud. But if she put the phone down she would be alone.

'Tell me who you are or I shall hang up,' Patsy threatened, adopting the booming voice which her mother had developed for her voluntary work with the Red Cross. Nanny had gone by then

Late in the Day

and Doreen came instead, plump and pink as peppermint rock. 'Elizabeth and Robert,' Lady Violet introduced her children. 'And Patsy, our problem child, tells lies and wets her knickers.' 'Well I never,' Doreen said with a grin. Doreen was her first friend, Patsy thought, the only person who had really loved her.

'I know who you are all right,' whispered the voice, eerily falsetto. 'Mrs M. Simpson.'

'Speaking,' Patsy said. When Doreen left Patsy went to Avon Towers, crying every night. 'Who is that?'

'It's me.' The voice quavered like the noises in her head. Was he drunk, swaying back and forth in some phone box? There was something familiar about it despite the artificial high-pitched tone. 'Shall I tell you what I'm doing?'

'Tell me at once who you are or . . . or I'm going to put the phone down,' Patsy said.

'Aaar . . .' said the phone.

'You need help,' Patsy said after a pause. Nobody could call her priggish or judgmental, she thought.

'You could help me . . . if you was to tell me the colour of your panties.'

'Oh, it's you,' said Patsy. 'Listen . . . there are clinics . . . like Relate . . . which used to be called Marriage Guidance. It's not your fault . . . people get damaged in childhood . . .'

But the phone had gone down.

There were dark leaves all along the ceiling now and each time she fixed her eyes on one it doubled, spinning like a Catherine wheel and dividing into two again. Soon there would be nothing but dark leaves. How could she put her phone down with leaves engulfing the ceiling and a blustery night that might last for ever?

The leaves were turning into black wings, gathering on the ceiling and fluttering so close she could no longer see the cream between them. 'You must cut down, Mrs Simpson, it's a crisis dosage,' Dr Walters said in her head. The whole room was swirling and the table tipped scattering pills across the hearth rug, turquoise and red and white like little jewels. She dropped to her hands and knees, searching and finding, sliding them down her throat in the scalding fire of whisky.

Suttee, Patsy thought, if only she could.

A sibilant whirring came from the receiver. Rex tumbled off the sofa and sniffed it. The pills ought to go back in the bottle but they kept sliding down the slippery brown glass outside instead of inside. Patsy pulled at a cushion and lay down where she was, on the back of the old grey sheep.

It had been difficult for Anna to ask Mr Austin for the afternoon off, when it was her first week working at Brandon Lodge. Despite Francesca's airy confidence, the interview and formalities for her appointment had all had to be gone through and today she had to drive her mother to Bexley House.

'Bring Mother just before five o'clock on Friday if you please.' Mrs Dewar's words had acquired oracular significance. She was after all offering Anna permanent release, a chance to repossess her own life. 'New things lie in front of moving feet,' an African proverb said, Nigerian was it? Were her recalcitrant feet moving at last?

'Then you can go up to her bedroom together,' Mrs Dewar went on, 'unpack her things and arrange them just as she likes. Supper is at six in the dining-room with all the other ladies and Mother can go straight to bed afterwards.'

'At six o'clock?' Anna queried nervously.

'Half past,' said Mrs Dewar. 'They've all had quite enough television by that time.'

It had been a difficult afternoon. Her mother allowed herself to be dressed, even assisted with the recalcitrant stockings. She did not protest or even speak when Anna packed her clothes and the photos of Bunny which was disturbing but also a relief.

'Perhaps you'd wait while Mother has her supper, Mrs Bolt?' Mrs Dewar said, assessing the situation with a practised eye. 'Help her into bed, get her settled for the night.'

'Yes of course . . . if you think . . .'

'One flight of stairs. The lift's over there if you want it.' But her mother was already toiling slowly up.

'Nice room they've given you,' Anna said, standing at the window. Mrs Dewar, having introduced her mother to the nine other old ladies assembled in front of the television next door, had retired downstairs. The bedroom had been partitioned from a larger room and was long and narrow with a washbasin in one corner. A plane tree outside the window gave a greenish tinge to the light, below was a wooden seat and a herbaceous border, rather overgrown. Her father's and Bunny's photos and the tarnished silver cups stood on the chest of drawers. Anna Blu-tacked the school groups to the wall behind. What was Cathy going to say? But why should she relinquish her own conscience in favour of her daughter's judgment? Anna scratched her itching wrists.

A bell tinkled in the passage. Her mother clutched her cane and followed the others into the dining-room. She sat down at one of the small tables, each laid for four, a pilchard and a slither of tomato on every plate and a central dish with a pile of white bread and butter and a bowl of red jam. Two young women in blue nylon overalls distributed cups of tea.

'Come along in, dear, Mrs Jennings is it?' one of them said.

'This all looks very nice,' Anna offered encouragingly as her mother did not reply.

'Always get fish Fridays,' the old lady by her mother remarked. 'Doesn't talk much, shy is she?'

'Fed up, more like,' said the old lady the other side.

By quarter to seven her mother was in bed, her face resolutely turned to the wall.

'Well, goodnight, dear. See you soon,' Anna said. Mrs Dewar met her in the hall downstairs.

'Better wait a bit before you visit,' she suggested. 'Till she's settled. Shall we say three weeks?' Years ago the headmaster at Olly's boarding school had said something similar.

'Sorry she's being a bit difficult,' she said.

'Don't worry, Mrs Bolt, we don't,' said Mrs Dewar with a silvery laugh.

It was a relief to get back in the 2CV which was almost a friend, Anna thought, deliberately disengaging her thoughts from Bexley House as she drove home. Olly was right about the emerald-green wings being easy to identify; he was thoughtful at times. Sometimes she wondered if a nursing training would suit him. She could have driven straight out to Stratton now the evenings were lighter but Patsy's phone had been engaged all day. Quite likely there was a simple explanation but you never knew with Patsy. Anyway she was too tired after Bexley House, exhausted.

She would phone first thing tomorrow morning.

A thundering on the back door woke Patsy. She sat up in the curtained darkness, a sliver of daylight filtering in between. A whirring came from the phone and she dropped it back.

'What is it?' Patsy said as the thundering came again. A turquoise pill, lodged in the neck of her dress, trickled on to the woolly mat. Her head felt drifty but rested. 'Rex?'

The thundering came again and she walked down the passage to the back door.

'You all right?' Anna stared at Patsy, who though uncombed and dishevelled seemed calm. 'Nobody came to the door.'

'Harriet's away for the weekend,' Patsy explained. 'Is it Sunday yet?'

'It's Saturday morning,' Anna said.

'Rex? Where's Rex?' Patsy's voice rose.

They found him behind the sofa. He was lying on his side with four legs stiffly extended. His black fur was cotton-wool soft to their fingers but his body was cold. Rex was dead.

Chapter Nine

'I want to thank you,' Anna said, sitting at Francesca's dining-room table on Sunday a week later, addressing envelopes to all the old girls of Avon Towers they could think of and locate. 'I mean for telling me about the job at Brandon Lodge, getting it for me really.'

She had realised facing Mr Austin and the committee at the interview that that was what Francesca had actually done. In fact there had been some chilliness at first and remarks about Jenny being 'let go'.

'By rights it should be me taking *you* out to dinner, Fran.'

'Nonsense,' Francesca said, looking youthful in pink and white check dungarees with her fair hair swinging loose about her shoulders. 'You got it on your merits, your curriculum vitae. I just told them you were reliable. Besides, what are friends for?'

'You're very generous,' Anna said, reproaching herself for the irritation with Francesca she often felt. 'I mean when I think how I mucked you about, said I didn't want the job . . .'

'You owe me one, don't forget because I shan't,' Francesca said lightly. She pinioned her blonde hair behind her ear and reached for the kitchen knife. 'Started already, haven't I? *My* lunch party end of May for the old girls, and I get *you* to address the envelopes.'

'Least I can do,' Anna murmured. The whole idea seemed pointless but harmless and Francesca was the expert at making life work. She seemed to be organising the English as a Foreign Language summer school virtually unaided.

'Lots of our old girls have done really well,' Francesca said.

'Married rich men, you mean?'

'Well, it's a help. I mean what we really want are *affluent* old girls,' Francesca said.

'Wasn't there a Penelope Mason who landed an oil-rich Kuwaiti?' Anna asked.

'That was Penelope Lee. Miss Snape's girls get everywhere,' Francesca said. 'Must be all those Kipling stories she read us in the evenings. Did I put Patsy on the list? How is she by the way?'

'She *was* a lot better, more herself,' Anna said and fell to wondering what that commonplace but intriguing phrase meant. 'But I'm afraid she's relapsed. Mark wants a divorce and it looks as if she'll have to sell OldPlace and it's upset her.'

'He has a point though,' Francesca said. 'I mean that great house must be worth thousands.'

'But difficult to sell in today's climate. She wants me to see Mark and sort things out. I keep telling her to get herself together and do it but she won't. She's got Harriet living there at the moment.'

'Poor Harriet! Poor Patsy! And that awful mother of hers, Lady Violet, world's biggest snob! Do you think Patsy will get to the lunch?'

'If I fetch her. It's all been too much,' Anna said. At the moment she was phoning Patsy every day. *Talking things through* was the fashionable panacea, listening the obligation of a friend. But Patsy's misery seemed to feed on itself and double with its expression. Anna had begun to wonder if endless listening didn't actually *delay* recovery.

'Is it warm enough to eat outside?' Francesca said, glancing at the window. The clematis Montana hung across the end of the garden like a pink-white screen carefully synchronised with pale pink tulips in the border.

'Oh, let's. I love picnics,' Anna said.

'Picnics?' Francesca's tone indicated this was rather more, a trolley loaded with cold poached salmon, green salad and tiny hot new potatoes, white wine chilled and misting in a silver bucket, underneath strawberries and Cornish cream.

'Fran, it looks marvellous,' Anna said. 'What are we celebrating?'

'Being alive,' Francesca said, tossing back her hair. 'Being lucky us.'

'Don't push it,' Anna said, picking up the silver bucket and following Francesca and the trolley up the concrete ramp. She wondered fleetingly what Mother was eating at Bexley House.

'Just as well you didn't come to lunch with me, Fran, you'd have got baked beans.'

'I always was a good cook,' Francesca said with justified complacency. 'Even Freddy conceded that. I don't think his girl manages anything more exacting than a tin-opener.'

Anna glanced at the backs of the neighbouring houses. Would two single women eating in the garden on their own be regarded with pity or envy by the established suburban wives? The summerhouse at the end of the garden, pale shiny wood like a log cabin, looked new and yet it also seemed vaguely familiar.

'When did you get this? Must have cost the earth.'

'Jack built it with the lads doing the woodwork course,' Francesca said. She parked the trolley and opened the summerhouse door, carrying out two white chairs and a folding table. 'Work experience. I paid for the materials, wholesale of course. If the weather's good we could have the Snape lunch out here.'

'You certainly have the right friends,' Anna said. A curtain of clematis cut off the view both from and into the park behind.

'You ought to have your own house and garden,' Francesca said, sliding the fish slice deftly between the segments of pink flesh. 'I'm always telling you and I shall tell Rupert too if I bump into him. Help yourself to lettuce, the mayonnaise is home-made. Jack's coming tonight.'

'When?' said Anna, glancing nervously over her shoulder. White raspberry blossom unfurled against the weathered fence. 'Tell me if you want me to leave early.'

'Jack won't come in if your car's outside,' Francesca said. 'He's very discreet.'

'Your midnight lover,' Anna said. 'It sounds marvellously romantic.'

'Don't get me wrong,' Francesca said. 'I mean we have this marvellous bed thing going, but we don't have much in common. Nothing at all really.'

'Do men and women ever have much in common?' Anna said. In the end she and Rupert had hardly seemed to speak the same language.

'Except sex,' Francesca said. 'And children? Not that Freddy ever took to his, the boys were my problem from start to finish. Might have been different if he'd seen them born. Have you ever heard of the triple orgasm?'

'Not until now,' Anna said coolly but Francesca was no respecter of reticence.

'Neither had I until Jack. He's got his own key, you know, just slips in, doesn't even switch on the light.'

'What about his wife?'

'That's Jack's problem!' Francesca said, gushing more white wine into Anna's glass.

'But suppose she leaves him or overdoses or something?'

'Tell me about it?' Francesca shrugged. 'People have to take care of their own lives.'

'Well...' But perhaps such considerations were obsolete when marriages were so unstable anyway, Anna thought. Moral codes worked out by the gentry and the church to contain the social dislocation of the industrial revolution had little relevance to e-mail and the Internet, the further dislocation of the technological revolution.

'I reckon I've had more sex since Freddy went than in the whole of my life,' Francesca said. 'Good sex too. Take this last week, do you know how many times I...'

'For God's sake, Fran...'

'You're so uptight, it's not good for you. Everybody needs love, keeps you in your right mind. Do you want to end up like that mad woman in the attic? I had this postcard from Hereward, "Let your childishness express itself and it will disappear."'

'Bhagwan?'

'Think so. Course it'll have to stop if Freddy comes back,' Francesca said, clattering the salmon plates together. 'I've told Jack, well it's only fair. Desmond too...'

'Desmond?' Anna murmured.

'The new DIY instructor. He's putting a fireplace in my sitting-room for the cost of the stone. Stone's not cheap, mind. Strawberries?' She handed Anna the little flower-shaped dish. 'Cream?'

'I don't usually.'

'Spoil yourself, a pinched look is no good at our age. Why are men so unreasonable? There's Freddy living with a girl young enough to be his daughter, as I don't forget to remind him, gets himself in a tizz because I've got a bunch of red roses with long straight stems in a vase in the hall. Well he could see they were hothouse ones. Very expensive. Sauce for the goose, I told him.'

Late in the Day

'Your strawberries are gorgeous,' Anna said.

'I get this extra kick feeding women really well,' Francesca said. 'I'll just take this in and get the coffee.'

'Good on you,' Anna said and lay back, staring up at the beech tree above her head. Women cosseting each other, comforting each other, might well be a regular feature of life as the century drew to its close, she thought. They had to learn to get along just as they had had to at school.

'Cream in your coffee?' Francesca asked, putting a huge dollop in without waiting for an answer. She always made fresh-ground Viennese coffee very strong.

'You know Owen Evans?' Anna said. 'What happened to his wife?'

'The one he left with six children? Or the young one who left him for one of her students at the University of West of England? My God, you never heard such a carry-on, Owen bursting into tears at staff meetings.'

'Perhaps he's the sensitive type?' Anna suggested and wondered why Fran disliked him so much.

'Only about his own feelings,' Francesca said.

A bat flittered in the twilight. 'Your summerhouse reminds me of the one at Avon Towers,' Anna said. 'You remember?'

'Course I do,' Francesca said, thinking of the lawn below the dormitory window, flanked by laurels which half concealed the summerhouse. Miss Snape's drawing-room opened on to the lawn too but the curtains were always drawn at night. 'All summerhouses are more or less the same. I used to meet Willy there, you remember, Willy, he worked in the garden?'

'Course I do, I was your go-between,' Anna said. Creeping out in her dressing-gown, tucking the note under the summerhouse door. Frightened to be seen by Miss Snape but more frightened to be excluded from the clandestine excitement. Heads bobbing at windows, curtains twitching, Francesca's love life was of consuming interest to the whole school.

'Let's go and see it,' Francesca said suddenly.

'See what?'

'Our old school, Avon Towers,' Francesca said, jumping up. 'It's years since I last went.'

'Wild goose chase,' Anna said, reluctant to dip herself into the past and feel the ebbing river of time suck at her feet.

Geraldine Kaye

'I like wild goose chases,' Francesca said, running down the garden. She had felt so restless recently, thinking so much about Willy which really wasn't like her. Was it Hereward's marriage or the estrangement from Hugo, she wondered? She hadn't seen Hugo or Lottie since the business about the abortion. When was the baby due?

It was almost dark now, squares of gold light chequered the neighbouring houses as she backed the car out of the garage. Further down a car was parked on the road, the driver's cigarette glowing in the darkness.

If it was Jack, Francesca took no notice, driving away towards the Downs, skirting them, sliding into the leafy roads of Sneyd Park where large houses still stood in large gardens, rhododendrons and cedar trees black under the moon. It was a long time since Anna had visited this particular area but she had been to an old girls' tea-party once, taken Olly three years old. 'So this is little Oliver?' Miss Snape had said, smiling. 'Perhaps he will be brilliant, you were the most brilliant girl I had through my hands.' Her opalescent eyes were shining with tears. 'I'm so sorry,' Anna said. 'So sorry.' It was five years after her leap to Richard and freedom.

'I thought you could see the top of Avon Towers from here?'

'Trees must have grown.' Francesca slowed as they approached the entrance. By the streetlight they saw the old green board, 'AVON TOWERS, Private School for Girls', propped against the stand of a more imposing black and white board which announced 'PARKSIDE HOUSING ASSOCIATION – Twelve luxury maisonettes with two and three bedrooms and private parking'.

'Whatever have they done?' Francesca wailed, edging slowly into the deeply rutted drive. The laurels had been savagely hacked back, a bulldozer and a cement-mixer stood side by side on the front lawn. All that remained of the nineteenth-century mansion was the rococo front porch and mountains of brick and rubble. 'It's barbarous. Knocking things down, destroying things, it's all anybody knows how to do nowadays. Know what'll happen, we'll be left with no houses and no one who knows how to build them.'

'It wasn't exactly a beautiful building. I suppose it wasn't much use in today's market,' Anna said softly. She felt slightly sick. They got out of the car and circumnavigated the dunes of rubble to the lawn at the back. Away to the left Brunel's suspension bridge hung across the gorge, its steel ribs jewelled with lights.

'The summerhouse *is* just the same as yours,' Anna whispered, trying the locked door and then putting her face to the window. A torn deckchair lay in one corner.

'She caught me *in flagrante delicto*,' Francesca said, feeling the cool dark air soft on her face. 'Well... we were only kissing actually. I know it was the sixties but Willy and me never went all the way. Perhaps that was the trouble.'

'What trouble?' Anna said.

'Miss Snape was so angry,' Francesca said. 'I'd never seen anybody as angry as Miss Snape that night before or since. She shut me in the tower all alone. Willy went to America, got killed in Vietnam. I had a letter from his father. It was awful getting expelled... I mean I know she let me come back when Papa endowed the new library wing... but Willy had gone, sacked of course, and somehow I couldn't settle down after what had happened. I begged Papa to let me leave and he did... but if I hadn't been expelled in the first place I'd never have got to Switzerland and nothing would have been the same.'

'Silver linings,' Anna said and thought of Jack waiting in the darkness. 'Hadn't we better get back?'

Chapter Ten

Francesca, arranging blue irises for the hall, congratulated herself on having achieved a quiet half-hour before her guests, the old girls of Avon Towers, arrived. Relaxation time but in fact she found herself thinking about Jack. He had been quite abrupt when she told him the key to the summerhouse was lost, as if losing the key was her fault. She preferred to finish a relationship first if she had to, it was best for morale.

She placed a final royal blue flower and swivelled round. The fridge was full of cold boned goose and ham, fruit salad and chocolate mousse, and every working surface was occupied with the quiches she had baked yesterday evening, covered bowls of asparagus salad, *champignons à la crème*, rice salad, green salad, cucumber in yogurt.

The day was perfect too, clear and warm. She had considered lunch outside but May was never reliable, an alfresco dream could so easily turn into a nightmare of showers and wet grass. Her living-room with its dining area was quite adequate and besides she wanted everybody to see the new fireplace which added a certain *je ne sais quoi* to the house. Francesca smiled, anticipating compliments flung like confetti.

Everything was ready. Antonio could open the wine when he arrived. It was to avoid that preoccupied hostess look that she had invited Antonio, a seventeen-year-old Italian on the hotel management course, to help her. His father owned two first-class hotels in Rome, so his presence at Brandon Lodge was mystifying, rumours of some problem over a girl easier to credit. He was strikingly handsome with his curling black hair and challenging gaze. In his white jacket he would give the occasion cachet, as well as getting some very good practice.

Late in the Day

The door bell rang as she put the irises on the hall table.

'Oh, it's you!' she said, startled.

'Do you mind?' Freddy said, preparing to take offence. He was standing on the doorstep with two large suitcases and a portable typewriter. His car, a battered Fiesta, was parked at the kerb. They stared at each other, both finding the other's attitude untoward. 'May I come in?'

'Of course, please do,' Francesca said, opening the door wider. She had visualised Freddy's return but never with the exasperation she was experiencing now. The summer school and today's Snape memorial lunch had occupied so much of her mind lately that Freddy was as unfamiliar there as an alien from outer space. 'It's just... I wasn't expecting...'

'I thought you would have realised it was on the cards... from my last visit?' Freddy said.

'Well, of course,' Francesca said, trying to recall the details of his last visit which had been a month ago. Freddy sometimes came for Sunday lunch which *the girl* didn't cook and occasionally they spent the afternoon in bed afterwards. But surely it hadn't been one of those occasions?

'It's just that I'm having a lunch-party. Twenty-two Avon Towers old girls.'

'Christ!' Freddy rolled his eyes to the ceiling.

'I had no idea you would be arriving, did I?' Francesca said. She looked at the suitcases which had sat on top of the wardrobe until four years ago. She had stood on a chair to dust them at spring-cleaning time. At least it seemed right that the suitcases should be back.

'Well, it can't be helped,' Freddy said, mollified. 'I'll stay up in the study if it's all the same to you?'

'It'll look rather peculiar, won't it?' Francesca said, wondering if the sudden appearance of Freddy at her elbow after an absence of four years would be less peculiar.

'It's *timetable* time,' Freddy explained.

'I see,' Francesca said. During the weeks when Freddy wrestled with next year's timetable, allowances had always been made for irritability. Probably *the girl*, a young teacher who had come to Freddy's school on teaching practice, was less accommodating. Did that give him the right to drop in unannounced, as if he had been on a weekend fishing trip? She had got used to living on her own. Besides, there was Jack even if the honey-time was over . . . and Desmond . . . and . . .

'Your car's rather in the way, I mean there'll be fifteen vehicles here by about twelve.'

'No chance you could cancel?' Freddy said, studying the name-badges on the hall table. There was a wary expression in his eyes, hazel eyes she had once called the colour of catkins. 'No, I suppose not.'

He glanced at his watch and started up the stairs, the suitcases scraping the paintwork.

'Would you like some coffee?' Francesca called after him as he disappeared into the study. She had already tidied the bedroom and Freddy couldn't know the blue toothbrush was Jack's. The front door bell rang again.

'Oh, Antonio!' Francesca said, seizing his hands. Freddy had often criticised her emotionalism. In the early days of marriage she had thrown plates. 'My husband has just come back after four years.'

'Oh, oh, oh!' Antonio said, squeezing her hands gently. His English was limited but his eyes were eloquent. Italians really liked women, Francesca thought, so few Englishmen did.

'Please will you do something for me?' she whispered.

'Si, si, anything.' *Would you open the wine boxes* was what Francesca had meant to say but instead she burst into tears.

Anna parked the 2CV by the barn. Driving to Stratton to fetch Patsy was the only way of getting her to Francesca's lunch and going out, seeing old friends, would be good for her, surely.

'Hello!' she called, walking in the back door of OldPlace and starting up the stairs. 'I knew you wouldn't be ready.'

Patsy was sitting on her bed in a black nylon slip, several dresses discarded beside her.

'I haven't got a thing to wear,' she said. 'Mark says I've got to sell OldPlace.'

'I know, you told me. Dare say you'll be able to work something out,' Anna said but Patsy went on staring as if she hadn't heard. Her hair showed two inches of grey at the roots.

'Are you going to see Mark for me?' she said.

'More to the point if you saw him,' Anna said. 'You've got to start sticking up for yourself, Patsy. Divorce isn't the end of the world. Now you can do just what you like.'

'But I don't *want* to do anything without Mark,' Patsy said.

'You never used to be so wet and sorry for yourself,' Anna said. 'Come on, wear your blue?'

Patsy raised her arms like a child as Anna slipped the blue dress over her head. 'I killed Rex,' she said.

'That's nonsense, he was an old dog with a weak heart.'

'He swallowed thirty Valium at least and a . . .'

'Oh, do shut up, we're going to be late,' Anna interrupted, burrowing in the cupboard. 'Have you got any white sandals?'

'Where are we going?' Patsy said.

'Francesca, after all this time. My dear, I'd have known you anywhere.' Soft arms folded round her in a rustling ambience of Chanel No. 5 and Quelques Fleurs. She had never been kissed so many times. 'And what a sumptuous spread!'

'I'm expecting Penelope Tabili,' Francesca said, visualising a really expensive plaque, green Italian marble with gold-leaf lettering. Penelope's marriage to a Kuwaiti oil magnate had made headlines in the national papers. Nearly all the name-tags had already been collected and hats, petalled and feathered, dipped and danced round the room in a private ballet. Brims were some protection from prying eyes and the unspoken question, 'Do I look as old as you?' One woman in a pale blue picture-hat had a woollen dog tucked under her arm.

Antonio circled expertly with white and rosé wine.

'Did you ever see anything so handsome? Is he one of Francesca's boys?'

'Whatever *do* you mean?' a high-pitched giggle.

Francesca smiled and went on smiling. So far she had no recollection of any face. Instead the moment of her expulsion filled her head, 'Francesca Alexander, there is no place at Avon Towers for a girl like you,' Miss Snape had said at morning prayers. '*Go!*' The assembled school had uttered an agonised moan for the real-life romance of Francesca and Willy, acted out with kisses each evening before their peeled eyes.

'What lovely eats, Francesca, when can we start?'

'Not everyone's here yet. Have another drink?' Francesca said. 'Antonio?'

* * *

'Where are we going?' Patsy said for the third time.

'Francesca's lunch in memory of Miss Snape,' Anna said. How many times would she have to say it? 'Out at Combe Dingle.'

'But wasn't she expelled?' Patsy said.

'Well... not exactly,' Anna said, wondering if taking Patsy was such a good idea. 'She came back for one more term, didn't she? I dare say we'll eat in the garden.'

'What garden?' Patsy said.

'Here's to Miss Snape. I was frightened of her actually. Bit of a dragon!'

'Me too. Did you know they'd pulled the school down?'

'But I saw a girl with a tasselled school cap last week.'

'Probably got it from the Oxfam shop.'

'What awful cheek!'

'Perhaps we may explore your lovely garden, Fran?'

'Please do,' Francesca said. 'And the summerhouse...'

'What have we come for?' Patsy said. The road outside was blocked with cars, an excited buzz came from the house.

'Have a name-badge, "Mrs Patricia Simpson",' Anna said, pinning it to Patsy's dress. It was a moment's respite before entering Francesca's chatter-filled living-room.

'But whose house *is* this?' Patsy was saying as the party flowed out into the hall, surrounding them.

'I remember you, at least I think I do.' A woman in a pale blue picture-hat peered tentatively at Anna. 'I'm Elfrida Bantock. It must be nearly thirty years?'

'Don't let's work it out,' Anna said and nervous laughter tinkled round her.

'How very nice to see you, Patsy dear,' Francesca said, embracing her.

'My dog Rex is dead,' Patsy said. Anna moved out of earshot, abdicating the role of keeper, besides Patsy might do better without her. The women already arrived were about their vintage. Had they come because they lived in Bristol or was there a time when school days became interesting again?

'Wine, signora,' Antonio suggested at her elbow.

'When can we start on your gorgeous spread, Francesca? I'm dying of hunger,' said a kingfisher-blue toque.

Late in the Day

'I'm afraid we have to wait for Penelope Tabili,' Francesca said standing protectively in front of the table, happy to postpone the decimation of her work of art.

'Oh, isn't she cruel?' the blue toque said, mock-rebellious.

'Who is this Penelope Tabili?' somebody whispered.

'Wasn't she Penelope Lee, buck teeth and good at lacrosse?'

'Surely *she* didn't marry an oil-rich sheik?'

'Penelope won't be long,' Francesca explained. 'But she's on all sorts of committees. Have another drink while we're waiting. Antonio?'

'Si, si.'

'You won't remember me but you remember Fido,' said Elfrida Bantock, presenting the woolly dog's paw. 'Shake hands.'

'I can't say I do,' Anna said, catching sight of terrified eyes under the picture-hat brim.

'He's a nightdress case,' Elfrida said, revealing his zip. 'We were only allowed a woolly animal at Avon Towers if it was a nightdress case. Mummy bought him specially and he remembers Anna Jennings who threw him out of the dormy window.'

'I certainly don't remember that.' Anna smiled wanly and circled away, subsiding into an easy chair.

'Of course it's a tactical error sitting down,' somebody said from an adjacent chair. 'You lose the initiative.'

'I've lost it anyway,' Anna said. 'Two glasses of wine on an empty stomach.'

'Olivia Porter,' her neighbour said. She was fortyish, slim in a pale grey suit, beautiful grey shoes and a sage silk blouse. 'Why are you looking so thoughtful?'

'I was wondering how many of us were divorced,' Anna said and felt betraying blood rise in her cheeks. 'The victim look?'

'How can you tell?' Olivia said. 'Personally it was trying to be a perfect wife victimised me. Now my married friends envy me.'

'I can see they might,' Anna conceded. 'The woman with the woolly dog, do you think she's married?'

'Obviously,' Olivia said. 'No woman with her own life to make would bother with that Fido routine. Besides, she's got that got-to-get-his-dinner look.'

'You're sure?' Anna laughed, exhilarated by the ease with which they had established a rapport but not quite convinced.

'Sure I'm sure! And single women are more competent. How

many married women can change a wheel or make out an income tax form? Far too many go straight from depending on mother to depending on husband and never learn to trust their own judgment. It's like skating or swimming: learn when you're small or you miss out altogether. Mind you, independence is scary!'

'Certainly scares me,' Anna said suddenly. 'But isn't that sort of competence more to do with doing a job than being married? Do you live in Bristol?'

'Keep a flat here as a base. Work overseas for the BBC.'
'Like Kate Adie?'
'Sort of,' Olivia said. 'What do you do?'
'Typing, word processing. I dropped out of university.'
'You could drop back, finish at the Open University?'
'Suppose I could,' Anna said doubtfully.

In the garden Elfrida Bantock had Patsy penned against the summerhouse. 'You write books, somebody told me?'

'Do I? I think I used to,' Patsy said.

'Patricia Simpson,' Elfrida said, examining Patsy's name-tag. 'Can I get you out of the library?'

'Oh, Francesca, when can we eat?'

'Rosé or white, signora?' Antonio's attention to empty glasses was assiduous and his eyes gleamed with mischief. Was he trying to get everybody drunk, Francesca wondered? Hats at rakish angles and two glasses broken already, in a minute twenty-one inebriated and hungry women might be unmanageable.

'Do you think this waiting is a good idea?' Anna whispered close to her ear as Patsy came in from the garden with a pinkish rosé stain down her blue dress.

'Whose party is this?' she was saying. The phone rang.

'Francesca Smith's party. Have some nuts?' Anna said.

'I don't like nuts,' Patsy said.

'Bad news,' Francesca clapped her hands for silence. 'Penelope Tabili can't come, so we'll get on with lunch.'

'Oh goody.' There was a surge towards the buffet table.

'Who is Penelope Tabili anyway?'

'Penelope Mason, dark hair and a squint, good at maths, you remember?'

'Looks like she got her sums right.'

Late in the Day

'Whose house is this?' Patsy asked as Anna steered her into the queue by the table.

'Hush,' said Anna. 'Francesca Smith's.'

'The shopkeeper's daughter?' Patsy said. 'Whoops!' A slice of roast goose slid to the floor. Fortunately Francesca, unable to witness the desecration of her laden table, had retreated to the kitchen.

'What are you doing?' she said to Antonio who was opening and shutting drawers staccato.

'Traycloth for signor,' Antonio said, slapping a tray on the kitchen table. 'Signor eat lunch?'

'Oh, Antonio, how thoughtful!' Francesca said. What a marvellous hotel manager he would be, so light on his feet.

'I think we all want to thank Francesca for this marvellous if sad occasion,' Elfrida Bantock began half an hour later. The food had had a calming effect. Patsy was asleep.

'Yes, yes, speech, Francesca, speech.'

'I'm afraid I'm no good at speeches,' Francesca said, charmingly pink. 'And Arabella Snape is our guest of honour. We're all Miss Snape's *gels*, aren't we? I want you all to drink . . .' Francesca paused as smiles modified for the solemnity of the moment. 'To Miss Snape who did her best for us all.'

'To Miss Snape . . .' a sibilant murmuring.

'As you know I have started a memorial fund,' Francesca went on briskly. 'So many of us want to commemorate Miss Snape's life, especially now the school has closed. I want to hear all your ideas at our next meeting in October which hopefully Penelope Tabili will be able to attend.'

There was enthusiastic clapping.

'Will there be a luncheon in October?'

'Poor Francesca . . .'

'But I was head girl,' Patsy said waking and extricating herself from her chair with some difficulty. 'Miss Snape said I was the best head girl she ever had.'

'Perhaps you should lie down for a bit,' Anna whispered, grasping Patsy's arm and propelling her towards the stairs. Five minutes later she lay on Francesca's large off-white bed with her eyes closed.

'Promise you won't leave me,' she whispered.

'I promise,' Anna patted her hand, irritation overlaid by

tenderness. Patsy *had* been an outstanding head girl, a lively young woman, a successful writer of romantic novels, a loving wife and mother until Mark's leaving turned her into a zombie.

'Please go and see Mark for me?' she whispered.

'Well...' Anna said.

'What's going on in here?' Freddy's expression relaxed as he recognised her. 'Oh, Anna, I wondered what was happening.'

'Don't we all?' Anna said, suddenly angry. 'You drop in and out like a yoyo, don't you know the rules?'

Freddy's smile faded. 'What rules?'

'*The* rules,' Anna said loudly. 'Rules which establish moral law. Because it's *legal* to discard your wife of twenty years for some teenage bimbo...' Anna was aware of Patsy's round black eyes '... doesn't mean it's *right*. Look at the miners, striking to maintain a job which is intolerable anyway, and the whole world weeps. Divorced women lose job, income and often their home in one swoop but who sends *us* food parcels?'

Anna dropped on to the bed. If she was being ridiculous, she didn't care. A burst of clapping came from the garden.

'Christ!' Freddy's eyes darted to the window like scared mice. He picked up his suitcases and made for the stairs.

'What are you doing here, Dad?' Hugo said, arriving at the front door. Behind him a van blocked the road.

'Getting out fast as I can,' Freddy said. 'They're raving bonkers.' He dumped the cases into his car. 'Get that bloody van out of it.'

'Did I do that?' Anna murmured, coming slowly downstairs as Freddy drove away. The party had moved out to the garden; only she and Antonio had witnessed his departure.

'Signor come, signor go,' Antonio said. 'No comprendo.'

'I want to see my mother,' Hugo said, coming back up the path with the rocking-horse carried between him and the van driver. It was painted black and white now with a thick grey mane and scarlet harness. Only extremity, threat of eviction and Lottie and the children wailing like banshees had got him there.

'I fetch,' Antonio said gleefully.

'Hey up,' said the van driver as they heaved the rocking-horse over the threshold. 'See you then, mate.'

'Hugo?' Francesca said. She turned quite pale. It was four months since she had seen him. 'The rocking-horse...?'

Late in the Day

'I need four hundred pounds for mortgage arrears, Ma,' Hugo said. 'Bastards are threatening to chuck us out.'

'Why didn't you ask your father?' Francesca asked partly for Anna's benefit.

'I know he wouldn't give it to us, don't I?' Hugo said.

'Four hundred?' Francesca said, pleased to buy this reprieve. She sat and wrote the cheque. 'How's Lottie?'

'Doing her nut about going to a bed-and-breakfast place. Crazy, I mean the cost to the tax-payer? You just bought my rocking-horse, Ma.'

'It's beautiful,' Anna murmured, setting it in motion.

'All my own unaided work,' he said with a smile so reluctant it was almost a grimace. 'Bye.' He disappeared down the road.

A few minutes later Anna collected Patsy. Downstairs Francesca stood at the front door, the first departures had precipitated a general exit.

'Goodbye, goodbye.' Francesca waved as they drove away.

'Signor not eat food,' Antonio said, coming down with the untouched tray. 'Signor gone. When come back?'

'When he gets sick maybe?' Francesca sat down on the sofa.

'Antonio get English cup of tea for you?'

'Thanks,' Francesca murmured. She was lying down when Antonio put the tray of tea beside her. He had taken off his white waiter's coat. She had never had anyone as young as this, she thought fleetingly.

'Washing-up finish,' he said. 'Antonio go now?'

'Please don't go, Antonio,' Francesca said.

PART THREE
Summer

Chapter Eleven

In the summer everything seemed better, spirits rising with the longer daylight, green leaves and bright cottons. Francesca allowed the pain and disappointment of not being allowed to take part in Hereward's wedding to slide away behind her. Antonio was *now* and she lived in the present. The lunch for the Snape memorial fund had covered costs but made no profit and for the moment her days were fully occupied with organising the English Language summer school, her nights with Antonio. He had proved extravagantly jealous and she was forced to break finally with Jack to avoid mayhem. Her four hundred pounds had bought reprieve for Hugo's house and she resumed her family visits with armfuls of garden vegetables for the children and the burgeoning Lottie.

Patsy was better too. The threat to OldPlace had focused her and she made a serious attempt to control her drinking and get off her pills. She started to go out, short walks down the lane and then short drives to the village. Mrs Bond, paid up to date by Harriet, was reassigned to cleaning. Anna phoned less often but was not allowed to forget her 'promise' to get in touch with Mark.

Anna found Brandon Lodge livelier than Brewsters. The stream of life certainly flowed through its noisy corridors, and the problem of her mother was safely if not happily resolved. On her first evening visit, her mother, already in bed, turned her face to the wall and refused to speak. How long was this silent protest going to go on, Anna wondered? It made visiting a pointless ordeal. But at least Cathy had congratulated her on the new job and if she was pregnant did not mention it. Pottery classes were over but Anna still babysat on Thursdays, so they could go out.

Changing things, taking the initiative, got easier, Anna

realised, in fact it was alarming the way you went into a roll. She had certainly displayed initiative over Bexley House, shouting at Miss Miles on the phone in a quite unjustified way. However the result had been a single room unexpectedly *found* for her mother. But were the other changes in her life things she actually wanted? It was Francesca who had engineered the job at Brandon Lodge for instance.

Now Anna was eager for further changes, but what did she really want? She was tired of negotiating her life round Mr Phillips's small tyrannies, tired of letting Rupert's reluctance to move continue indefinitely. She wrote to him on the office word processor suggesting they meet to discuss the sale of Rose Lodge. Then she made an appointment to see Dr Wilding about the rash on her wrists. No doubt he thought all skin problems were stress-related just as Rupert had, but despite her job and her mother's improved situation the rash was no better.

Dr Wilding studied her wrists before proceeding to judicious questions. 'I could give you some ointment but a reaction like this suggests...' His eyes met hers. He was a handsome man in a well pressed lovat suit. A GP had to look impervious to life's reverses to inspire confidence, Rupert always said. 'It suggests things are not quite right,' Dr Wilding went on. 'The quality of your life depends on you, Mrs Bolt. Only you can change what's... not quite satisfactory.'

'How do you mean?' Anna said, blushing.

'Do you get out enough, meet people? Got to give us shy fellows a chance, you know?' He tore the prescription off with a wink and a flourish. Anna smiled weakly. Did all medical heads indulge the fantasy of the healing penis? Being patronised was irritating, but she supposed he meant to be kind.

Anna had come to depend on the kindness of strangers.

She allocated Saturday, the only possible day now she was working, to the dire task of cleaning up her mother's flat, asking Briony, who had finished finals, to help. Was she making a point, Anna wondered, or was it just that Briony could cope?

'Mr Magic and all, how efficient!' Briony said, turning round to the large box in the back of the 2CV which was piled up with spray cleaners, bleach, plastic bags and a variety of cloths and paper towels.

'Clearing out my mother's flat is not exactly a fun day!' Anna said as they drove towards Hotwells, admitting to herself that buying such a quantity of new cleaning stuff had been oddly enjoyable. 'Just something which has to be done.'

'Yeah-yeah,' Briony said.

'I ought to have done it before, but I was afraid Mother might insist on coming back. Fortunately she hasn't, well she won't speak to me at all actually,' Anna sighed. 'I sometimes think I lack compassion.'

'Leave it out! Scolding yourself is boring!' Briony said. 'I wasn't expecting a fun day. Anyway how is the old boot?'

'Not too bad but I don't care much for that expression,' Anna said. 'At Bexley House it's all so regimented, they make them all get dressed every day, probably good for Mum. I'd better take her some more clothes. She's talking to the others now but she stops as soon as I appear.'

'Lets you out then, doesn't it?'

'Mrs Dewar thinks it'll pass. At first I just hovered about, then I got silver polish and buffed up Bunny's cups. Honestly they look dazzling.' Anna caught Briony's eye in the driving mirror and smiled too but her eyes felt prickly. 'What I mean about compassion is I don't *want* to visit, I have to *make* myself.'

'You'd have to be nuts to *like* visiting somebody in an old people's home who refuses to talk to you, even if she is your mother. Let alone doing a shitty job like cleaning out her flat,' Briony said. 'Watch me when Mum goes gaga!'

'Harriet's been very good. Have you been in touch?'

'Yeah-yeah. She carried on about some guinea pig.'

'In Gambia they manage to love their old people, give them the best food and everything,' Anna said.

'Children should get the best food,' Briony said. 'Africa's the pits if you ask me ... genocide and military dictators with beds of gold. Bet they wish for old colonial times.'

'Bet they don't,' Anna said.

She stopped the car by her mother's flat and sat gathering strength. The dingy grey of the net curtains still reproached but that was the next tenant's problem now.

'Come on,' Briony said, hauling the box of cleaning stuff from the back.

Anna could feel the beat of her heart as she approached the front door. Unlocking it felt like a violation; for an instant she expected her mother to be standing there with her silver-knobbed cane raised. The air smelt stale, the apples in the blue and white bowl had turned brown as conkers.

Briony sniffed. 'What's that frightful pong?'

'Afraid I didn't clear the food out,' Anna said, dropping weak-kneed into the wicker chair. 'Forgot.'

'Let's get organised,' Briony said. Her voice was firm but unexpectedly sweet in the gloom of the half-drawn curtains. She struggled with the sitting-room window which stuck at first, not having been opened for years. Anna heard her mother's voice, 'Nothing but petrol fumes and muggers.'

'Chuck all the food in the dustbin,' Briony went on. 'Then we'll put the maggoty sofa out on the pavement and you phone the cleansing department to remove it while I do the kitchen.'

'Right,' Anna said, galvanised to action.

By midday the worst of the clean-up was over. Bathroom and kitchen scrubbed, smelling powerfully of bleach. A suitcase of clothes stood inside the front door ready for Bexley House, flanked by a plastic bag for the Oxfam shop and three more for the dustbin. The sofa stood up-ended outside the window, making room for the bed which had also proved maggot-infested.

Briony hoovered the sitting-room, her head turbaned in a duster. The small spare room had been a repository. Anna knelt in front of her mother's bureau. In childhood she and Bunny had never been allowed to touch it. Now she must work her way through the layers, Bunny's school reports, her notes from Newnham, birth certificates. At first she glanced at each and tore it across, photographs of unknown children, Father's birth certificate, letters from the bishop.

Anna stopped reading, extracted her mother's vital documents and piled the rest into plastic bags in handfuls. The riding switch her mother had beaten her with lay at the back. 'You're a very naughty girl,' Mother had chanted as she switched, her round eyes simulating fury. Father was visiting round the parish, Father was CND and hated violence. 'Give you the stick, did she?' Mrs Robb said cleaning next day, her eyes curious. 'Our dad give it to us reglar, didn't do us no harm.'

Anna tried to snap the switch in half but only succeeded in bending it. Her throat felt dry and tight as she thrust it into the bag. Was her switching mother, symbol of retribution for naughty

Late in the Day

girls, the reason she didn't know what she wanted, hadn't the confidence to decide? Unfinished business, Miss Miles said, but it was altogether too late to finish it now.

At midday she bought filled croissants from the delicatessen up the road and she and Briony climbed out through the window to the neglected back garden, long grass and overgrown shrubs.

'People upstairs won't like it,' Anna said, glancing at the windows as she peeled the plastic off her croissant. 'Seem to think the garden's their private domain. What about you, love, applied for anything?'

'Give us a break!' Briony lay in the grass. 'Just done finals. Anyway there aren't any jobs, except nude modelling.'

'Could you do an MA? Everybody needs a purpose.'

'Wouldn't get a grant. I might go abroad,' Briony said, staring at the sky.

'Lucky you!' Anna said.

'Loads of people your age do Voluntary Service Overseas!' Briony's eyes came back to her. 'Why don't you have a go? Meantime move into this clean and salubrious flat?'

'Belongs to the church,' Anna said. 'I had to tell them Mother had gone into Bexley House, they want it for the next clergy widow.'

'But if you just moved in, it'd take them months to get you out,' Briony said, experienced in squatter law. 'Quite likely they wouldn't bother. You're a clergy orphan, aren't you? Bet if I could get your sad story in the *Evening Post* . . .'

'Are you quite unscrupulous?' Anna said.

'Survival skills,' Briony said. 'What you need nowadays.'

'Shall we have a drink later?' Briony seemed reluctant to part though it was already after six.

'Well, I need a bath and I'm very tired,' Anna said.

'But you can't stay in Saturday night. See you at the Beagle nine o'clock?'

Leaving the loaded car parked in Cliftonwood overnight was asking for trouble. Anna dragged the case to the front door.

'Been busy, looks like?' Mr Phillips's voice came from the basement.

'Just clearing out my mother's flat.'

'Sad!' he said leaning over the banisters to watch her ascending legs.

The house was quiet. Anna made for the bathroom. She opened the bath cubes Olly had given her last Christmas and lay down in the jasmine-scented water. Footsteps and a tap on the bathroom door.

'Got to be over Sneyd Park eight o'clock. Must have a bath,' Miss Baker said. 'Leave us a bit of hot water?'

The Beagle on Saturday night was busy. Anna carried her drink to a corner, studied a bull-fighting poster through the smoky pall. Briony's entrance minutes later caused a lull. She had washed her hair and threaded it with blue glass beads.

'I like it!' Anna said. 'What you drinking?'

'Spritzer, if you're paying,' Briony said, grabbing a table as Anna returned. 'What's wrong with your wrists?'

'I went to see Dr Wilding. He gave me this ointment stuff, and said . . . well he said I ought to get myself a man,' she added with a self-deprecating smile.

'Flagrant sexism and you can't even see it?' Briony fumed.

'I suppose . . .' Anna murmured, uneasily aware that despite her irritation she had been flattered by Dr Wilding's view of her chances. She had dreamed of Rupert since.

'Telling you you need a good screw. Yuck!' The beads swung like spaniel's ears as she glared at the next table.

'Do hush up,' Anna whispered. Owen Evans sitting at the bar, was gazing fixedly at Briony.

'What bugs me is you're so conditioned to being treated as a second-class citizen you don't even notice,' Briony said.

'We're pioneers, your mother and me, first generation where half of all marriages break up . . .'

'That why Mum starts falling to bits?'

'People don't choose the way they react to trauma,' Anna said. Owen had left his stool and was pushing towards them.

'Piss off,' Briony said distinctly.

'Excuse me. I think we met somewhere?' Owen swayed and landed in the chair between them. 'May I join you ladies?'

'Christ,' Briony said. 'Who *is* this?'

'May I introduce Owen Evans. We both work at Brandon Lodge,' Anna said.

'Get you a drink?' Owen levered himself on to his feet.

'No way,' Briony said.

'How kind of you,' Anna smiled. 'Half of shandy, please.'

'Are you sure?' He seemed unaware of Briony's hostility.

'I'm going,' Briony said.

'Going?' His face crumpled with disappointment.

'Do you have to be so rude?' Anna said as he went to the bar.

'Makes me sick when you can't go into a pub without some old git trying to buy you a drink.'

'Isn't that ageist?' Anna said. 'And sexist.'

'Here we are,' Owen said, depositing crisps and pickled egg, grinning with delight at his own munificence.

Briony jumped up. 'I'm picketing at the Watershed.'

'What's the film?' Anna said.

'Forget but it's degrading to women. Cheers!'

'Lovely girl,' Owen said sorrowfully as the door slammed. '*You* might as well eat the pickled egg.'

'Well...' said Anna who had never cared for pickled eggs. 'Thanks for the shandy.'

'You got her telephone number?'

'Sorry.' Anna shook her head.

'Bet you bloody have,' Owen muttered, sinking his full red mouth into his beer.

Anna glanced at the door and planned her exit.

'My wife just left me,' he said suddenly. 'For one of her students. What she see in a fucking twenty-year-old?'

'I'm sorry,' Anna said as heads turned curiously. How could she leave when his eyes were brimming with tears?

'Sorry she says... Jesus Christ!' He flung back his head with a loud neigh of laughter. The barman clicked his tongue.

'I'd better be going,' Anna said.

'No.' He grabbed her wrist. 'Something to show you.' He pulled a tattered exercise book from his pocket. 'My poems. Have another drink?'

Why didn't she just walk out, Anna wondered, as he lurched away with the glasses. A violent altercation broke out at the bar. She could see the curly fringe of Owen's head as he was seized and manhandled along the passage by two young men.

'And don't come back, sir, you're not welcome here,' the barman shouted. 'Persona non grata. Got it?'

'Oh, do be careful...' Anna grabbed the exercise book and hurried down the passage. The young men were coming in again.

'Animal,' one of them said, swaggering a bit.

'Are you all right?' Anna said. Owen sat on the pavement.

'Blood.' He dabbed his forehead. 'They assaulted me and you're a witness. I shall ring my solicitor.'

'Whatever did you say?'

'What do I ever say?' Owen shook his head ruefully, staring down the street, still brimstone yellow in the evening light. 'Banned from pubs all over Bristol. Where's my car?'

'You can't possibly drive,' Anna said. 'Look, you'd better come back with me. I'll make you some coffee.'

It was further than she realised and Owen leaning on her shoulder was more drunk. Students in jeans spilled from doorways, beer in hand, rock music thumped from open windows. Somehow she got him upstairs. Fortunately Mr Phillips didn't seem to be about.

'You'd better have coffee with lots of sugar,' she said, putting the kettle on. Give a drunk coffee and you get a caffeinated drunk, Rupert said, but what could she do? Owen submitted to her dab of antiseptic but, feeling no need to dispel the mood he had expensively purchased, he declined the coffee.

'I really loved that woman,' he said to the furniture.

'I'm sorry,' Anna said but though he gradually sobered his desire to share his grief didn't diminish. She had never known a man so deficient in stiff upper lip. Was it to do with his American origins? 'Divorce is awful,' she said. 'A sort of murder. But you do get over it.'

It was dark when Miss Baker's voice sounded in the street. 'Ciaou.' A car door slammed. Her heels tapped up the stairs.

'Did you say your car was parked in the Mall?' Anna said.

'Chucking out time?' Owen said. 'What about my poems?'

As Anna closed the front door there was a rustle from the basement stairs.

'Oh, Mr Phillips, my friend had a nasty fall. He needed first aid.'

There was no answer, just a faint click.

In Bedminster, Briony curled under her duvet. You had to free yourself from heterosexual conditioning, Joyce had said at the consciousness-raising group, but Briony had to admit she quite like screwing blokes and it seemed well . . . natural.

Natural was a red rag to Joyce, nothing was natural, everything conditioned. You had to think your way through the brainwashing. Briony thought about making love to Joyce and then switched to Susie. It went better with Susie . . . with Jasper better still . . .

Chapter Twelve

Distant church bells announced Sunday. Anna stretched gently, testing discomfort in her back and arms from the final clean-up of her mother's flat the previous day and the disastrous evening at the Beagle.

A faint scratching alerted her, and her eyes went to the door where a square of beige envelope had appeared. The note on lined paper in Mr Phillips's spidery handwriting gave her the month's notice to which she was entitled, and hoped she would leave the flat as clean and tidy as she had found it.

Anna dressed slowly. Should she go down to his basement and try to explain? Wasn't it high time she moved anyway? She was making coffee when she heard a knock on the front door and, peering out, saw a circlet of grey hair and a double bunch of freesias.

'I've come to apologise,' Owen Evans said as she opened the front door. His hands pressed together in an attitude of prayer. 'Mea culpa, please accept this small token of my esteem. I think I had a little too much to drink last night.'

'You certainly did,' Anna agreed. 'You'd better come in.' His eyes were merry as he followed her upstairs, her plaster still on his forehead, a naughty satyr with an irritating lack of hangover. Evidently his body was used to dealing with excess alcohol.

'Thank you for being so kind, so understanding, so . . .' Owen seemed to be enjoying himself. Did he think women found barefaced effrontery in men irresistible, Anna wondered and then wondered if she did.

'My landlord has just given me notice,' Anna interrupted, handing him the note.

'What did I do?' Owen moaned. 'I'm a Jeremiah . . . but I

Late in the Day

mean we didn't *do* anything, did we?'

'Quite,' Anna said. 'Would *you* like to tell my landlord that? He's rather particular ... and male visitors aren't allowed at night. It's his house and his rules OK.'

'What about gross infringement of your personal liberty?' Owen demanded. 'Where is he? Let me explain.'

'Please do,' Anna said. 'You'll find him in the basement.'

Five minutes later voices sounded in the hall and Owen tapped on Anna's door.

'Crisis over!' he said, eyes bright with triumph. In the right mood he was charismatic, Anna thought. 'Mr Phillips quite understands I wasn't myself, this crack on the head. You can stay after all.'

Anna's gaze followed his round the room and suddenly she knew she didn't want to stay. Couldn't. She was sick of Mr Phillips, his intrusive curiosity and his power to throw her out, sick of being manipulated. She could move into her mother's flat and she would.

'Aren't you going to offer me a coffee?' Owen said.

Anna glanced at her watch. 'I've things to do.'

'I was going to ask you out to lunch,' Owen said. 'We could really get to know each other, I could tell you about myself.'

'You already did,' Anna snapped, sick of listening to other people's problems. Enough was enough.

Owen blinked. 'Hey, wisecracks so early in the morning, what a termagant! Bet you're amazing when you're really angry. I go for passionate women, always have. How come you haven't told me anything about *yourself?*'

'Chance'd be a fine thing,' Anna said.

She was never quite sure of the morality of what she did next. But she had to do it while the roll lasted. She phoned Briony ostensibly to borrow a campbed and Briony arrived within the hour with two young men, Ringo and Jasper. Their ancient van transferred Anna with her cases, mobile phone, her geraniums and even the freesias from the streaky pink flat in Cliftonwood to her mother's flat in Hotwells in under an hour.

Anna was so exhilarated by this irrevocable action that she insisted they detour to Sofa, a charity which supplied secondhand furniture at low prices, and bought herself a bed and settee. Briony topped this with a large bunch of Sweet William and the young men supplied cans of beer for an impromptu house-warming.

It had all been so easy, so trouble-free, she thought, as she composed a suitably pusillanimous letter of explanation to her new landlords that evening. Perhaps thinking about things just complicated them. Action was what mattered.

Later she phoned Olly and explained the new situation.

'Poor old Grandma,' he said. 'Bet she's fed up?'

'She's fed up with me but I'm sure she'd like to see you,' Anna said. 'I've got a campbed and a settee if you want to come down. Anyway what's new with you?'

'Had to take some wine down to Pinewood Studios last week,' Olly said.

Anna took a deep breath. 'What about your A-levels?'

'Took one,' Olly admitted. 'Overslept the other one. Anyway don't know why I bother.'

'It's important, education, finishing what you started,' Anna said. 'You don't want to drive a van all your life?'

'Look who's talking,' Olly said.

Since the journey to Brandon Lodge involved two buses, Anna drove herself the two miles each morning. The job was easy enough once she had mastered the office routines and she enjoyed the house itself, large and gabled, built a century ago by a coal owner from Winterstoke and planted round with yews, cedars and ilex. How come people had such confidence in property and the permanence of the social order then, she wondered? Behind the house was a conglomeration of single-storey classrooms accumulated during the last twenty years and a distant sports field. It was a lively, noisy place to work.

She saw less of Francesca than she had imagined since Fran seemed to be responsible for much of the day-to-day life of the college, as well as organising the English Language summer school, necessary, Fran said, to cover the cost of repair to the roof in these grant-cutting times.

By now Anna was on nodding terms with most of the lecturers and chatting terms with Owen Evans.

One Monday morning she got in touch with Mark and they arranged to meet for an early evening drink.

So far so good, Anna decided cautiously.

Late in the Day

* * *

Harriet sat in the head's office and stared at the telephone. It was half past three, and an intrusive yellow sun poured in through the wide open window. Outside children streamed towards the gate waving paintings and coloured school bags.

'Sorry to keep you like this, Harriet,' Mrs Gregory said. 'It's just the education department promised to get back to us. I expect they're busy. Aren't we all?'

Harriet smiled bleakly.

'Miss... miss?' A small girl bobbed outside the window, her fingers gripping the sill. 'Will you get the sack, miss?'

'Run along now, Jessie, your mum's waiting,' Mrs Gregory said, moving to close the window as the child scurried away.

Presently the school grew quiet, the only sound the whirr of the vacuum cleaner, the occasional scrape of a chair leg.

'At least we're not expecting an irate parent,' Mrs Gregory said to relieve the tension. 'You can take it from me disruptive children always have exceptionally self-righteous parents. Let's have a cup of tea, shall we?'

'Darren said something about new foster parents?' Harriet said.

'Won't last,' Mrs Gregory said, arranging the cups. 'Give it a week and he'll be back at Fernleigh. That child ought to be in a special school. The times I've suggested it. Bureaucracy. They don't look ahead. Money spent on the child now would be an investment... I mean what does it cost to keep a man in a high-security prison?'

Harriet's eyes filled with tears, not for the guinea pig's scream or the smack she had given Darren, witnessed by the entire playground, but for the whole world and its millions of hungry and distressed children and most of all for herself. Briony said it was politically OK to weep if you felt like it.

Harriet sniffed.

'Oh dear,' said Mrs Gregory. 'Like a chocolate biscuit? It isn't fair, you having to hang about like this. I told them time and again Darren ought to be at a special school. What was he doing to the guinea pig anyway?'

The telephone began to ring.

It was just six o'clock when Anna secured a parking place in Charlotte Street, a minor triumph which winged her step as she hurried down Park Street towards the College Tavern. What was she going to say, she wondered. What were the right words for this situation? Habits of speech, attitudes, seemed to change all the time. What was appropriate behaviour had become as mysterious and random as a pinball machine. Olivia Porter had said single women were more competent, had a better grip on managing their lives. But Anna didn't feel in the least competent and Olivia's answerphone being on seemed to indicate she was away.

At least College Tavern was a good choice, conveniently divided into semi-private wooden cubicles. Mark in his charcoal office suit, tie slightly loosened and nursing a gin and tonic, waved from a corner as she came in the door.

'Anna, it's been a long time and you're looking good. Great gear,' he said, holding her hand longer than was necessary and glancing down at her red and blue trousers. 'What are you drinking?' His eyebrows rose above large, slightly bloodshot grey eyes. 'Gin and tonic?' He had lost a good deal of weight in the five months since they had seen him at the White Hart. Had he seen them? Did he think of that day as the day of his deliverance, she wondered?

'Thanks,' she said and waited for his return, anxious to get the talk on track rather than slip into exchanging social pleasantries. 'I expect you realise this is about OldPlace,' she said as soon as Mark returned with two gins. 'I'm here because Patsy asked me to come.'

'How is she?' he inquired, his voice and the angle of his head suggesting a suitable degree of concern.

'So-so,' Anna said. 'Miserable of course but better than she has been. What did you expect?'

Mark clicked his tongue and sipped his gin. 'Ask a silly question, eh?'

'Quite,' Anna said. 'She asked me to come because well ... you won't talk to her. I mean she's a very vulnerable ... you heard about Rex?'

Mark nodded. 'Briony told me. Poor old chap, it's a shame. Apparently Harriet was away?'

'Young women Harriet's age don't reckon to spend all their time mummy-minding,' Anna said.

'Course not,' Mark said.

'For someone like Patsy, all that verve and sparkle, well it demands an audience, doesn't it?' Anna said.

'Don't I know it?' Mark said.

'I mean it really is difficult for her to be alone,' Anna went on. 'I don't know how to say this, Mark, I'm not blaming you or anything ... but since you left, OldPlace is her whole life, all she's got.' Was that true, Anna wondered? It seemed true but what did you really know about another person? 'I mean it's what keeps her going.'

'I dare say, but what am I supposed to do?' Mark said, smiling and apparently composed.

'I rather thought you'd done it,' Anna said tartly.

He shrugged, 'As a go-between you have to try to see both sides, Anna. I made that house. OldPlace was derelict. I rescued it, nurtured it, loved it like a baby ... and now it's worth megabucks and I need somewhere else to live and the money to buy it. Two of us in Judy's pad is a squash to put it mildly.'

'Tough!' Anna said.

'Come off it, Anna love. *Judgmental* doesn't suit you. What do you think it's been like living with Patsy all those years? What do you take me for? Anyway it's all in the hands of my solicitors now. OldPlace has to be valued and both parties are entitled to half the dosh. That's sex equality, kid, that's the way you wanted it and that's the way the law now sees it.'

'But you've got your profession, the company you started ... Patsy hasn't anything but the house.'

'Architects have been pretty much out of business since the recession. Even now there's very little building going on. Simpson and Cape is deep in the red. Between you and me it's reached the point of no return ...'

'Oh God!' Anna was floundering now. 'But Patsy hasn't any money. She's borrowing off poor Harriet half the time. I mean, say OldPlace is valued at four hundred thousand pounds, how can she possibly pay you half when she hasn't got it?'

'She'll have to sell, won't she? I shan't press for payment right away,' Mark said. 'And she must get a job, she can type, can't she? Bit of hard graft never did anybody any harm, take her mind off herself and her problems.'

'It's not like you to be vindictive,' Anna said, glancing round the bar. Nobody else looked more than thirty. 'Get real, Mark! Patsy is a woman of forty-six with no qualifications and a drink and pill problem, who's going to give her a job if and when the recession really is over? Have a heart.'

'What about her writing? She did very well at one time, money rolling in,' he said, avoiding her eyes. 'Once a writer, always a writer. Had everything on a plate, that's Patsy's problem!'

'But she hasn't written anything for twelve years,' Anna said. 'Who are you trying to kid? Suppose something happened... I mean Rex died of an overdose, Patsy's pills over the floor, how would you feel if...'

'All right, all right.' Mark downed the rest of his gin. The timbre of his voice seemed to alter, perhaps he wasn't as ruthless as he pretended. 'You can be very persuasive, Anna. Twist me round your little finger, you ladies, know what I mean?' She caught his eye and knew he remembered that night, the Robertsons' party. 'Listen, I'm talking right off the top of my head now. Suppose I was prepared to consider...'

'What?'

'Some sort of compromise...' he said slowly. 'If Patsy let me have a bit of the land, say the five acres of old orchard behind the barn and maybe... ten thousand pounds in her own time... then I might consider the offer.'

'What's the point of that?' Anna said. 'You wouldn't have anywhere to live and Patsy hasn't got ten thousand pounds.'

'Don't worry about me,' he said. 'Bit of money we could rake up a mortgage on a bigger flat one way or another. Fact is I don't want to see the poor old thing lose her precious house, do I? Not when it comes to it. After all she was my wife... we used to love each other, least we thought we did...' His smile wrinkled the corners of his grey eyes. How attractive he still was, Anna thought, his shrewdness, his business acumen part of his sex appeal.

'Well thanks anyway,' she said. 'I'll let Patsy know right away. The orchard and ten thousand. I can't speak for her obviously but... I should think she might like the idea. I take it you'll be putting all this to your solicitor and she can expect to hear?'

'Got it in one,' Mark said. He stood up, taking her hand and holding it. 'Let's have another drink some time, shall we?' he said. 'Give me a ring and don't leave it too long?'

'Thanks,' she said, knowing he knew she never would.

* * *

Late in the Day

It was half past seven when Anna collected her car, picked up a tomato and anchovy pizza and a bottle of sparkling wine from a late-night Gateway and drove out to Stratton. She had promised on the phone she would and what could be nicer than driving out through Somerset countryside to visit a lifelong friend with news which surely held no threat to the messenger.

The meeting with Mark still filled her head. It had been a success beyond all expectation. But why would Mark give up any claim to OldPlace for ten thousand pounds and five acres of mildewed apple trees when his own affairs were apparently so dire? It was out of character and that bugged her. How many times had she heard people call him a two-faced bastard? Was he up to something and if so what? She wasn't going to pretend to have fixed him with her brilliant negotiating skills. Anna scratched at her wrists.

People did act out of character sometimes, especially if they felt guilty. Mark was devious but maybe in his way he was still fond of Patsy or at least felt responsible for her. You never knew with Mark; perhaps he didn't know himself.

'No Harriet?' she said, parking by the barn where the Mini usually stood. Patsy had walked out to meet her.

'Patrick I expect,' she said dismissively. Anna meeting Mark had pushed everything else out of her head. 'Good news?'

'I think so,' Anna said carefully. She put the pizza in the Aga, slammed the door and followed Patsy into the sitting-room. 'What's different here?'

'Walnut tallboy's gone,' Patsy sighed. 'Sold it last week. They wanted to cut my phone off. Harriet didn't even notice. Anyway how was Mark?'

'OK,' Anna said, made more cautious by the intensity of Patsy's gaze. 'I can't quite make it out. At first he seemed determined you should sell OldPlace, wanted his pound of flesh and no messing. But then we talked and he sort of changed . . . softened, like it had all been an act. Suddenly he said he'd accept ten thousand pounds from you plus the old cider orchard and let you keep the house.'

'The old cider orchard?' Patsy said, mystified. 'What's he want with that? I mean it's useless, isn't it?'

Anna shrugged. 'Evidently not to Mark.'

'Come and see!' Patsy jumped up and they walked out across the cobbled yard. A five-barred gate in a hawthorn hedge gave on to an orchard of gnarled and ancient trees.

'I suppose it's flat,' Anna said. 'What about access?'

'How suspicious you are! Don't you know a good deed in a naughty world?' Patsy said, her dark eyes glowing. 'We used to talk about getting planning permission in the old days. It was possible then but you'd never get it now with the new legislation about green belts and a Labour-controlled council. There's a track to Clegg Farm; old man Clegg lets his pigs in the orchard at windfall time. Maybe I should charge him now, what do you think?'

'Well, it's up to Mark, isn't it? Least it will be if you're going to let him have the cider orchard, that is. Unless you think he's up to something, I mean you know Mark better than I do.'

'Course I do.' Patsy's expression sweetened. 'He wants to come back here eventually, it's obvious, isn't it? Maybe he doesn't quite realise himself yet but it's wearing thin with that Judy girl. Mark always loved OldPlace. He created it really . . . well resuscitated it anyway, saw its potential. Of course he doesn't want me to sell it because sooner or later he's coming back.'

'He didn't say anything like that,' Anna said, worried now. Patsy's moods and expectations were so volatile. 'In fact he said it would do you good to get a job and earn your own living and maybe he's right?'

'Well he would say that to you, wouldn't he?' Patsy said, feeling a new vitality surge inside her. In the end it was all going to be all right but she had to be patient. 'You have to read between the lines. Glass of bubbly?'

'Thanks. But do be careful, Patsy. I mean I don't know anything about property and deals but he could be stitching you up.'

'Course not. You don't know him like I do.' She opened the Aga door. 'Pizza's ready.' She banged the hot tin on to the kitchen table. 'Grub up!'

Half an hour later the Mini puttered up the drive. Harriet got out looking pale and carrying a cardboard box.

'I've been suspended,' she said in her little-girl voice. 'Full pay pending an inquiry.'

'Suspended?' Patsy said.

'Why?' Anna said after a pause. A chirruping was coming from the cardboard box. 'Whatever's that?'

Late in the Day

'A guinea pig,' Harriet said. 'Darren kept hurting it and I smacked him and they suspended me.'

'Never mind, my darling!' Patsy cried, flinging her arms round Harriet. 'We'll get the very best lawyer in Bristol.'

'What with, Mother?' Harriet said.

Chapter Thirteen

'Oh, it's you again,' Anna said when Owen knocked on her office door late one afternoon. She was puzzled since he had knocked that morning, paced her office restlessly and gone away without a word. He was wearing a different shirt this afternoon, a dark-carrot colour.

'Something bothering you?' she suggested after a pause which had gone on too long.

'Why should anything be bothering me?' Owen said, fixing her with fierce blue eyes. 'Because I come to see a woman I admire and for whom I wish to express my admiration, why does something have to be bothering me?'

'Course it doesn't,' Anna said, irritated to feel herself blushing. What he had said could be construed as a pass and discreet recognition was required. People needed each other and surely in middle-age that could be recognised. On the one hand she appreciated an unvarnished approach, no fuss about being *in love*, no step by step or feigned surprise. On the other hand, though she couldn't help finding him attractive, Owen was conspicuously trouble.

'Er... would you like a coffee or something?' she suggested, frozen like a rabbit in his indignant gaze.

'Depends on the something,' Owen said, allowing himself a small smile. 'I was wondering how you were about opera? The Welsh National is on at the Hippodrome. Queues a mile long... but I could get a couple of tickets for Saturday night, *Marriage of Figaro*.' He tapped the side of his nose and grinned. 'Friends in high places.'

'Lucky you, sounds great,' Anna said. 'I'd love to come.' She paused. Wasn't Owen always talking about the six children he

Late in the Day

had to feed? 'Shall we go Dutch? Tickets are expensive.'

'Certainly not,' Owen said louder than was necessary. 'I suppose I'm entitled to a fraction of the fruits of my labours. If I ask a woman out I pay. You a feminist or something?'

'Well OK...' Who was she to look a gift horse in the mouth, she thought. 'Thanks anyway, I'll look forward to it.' But why hadn't he asked her that morning, Owen could hardly be accused of being shy, was she perhaps his second choice? 'I've moved house by the way. Gone into my mother's flat.'

'Congratulations!' he said and his eyes brightened. 'See you in the foyer at half past seven then?'

'Fine!' Anna said. Which shoes, she began to speculate at once, she couldn't walk far in the smart black sandals. Would he want to drive her back, did she want him to or did she just want him to want to? And why did the stretch marks on her belly, shiny and white, have to come into it?

Going home to the Hotwells flat each evening was still an adventure. Anna unlocked the front door, smelling pinks bought from a shop and honeysuckle picked from the garden, switched on the kettle and listened to the silence round her. Mr Phillips's tenanted house had never been quiet at six o'clock.

Later in the evening she phoned Cathy. 'I was just going to phone you, Mum, matter of fact,' Cathy said. 'Honestly. How's Grandma's flat?'

'*My* flat, it's *my* flat now,' Anna said.

'But wasn't it absolutely filthy?'

'We cleaned it up beforehand, Briony and me.'

A pause and then Cathy said, 'If you'd told us we could have helped...'

'I did think of it but the flat was so squalid for the children...' My three grandchildren, Anna thought.

'You could have let me know you were moving though,' Cathy said after a pause. 'I mean you didn't discuss it or anything.'

'Had to be my decision,' Anna said.

'You could at least have mentioned it, I mean anything could have happened.'

'I did tell you the next day,' Anna said. Whatever she did or said it was never quite right for Cathy. Was *she* rejecting or was Cathy difficult, over-dependent? Olly was less competent at life but kinder with his shy sideways smile. One cut one's teeth on one's first child. 'Anyway you'd got my number. I kept the phone switched on in case you'd needed me.'

'Have you told Grandma?' Cathy said casually.

'No. Well she isn't speaking to me at the moment.'

'She speaks to me all right, I'll tell her if you like?'

Anna hesitated. 'Better leave it for the moment, love.'

'If you say so . . .' A pause and then Cathy went on chattily. 'I took Gilbert in last week. Grandma was thrilled to bits. So was Gil, showing off his clever walking to all the old dears. He yelled like crazy when I took him off home.'

'Poor Gil,' Anna murmured, deciding not to notice she hadn't even been told Gilbert was walking. 'Anyway what were you going to phone me about?'

'Babysitting Saturday night? Pitmans are having a party.'

'Sorry,' Anna said with a certain satisfaction. 'I can't.'

'Oh!' Cathy was taken aback. 'Something happening?'

'Well I'm going to *Figaro*, the Welsh National Opera at the Hippodrome with Owen Evans, one of the lecturers at Brandon Lodge. Sorry.'

'Oh . . .' Cathy said. 'Can't be helped. Dennis'll just have to go on his own.'

'Maybe you can get somebody else?' Anna suggested. 'Sorry, darling.'

'For God's sake stop saying *sorry*,' Cathy said and hung up.

Patsy lay extended on a deck chair, squinting at the pear tree through half-closed eyes. It was Friday afternoon and hot. Nearby the guinea pig sat quietly in the shady run Harriet had constructed for him. She had also neatly splinted a broken front leg with half a toothpick and a roll of sticking plaster. Once or twice Patrick phoned. Once or twice Harriet suggested they should try and let the cottage but Patsy didn't want strangers around. Displaced persons, she thought sleepily, all three of us. Since her suspension Harriet had undertaken the care of the garden, scything and then mowing the lawn and persuading one of Mrs Bond's unemployed cousins to repair the pond and wall. Children no longer invaded and the garden was at peace.

Patsy was at peace too. She had formally accepted Mark's suggestion, giving her sole possession of the house, OldPlace, and contents in return for the orchard, ten thousand pounds and an undertaking to make no further financial claim on him. When the documents were prepared, she went into the solicitor's office and signed them at once. She had no money but she could sell the furniture piece by piece if necessary and OldPlace was hers. Simpson and Cape was going bust anyway, somebody said.

'Where are you going, darling?' Patsy said, looking up as a shadow fell between her and the sun.

'I told you, Mother,' Harriet said. She had on a pink and blue cotton dress instead of her usual jeans, a zip-bag in one hand and an envelope in the other. 'I'm spending the weekend at the flat. Don't forget to put Monty back in his hutch. OK?'

'Of course,' Patsy said, offering a smile but adding before she could stop herself, 'You will come back, won't you?'

'Yes,' Harriet said flatly. She held up the envelope by one corner. 'I'm resigning my job!'

'But what about your suspension, won't there be a fuss? Don't you have to go before the governors next week?'

'Not if I resign!' Harriet said.

'But sweetheart...' Patsy pulled herself up to a sitting position. 'Your whole life is ahead of you... your career. I think I should speak to Mr Bradshaw, everybody says he's...'

'Let's talk about it later, shall we?' Harriet backed away. 'See you Sunday evening. Don't wait up.'

The Mini scurried down the drive. How she hated living at OldPlace and her absence had created a dangerous vacuum, Patrick said, which loads of girls would be happy to fill. Harriet pulled up at the pillar box and posted her letter. Somehow she had to get away.

Later that evening Anna's doorbell rang. Cathy stood on the doorstep with a potted marguerite and a determined expression.

'My dear, why didn't you tell me you were coming?' Anna said. 'What will you have? Glass of wine?'

'No drink thanks, I'm driving,' Cathy said. She wore much-washed jeans and a blue check shirt, her hair tied in a ponytail by what looked like white tape.

'Tea then?'

'OK.' Cathy's gaze took in the geraniums, pinks and honeysuckle, a box of chocolates. 'Coals to Newcastle!' she said, depositing her marguerite pot on the table with a clack.

'Can't have too many flowers,' Anna said, kissing her cheek. 'Thanks, darling. New shirt?'

'Oxfam shop,' Cathy shrugged, her eyes circling the room. 'Looks nice now.' She sounded surprised. 'You did a good job, you and Briony. Have you sorted out about the garden?'

'Not really.' Anna moved into the kitchen and switched on the kettle. 'People upstairs say I'm not entitled to use any part of it but I may not be here very long.'

Cathy's head turned quickly. 'Think they'll evict you?'

'Not that,' Anna said, dropping tea bags into mugs. 'I want a place of my own. I'm seeing your father next week to talk about selling Rose Lodge.'

'He's not going to like that,' Cathy said.

'He doesn't have to *like* it,' Anna said, pouring in boiling water. 'He just has to do it.'

'But you don't want to live there, do you? I mean you couldn't afford . . .' Cathy's voice trailed off.

'Course not. I just want my half.' Anna was pleased and surprised by the firmness of her voice. 'Half the money, so I can get a place of my own.'

'Solomon's baby?' Cathy said, flicking out her tea bag. 'This guy taking you to the opera . . . er, Owen Evans?'

'About time I worked at my musical education,' Anna said cheerily.

'You don't give a fuck about your musical education,' Cathy said. 'And neither do I. But I mean . . . will he come back here?'

'I haven't really thought . . .'

'You can say that again!' Cathy said putting down her tea. 'You have to buy condoms at the chemist. I mean what planet are you on, Mum, going out with people and bringing them back here when you don't know the first thing about them? You have to be careful nowadays, *very careful indeed* all the time. I mean you're not in bad nick for a woman of your age.'

Cathy's voice cracked slightly and she opened her handbag and dropped two packets of condoms on the table.

'Thanks,' Anna said.

'You've got to insist, Mum,' Cathy said blushing and urgent. 'Absolutely insist because they don't like it and they get all uptight and stuff, and carry on and act up, say why don't you trust them and anyway this is their first time even, all sorts of bullshit. You have to insist, Mum, whatever they say. Promise me?'

'Well thanks,' Anna said, fingering a silver-coloured packet and then pushing it away, upset but not sure why. Was it something to do with role reversal? It was all so difficult, maybe she had been out of life too long to get back. She didn't understand sex any more, she didn't understand anything any more. Her own fault of course. She read the papers but she didn't take in the way things were. Going to the opera with Owen Evans, that was living, wasn't it, the stream of life? But perhaps it was also too much, more living than she really wanted.

'I'm not stupid, you know, and I was married to your father for twenty-two years, don't forget,' Anna went on. Twenty-two times fifty-two times two or three times a week, she couldn't do it in her head, but it must be around three thousand. Could she really have had sexual intercourse with Rupert three thousand times and be unable to remember a single occasion? Well there was the time he tore her spotted nightie and that time he hurt her on purpose and the night Cathy was conceived. 'I can and do look after myself,' Anna finished.

'Oh yes?' Cathy said. 'Like hell.'

'And well... sex is private,' Anna said. 'And I'm not sure it's really your business.'

'Of course it's my business,' Cathy said, her eyes filled with tears. 'Like it was your business when I was sixteen and clueless and mixed up and madly in love with that awful boy and you were so *good* about it all.'

'Was I really?' Anna said, amazed.

'Course you were, but you're such a bloody drongo now. I bet you hadn't even thought of getting condoms or safe sex or anything and I don't want a mother who is HIV positive if it's all the same to you.'

By Saturday evening Anna had had her hair done and visited Bexley House, buffing Bunny's silver cups and talking to her mother's silence. She returned to the flat and took two short cocktail dresses, one green and one black, from the cupboard, and considered which to wear. They were both five years old, left over from the days when she and Rupert went to parties in Stratton and the villages round, Mark and Patsy's parties at

OldPlace for instance. No doubt both dresses were too short or too long for current fashion but Anna was not sure which.

Francesca would know. Francesca would be only too delighted to lend her, probably even give her, something expensive, stylish and really up-together. But Anna found that solution too diminishing. She considered her legs in the wardrobe mirror, at least they were all right. She decided on the green and laid it on the bed with fresh tights and the smart sandals. Odds on Owen wouldn't notice anyway. She made herself a cheese sandwich and tried to feel *cool*.

She considered driving herself. It would increase her options but parking on a Saturday night in the city centre was too much hassle. She could easily walk from Hotwells, and back if Owen didn't offer her a lift. But probably he would and probably she would accept. She didn't want to think further than that. Besides wasn't it a bit ridiculous, vainglorious even, to go about thinking everyone was *after* you?

Owen was waiting in the foyer. He had had his hair neatly cut. 'You're late,' he said, steering her towards the bar. He had clearly had a drink already.

'Lady's privilege?' Anna said brightly and wondered if she even liked him.

'What'll you have?'

'Orange juice, please.'

'Yuck!' Owen said, departing to the crowded bar.

Anna gazed round. People said Bristol was a village, you kept bumping into people you knew, but she never did. People also said there was a lot of money in Bristol. So who were all these elegant and well-dressed strangers? Old Bristolians, yuppy Bristolians, opera lovers from the Somerset squirearchy, loyal Welsh patriots from across the Severn Bridge?

'Er ... Mrs Bolt isn't it?' A woman in cream silk stood at her elbow. 'I remember you so well from the Stratton days.'

'Oh yes ... Mrs er ...'

'Clarke, Belinda ...' the woman said, smiling forgivingly. 'Can't expect you to remember ... this is my husband, Neil.'

'How do you do?' Neil said.

'You remember Mrs Bolt, Neil?' She laughed uneasily. 'The doctor's wife, used to be, Dr Bolt at the health centre?'

'In Stratton,' Anna said. Divorce might be commonplace but it was still uneasy socially ... just like death.

'Ah!' said Neil. 'Yes, of course. Long time no see!'

'If you're on your own?' Belinda said. 'Feel free . . .'

'Oh no. I mean my friend is over there,' Anna said.

'Nice to have met you anyway . . .' Belinda said, peering after Anna as she moved towards Owen approaching with drinks.

'Who was that you were talking to?' he asked, steering her to one side with a proprietary air.

'People from Stratton,' she said. 'Patients of Rupert's.'

'You never told me you had been married to a doctor,' Owen said suspiciously.

'You never asked,' Anna said.

The theatre was packed. In the foyer people unable to get tickets clamoured and waited. Owen it transpired had secured two seats at the front of the dress circle. The babble of talk hushed as the orchestra began the overture and the audience relaxed into the world of Mozart.

'How was it for you?' Owen said, holding her arm as they made their way out afterwards.

'Marvellous,' she said. 'Thank you very much, Owen. It was a really lovely evening.'

'Not over yet,' he said. 'Parked in Queens Square.'

'Well . . .' Anna said but he was already propelling her across the traffic lights, at least he wasn't drunk. Cars backed out of parking meters and taxis swirled in the darkness. A few minutes later Owen navigated carefully round the centre, turned up Park Street and left towards the Hotwell Road.

'Turn right here. Third house along. Thanks again for a marvellous evening,' she said as he drew into the kerb. Her voice sounded breathy and nervous.

'Aren't you going to ask me in?' Owen said, already out and locking the car doors.

'Well . . .' she said. 'Just for a minute but I'm tired after all that emotion.' She unlocked the front door. Her mother's startled image vanished as Owen slammed it behind him.

'Why don't we just stop arsing around and go to bed?' Owen said, taking off his jacket. 'Bet it's what Wolfgang Amadeus did.'

'Oh, I don't think . . .' Anna said, flustered.

'What did you move to this flat *for*, then?' Owen said.

'Not *for* anything, certainly not for your convenience!' Anna said.

'Just a coincidence was it? Stop mucking me about, Anna. When I think what I paid for those bloody tickets.'

'Whose fault's that?' Anna thumped her fists against his chest as his arms came round her but suddenly she stopped. Her body was already responding, ignoring her reservations. It seemed to know her better than she did. She laughed aloud. 'What the hell, you great unreconstructed barbarian bastard, you!'

'Can't argue with that!' Owen said.

Chapter Fourteen

Harriet will be back tomorrow, Patsy thought, waking on Sunday not to distant bells, but to shouts and a high-pitched mechanised buzz coming from the orchard.

Patsy flung on her dressing-gown and opened the back door. Two unfamiliar cars were parked by the barn. She flew across the cobbled yard to the gate.

'What's going on?' she shouted. Four green-helmeted men, two of them perched on ladders, turned to look at her.

'Choppin' down they old trees, missus,' one of them offered. 'Buildin' starts Monday.'

'What building?'

'Green Orchard Estates. Twenty-one luxury houses.'

'What Green Orchard Estates? They can't ... haven't got planning permission. It's a mistake, must be ...'

She ran back to the house and phoned Mark's number. The receiver was lifted but nobody answered. Outside the whirr of mechanised saws started up again like a swarm of angry bees. She phoned Anna's flat.

'What can I do?' Patsy screamed into the phone.

'Well ...' Anna sounded half asleep. 'Well ... you could phone the police?'

'Who the hell was that?' Owen called from the kitchen where he was making morning tea.

'Friend of mine, Patsy,' Anna said.

'At this time on a Sunday morning?' Owen said, returning with the tray. He had wound a towel round his waist, his body and arms were thickly covered with monkey-coloured hair. 'Woman's not human.'

'She's got human problems,' Anna said.

'Who hasn't?' Owen said, his eyes bright blue and satyr-like. 'You still angry with me?'

'Yes,' Anna said sternly and wondered was she playing up to him, an amateur Miss Whiplash.

'You're sensational when you're angry,' Owen said, his hand on the duvet. 'Fantastic. You don't mind if I come back in?'

'Yes, I do!' Anna said. 'And paying for the tickets last night did *not* entitle you to share my bed incidentally. Especially when I had offered to pay for myself.'

'You certainly did,' he said, insinuating himself beside her. 'I distinctly remember. I behaved disgracefully, treating you like a two-bit whore. Not that I've had much truck with your actual professional, know what I mean? Got you going though, didn't I? My second ex-wife Bethany . . .'

'We're not talking about your second ex-wife Bethany . . .'

'If you'd just let me explain.' Owen grinned engagingly. 'And it worked, didn't it, my full frontal attack?'

'Are you winding me up?' Anna said, exasperated.

'Certainly not,' Owen said. 'Drink your tea and we'll start the day again, shall we? How's that for a brilliant offer?'

'Well . . .' she said aware of a tweak in her lower abdomen as his hand brushed her thigh. Last night despite her uncertainty her body had sprung into its exercise like a well-trained horse. Owen was certainly vigorous in bed but was he what she wanted? The trouble was you had to commit yourself before you really knew. 'You might have matched the cups with the saucers.'

'I expect I'll get *au fait* with your domestic arrangements in due course, ma'am?' he suggested.

'Have you got another condom?' Anna said a moment later.

'Not as such, but I could just . . .'

'No, you could *not*,' Anna said, stretching a long arm. Sex with condoms but without strings, she thought, no commitments. Sex with no past or future, well no past anyway. What did it signify, matter, mean in the millennium? *Brave New World*. Had Huxley changed society with his imaginings half a century ago? The writer as prophet, sex and soma useful to keep the underclass happy. Sex in her mother's flat where no such thing had happened in years and maggots curled in the mattresses. Disgusting behaviour for a clergyman's daughter. 'Get thee to a nunnery.'

After so long, after so long, aff . . . terrr . . .

Late in the Day

'OK?' Owen said some time later.

'OK,' Anna said and added because she could, though she knew it was hardly fair, 'but too damn quick.'

'I expect you're out of practice?' Owen said, defensive. 'Just give us a breather, be all right next time, I promise. Quick quick, slow, like a foxtrot, know what I mean? Let's talk about you while we wait. Any children?'

'Two,' Anna said. 'Cathy and Oliver, both grown up.'

'Two?' he repeated like an admonition but his eyes had already wandered. 'Six I've got, six kids in this day and age, can you beat it? A house with six kids, what sort of life is that for a thinking man? No wonder I went off with Sylvia.'

'In the part of Africa I know the men live in a sort of long house and each wife has a hut with her children. Husbands drop in at night if they feel like it.'

'Sounds like a good system,' Owen said. 'Isn't as if she even liked it.'

'Liked what?'

'Making love. Making babies. Bethany. Married fifteen years and made six babies and she never came. Not once. Hour after hour, I worked away at her. Read all the books, tried everything. I was totally in love with Sylvia, mind.'

'How come we always end up talking about your ex-wives?' Anna said.

'Jealous?' Owen said, finding the notion interesting.

'Time to get up,' Anna said. 'I've people coming for lunch.' *People* sounded less provocative than *my ex-husband*.

'OK, OK, I can take a hint. Pity though, when we could have spent the day in bed, worn each other out totally?'

'Thanks, but no thanks,' Anna said.

When Owen had gone she opened the windows and tidied the flat. She and Rupert had not shared a meal since she left Rose Lodge four years ago. It was two years since she had even seen him. It could hardly be coincidence that she had let Owen stay last night. Freud didn't believe in coincidences, did he? What then, a secret levelling of scores or an attempt to defuse the Rupert occasion? If so it had been a success.

The food should be adequate but not that special, she had decided several days ago. She was only asking for what was legally and morally hers but what she had been too reduced, too insecure, to ask for until now.

The doorbell rang.

'Hello! You found it all right then?'

'As you see, flew straight as a homing pigeon,' Rupert said, stepping into the passage and pecking her cheek. He looked different. His jacket, she noticed, was new, so was his shirt, his cravat vaguely familiar, his eyes blue as bonfire smoke extremely so. His hair was appreciably thinner, as was his figure. He looked fitter but more tense, a natural corollary, she supposed, to living with a much younger wife. That she looked different too was a reflection best avoided.

'I still think you ought to have let me take you out to lunch,' Rupert said, smiling his most engaging smile and following her into the sitting-room where the small table by the window was already laid.

'Cider, OK?' Anna said.

'Fine!' he said cheerfully. 'But we could have tried the Restaurant de Gourmet, for instance?'

'I don't go to places like that nowadays,' Anna said with a small grimace because it sounded self-pitying. 'Do you?'

'Not as a rule,' Rupert said. 'But this is a special occasion.' He raised his glass. 'The first of many, do I dare to presume?'

'Oh, I don't know,' Anna said, jumping up. 'Excuse me ... the potatoes.' She was happy to leave for a moment. Rupert could charm the birds from the trees when he chose but his charm did not survive familiarity. Not having seen him for so long Anna experienced again something of its initial impact. She dished up the new potatoes and brought them in with the ham and salad.

'Looks delicious!' Rupert said.

Over lunch he talked carefully about the village, the practice, the various patients who had given birth, been hospitalised or died since she left. It was the conversational exchange of strangers, she thought sadly, 'strangers in law' was what they had become in life. He didn't mention her letter and neither did she.

'I'll make the coffee,' she said, clearing the table and returning a minute later with the tray. 'It's only instant.'

'You always made a smashing cup of Nes,' Rupert said. 'And you've got this flat looking really good. Delightful.' His eyes considered the Francis Danby poster she had bought, an attempt to introduce cool green trees into a flat which looked on to urban pavement and the grey terrace opposite. The geraniums from

Late in the Day

Brewsters flourished pink and scarlet on the window sill. 'You always were a wonderful home-maker.'

'Not wonderful enough evidently,' Anna said. Rupert had always confused flattery with kindness, but she wanted to avoid reproach. Time did heal if you let it and people could not help the way they felt or did not feel. The early days of separation when his occasional letter lying on the mat had made her heart thud with anger and distress were long past.

'I wouldn't say that,' Rupert murmured. 'That's a pretty skirt by the way, suits you.'

'I read somewhere that rows over housekeeping are the greatest apparent cause of domestic violence,' Anna offered into an awkward silence. 'Don't you find that odd?'

'Not at all,' Rupert said, improvising different voices. '"Where's my tea?" "What time do you call this then?" "Wham!"'

'You were never like that,' Anna said. 'Olly's just done another A-level, Economics,' she added, omitting to mention that he had overslept for his second subject.

'Great stuff,' Rupert said. His euphoria had enchanted her at first, nothing seemed to get him down. Later she had seen it as emotional shallowness. 'He'll get there in the end.'

'Get where?'

'Wherever it is he wants to get,' Rupert said, his tone indicating that the subject of Olly between them had long since been exhausted.

'About my letter?' Anna said abruptly.

Rupert put down his coffee cup. 'Ah yes, came at a rather inopportune moment, matter of fact.'

'Oh?' Good timing was a wifely obligation, Anna thought, but it couldn't be extended to ex-wives.

'Yes. Deirdre's grant has been cut to the bone and the overheads of the practice have gone up considerably ... go up every year ... and the house needs ...'

'Didn't you and Deirdre go to Majorca for three weeks?'

'I thought that would come in somewhere,' Rupert said. 'I work damn hard and everyone's entitled to a holiday.'

'Course you are,' Anna said, glancing at the window. You couldn't see the Hotwell Road but you could hear it all day and much of the night. 'You're entitled to your own house too. And so am I.'

'You want me to sell Rose Lodge, is that it?' Rupert said, colour rising in his face. 'When I've worked all these years to pay for it? I mean the house and practice are inseparable...'

'I don't see why,' Anna said. 'When you work from the health centre.'

'I should go and live on the Stratton council estate, is that it? I only bought Rose Lodge because you wanted it, wasn't my sort of place, too bourgeois. The twenty-year mortgage is only just finished. My God, twenty years of my life have gone into that house, now you want me to sell it?'

'A good many years of my life went into Rose Lodge too,' Anna said, trying to keep her voice steady. 'And we *both* wanted it, Rupert. You never do anything unless you want to.'

The house had seemed so solid, a bulwark against whim and adversity. She had felt the need of something more dependable than Rupert's promise with two small children. She still loved him then. His reaction to the mortgage was bizarre, his first intimation of mortality, the end of his maverick youth. At the Bristol and West Building Society, his eyes dived like swallows after the clicking heels of the attendant clerks and within a week he was involved with a girl called Holly, who lived in Southville.

Not that she was angry with Rupert now. She had always had this problem. How could you say to anybody 'You may not make love to that woman'? What gave you the right? Did making scenes improve the situation? Anna had done the only thing she could do, sat it out. Lipstick came out in the wash, Rupert declared, more euphoric than ever. All Anna had to do was look after the children and mind her own business. He was never going to leave her. He never deceived her either, he needed her to know. It hurt but far worse was the way it filled her mind with speculation: what, where, when, now?

As the children grew up the game was less and less worth the candle.

'I'd give you Rose Lodge if I could,' Rupert said with a dramatic sweep of his arm. 'Is that what you want?'

'I just want my half,' Anna said. 'My solicitor says you could take out a second mortgage.'

'Good grief,' Rupert said, astonished less by the suggestion itself than by the fact that Anna had made it. During the marriage she had left all financial matters to him. 'Have a heart, I've only just paid off the first one. I should have thought this flat would suit...'

'That's because you don't live in one,' Anna said. The carapace of reasonableness from which she had always tried to relate to Rupert was disintegrating fast. She felt angry and free. 'You can't be that short of money. Cathy said you gave a talk on Woman's Hour?'

'"You and Your Baby", a series of six talks actually,' Rupert conceded. 'Deirdre's idea but the fee's peanuts.'

'What about your research?' Anna said. Hadn't he asserted that Deirdre rekindled the part of him she had maimed?

'What time do I get for research?' Rupert said testily. 'Eighty-five patients I saw on Friday. Eighty-five. Whoever they sign up with, all the frail geriatrics, hypochondriacs and depressives gravitate to me.'

'You're a tonic in yourself,' Anna said, remembering how she had tried tactfully to deflect them. 'You make people feel better, you always did.'

'I've missed you, Anna,' he said. His hand moved towards her, a blue cuff and a bright gold cuff link. 'Do we have to have a divorce like other people, all bitter wrangling? What's the hurry about your getting a house all of a sudden?'

'It's not all of a sudden,' Anna said. 'It's four years since we split and I'm looking at houses, I want to get a house of my own.'

'What house?'

'Just a house.' She didn't want him even thinking about any particular house until it was safely hers. 'I've told Mr Hill, my solicitor.'

'Have you indeed?' Rupert looked at her for a long moment. 'Things all right otherwise?'

'Everything's fine,' she said. The cravat, she realised, was one she had given him for Christmas years ago, still new. Had he opened the gift box for the first time today?

'We ought to see each other more often,' Rupert said. 'I'm still very fond of you.' He leaned forward and his eyes gleamed. Was he going to try to make love to her? Could he smell sex subliminally in the atmosphere? He was not an unkind man, she thought, gazing at his hand spread like a starfish on her knee, just spoilt and manipulative.

'It won't do,' Anna said, getting up. He knew nothing of her life now and cared less. 'It's four years and I'm entitled.'

'Shylock was entitled,' Rupert said.

'You always exaggerate. It's not a matter of life and death,' Anna said. 'Just keeping the car longer . . .'

'Majorca's peanuts out of season.'

'Then you'll still be able to afford it,' Anna said.

'I always thought of you as magnanimous,' Rupert said.

'I'd rather you didn't think of me at all,' Anna said. 'I don't need it. Look, Rupert, I didn't want to leave Rose Lodge but I had to, I didn't want to get divorced but I had to, I didn't plan to spend my declining years on my own but if I have to I'm damn well going to spend them in my own house. OK?'

'Turn the volume down, will you?' Rupert said. 'And you must have this particular house right now?'

'Yes, yes, yes,' Anna shouted.

Parking the Mini at OldPlace on Sunday evening, Harriet stared at the lines of felled apple trees in the orchard.

'What on earth's going on?' she said. Patsy was prostrate on the sitting-room sofa.

On Monday morning Harriet phoned and then went down to the planning office. She did not return until late afternoon.

'Did you sort it out?' Patsy said.

'Sort out what?' Harriet said. 'Planning permission for the orchard was applied for and granted more than three years ago. The application's signed by you and Dad.'

'How can it have been?' Patsy whispered. 'An adult person doesn't sign things and not remember.'

'You were probably drunk, Mother,' Harriet said flatly.

'And Mark sold it to Green Orchard Estates?'

'Dad *is* Green Orchard Estates,' Harriet said.

'What can I do?' Patsy whispered.

'Well . . .' Harriet said. 'You could go to court and say Dad got you drunk and pressured you to sign the application?'

'I couldn't,' Patsy said.

'By the way,' Harriet said. 'Patrick and me, we're going to Hydra for a holiday soon as we can fix it up. Patrick's had this legacy . . .'

Patsy was appalled. That evening she phoned Anna with a tearful account of how planning permission for Green Orchard Estate had been granted three years ago.

Late in the Day

'I did say Mark might be stitching you up,' Anna said.

'It was you stitched me up,' Patsy said.

'Me?' Anna took a deep breath. 'Listen, Patsy, I only saw Mark because you begged me too. I don't know anything about business, do I? It's you who needs to understand Mark's business affairs and stand on your own two feet. You should have got together with your two solicitors and worked through the Old-Place situation. All this drama and weeping and being sorry for yourself, it's a waste of space. It's also very boring for your friends.'

'Boring?' Patsy said. 'I suppose some people would find the sinking of the *Titanic* boring?'

'Mark is not the *Titanic*,' Anna said. 'Please get it into your head it is not *cute* to be ignorant about money and business and it is not *cute* to trust the untrustworthy, it is silly. You're just fixated on Mark and his bullshit and it's pathetic and ridiculous. He's not worth it. Let him go. And for God's sake get your finger out and stop phoning me and moaning,' she added, slamming the receiver down harder than she meant to. Her heart was pounding. The switching mother, she thought, have I become the scourging, punishing mother?

Chapter Fifteen

It was hot that summer, day after day of clear blue sky. 'Who needs the Mediterranean, day like this?' people said sunbathing at lunchtime on College Green.

On one such morning, as Anna drove towards Brandon Lodge, she was thinking about houses. Her meeting with Rupert a fortnight ago had sharpened her interest in For Sale boards along the route. There did not seem to be much movement. Rose Lodge might take years to sell.

As he had promised Rupert had had the house valued; apparently it was currently worth two hundred and forty thousand pounds. Francesca urged Anna to get a valuation herself but Anna was content with the prospect of half that sum minus the costs of conveyancing and solicitors' fees. Besides she did not want to delay things. Already agents were deluging her with printed information about modest properties in the Bristol area. She was also entitled to a share of the furniture. Did she want the mahogany bureau she had bid for so recklessly for instance or would it be better to make a fresh start? Olly might like to have his old bedroom furniture.

Unfortunately she also had Owen on her mind. He had visited her unannounced the Tuesday following the opera weekend. She had cooked him an omelette and they had gone to bed.

'Not bad for forty-nine?' he had said, combing his fingers through his furry chest. 'You ready to go again, ma'am?'

'If you have a bath first,' Anna said, rolling out of range.

'A bath?'

'One of those things with hot water and soap.'

'I'll have a bath after if you like, that do?' Owen said.

'No, it won't. You need a bath now.'

Late in the Day

'But I had one.'

'Not recently, you didn't,' Anna said, sitting up on the far side of the bed. 'I just don't care for making love with a man who smells like over-ripe Stilton.'

'Fuck me!' Owen said, astonished.

'No thanks.'

'My God, you're wonderful when you're angry. Like a woman of spirit, always have, especially when I'm not married to her. First time I've done it with a liberated woman, matter of fact. If I have a bath will you let me stay the night?'

'Liberated?' Anna had said, vaguely gratified but not sure she deserved the soubriquet.

Owen hadn't seemed offended when she declined his offer to visit again on Saturday because she was babysitting. But she had not seen him on his own since. He nodded moodily across the staffroom but made no attempt to speak to her. Her initial relief had turned to a gnawing anxiety, *love* it was not but it was something. There were lots of kinds of acceptable sex and you had to start somewhere. Had he just wanted to prove he could make her? She dreamed about him twice and her weekends had been empty. He was over-sensitive, egotistical and altogether too much of a good thing, but he was also a feeling person, nobody could call him hard-boiled and now they had started, better in her bed than in her head, Anna thought disconsolately.

Was he upset at being told to have a bath, offended by her babysitting or had he just gone off her?

As she went through the gates of Brandon Lodge and parked on the off-white gravel of Francesca's extension, her eyes automatically located Owen's Fiat, poignant with significance now. Would she ever travel in it again, she wondered, crossing to her office and switching on her word processor. Suddenly Owen's head poked round her door.

'How about a ploughman's later?' he muttered.

'Sounds like a good idea,' Anna said coolly. Was everything all right after all? What a fool she was imagining things.

'Old Oak, half past twelve?' Owen said. 'By the way, *sir* wants to see you at once.'

'Right.'

Mr Austin's door was closed.

'Come,' he said as she knocked. His pale face was tense. 'Ah,

Anna, trouble with the summer school, I'm afraid. It was always on the cards of course, a hitch, something like this, it's the name of the game. I told Francesca a dozen times, anyway she's asked me to have a word. It's, er . . . a bit of a crisis and we wondered if you could help?'

'Me?' Anna said. 'Course I'll do what I can but . . .'

'Perhaps you could start by telling me, er . . . a bit about yourself?' Mr Austin smiled encouragingly. 'Francesca says she believes you got a scholarship to Cambridge University?' he added, his voice heavy with the reverence of the red-brick graduate.

'Well . . . only an exhibition actually,' Anna said. 'I read English at Newnham but . . .'

'Splendid!' His expression was respectful as he leaned back in his chair. 'Just the lady we need. As you know we have this English Language summer school starting in two weeks and two teachers have dropped out at the last minute. Can't be helped, an appendix and a nasty virus . . . I was hoping you could help out?'

'Help out how?' Anna said.

'Teaching, of course,' Mr Austin said, smiling with relief. For a moment it had looked as if he might have to teach himself.

'Teaching? But I'm not qualified or anything,' Anna said, too surprised to remember that neither was Francesca.

'If you were at Newnham College, Cambridge that's quite enough for me,' Mr Austin said. 'And more to the point quite enough for our fifty-seven overseas students.'

'You want me to teach fifty-seven overseas students?' Anna gasped, her knees dissolving to jelly. Why hadn't she told him she'd only stayed at Newnham for two terms? 'I don't see how I could possibly . . .'

'Not fifty-seven, course not,' Mr Austin said. 'Students are divided into groups according to their attainment level. Each group will be approximately ten.' His smile had rapidly mutated from anxious to benign; he was confident she could not resist the combined pressure of himself and Francesca.

'Well, I'll have to think it over,' Anna prevaricated but Mr Austin seemed not to hear.

'You will only be responsible for your ten students and of course Francesca and I will give you all the backup you need,' he went on. 'The course books are in this cupbord, help yourself.

Late in the Day

There's a memorandum about the syllabus and you'll be free to use the language laboratory whenever you want, providing it's free, of course. Working with students, right at the chalk-face, nothing like it, you know ... the stimulation ... the challenge.'

'I like to be straight about things,' Owen said, putting a pint of beer and an orange juice on the table of the Old Oak some hours later. 'Cheese or ham with your ploughman's, ma'am?'

'Cheese, please,' Anna said. 'And we'll go Dutch.'

'Just as you like,' he said, gulping beer like one just rescued from an exceptionally arid desert.

'But the thing is I have absolutely no teaching experience and I dropped out of Newnham after two terms,' Anna said.

'You didn't tell Austin that?' Owen said.

'You think I should have?'

'No way,' Owen said. 'Never put yourself down, plenty of people ready to do it for you. Anyway nothing to it once you get through the first day. Couldn't you use the extra dosh? I know I could but the bastards wouldn't take me on. Your friend, Francesca, that is.'

'Well yes, the money would be useful,' Anna said, aware of the shabbiness of her flowered skirt – there was actually a hole in the pocket – and the money from Rose Lodge might not be available for months. But such considerations were hardly credentials for teaching English to ten overseas students who had paid good money for the privilege.

'Don't worry, you'll do fine. The world is full of highly qualified incompetents,' Owen said. She had forgotten how seraphic and blue his eyes were at close range. 'Rely on the inspiration of the moment, I should. A pox on all that paper qualifications crap, you speak the language well and fluently, don't you? Look out for number one, that's my philosophy.'

His smile faded as it occurred to them simultaneously that his philosophy had signally failed him. 'She got the house, you know, Bethany, stripped poor Jack naked.'

'Generosity has to be its own reward,' Anna said, already too familiar with the details of his marital catastrophes. 'And she did have your six children.'

'That was her line,' Owen said, swallowing more beer. 'My God, I really loved that woman.'

'Bethany?' Anna said.
'Sylvia. Do you think she ever really loved me?'
'I don't think about it at all,' Anna said irritably. 'The subject of your ex-marriages is exhausted, far as I'm concerned. And you carrying on about you when I'm trying to decide whether to have a go teaching at the summer school is driving me flaming mad.'
'Phew!' Owen said, getting up with the glasses. 'What a tigress! Let me get you a proper drink.' Heads turned their way. Owen thrived on public attention and his grin was puckish.
'Orange juice, thanks,' Anna said.
'You're gorgeous when you're angry,' Owen said in a loud whisper as he came back with the drinks. 'Absolutely splendid, really turns me on. But you know what it means when women get all uptight? You need it much as me and aren't getting enough. Well-known fact.'
'Really?' Anna said coolly. 'You're the expert?'
'Matter of experience. Just like to get things clear, know what I mean?'
'I'm not sure I do,' Anna said. 'Quite.'
'Like to know the ground rules. The days when I can see you for instance. Tuesday suits me, say Tuesday and Saturday? Thanks, Jock,' he added as the barman brought the ploughman's to the table.
'Any port in a storm?' Anna said. 'What do you mean ground rules? Am I being thick?'
'Not specially,' Owen said. 'It's just I don't come on with *chocs* and *pretty packaging*.'
'And theatre tickets?' Anna said.
'Can't afford it with six children.'
'Quite,' she said.
'Take the mick if you want, but I'm talking about our mutual need and convenience. Why don't we look it in the eye and work out an *arrangement* which suits *us*?'
'Well...' she said doubtfully. She had never heard it put quite so plainly. Not a scrap of crap as Olly would say. A sensible arrangement was something she had thought about herself, but when it came to it she wasn't sure she wanted to be somebody else's sensible arrangement. Not that she hankered for chocs exactly...
'Just like to get things settled,' Owen went on inexorably.

Late in the Day

'Would twice a week suit you?' He took a red diary from his jacket pocket. 'How about Tuesday and Saturday?'

'What?' Anna said, cornered.

'Your place or mine? Better be yours, mine's such a tip. Women got all the aces these days, move out and take their housekeeping skills with them and then where are you?'

'My place then,' Anna said. 'But Saturdays I often babysit for Cathy. Actually I think one day, say Monday, would be enough to start, don't you? See how it goes?'

'All right, Monday,' he said. 'My third ex-wife Sylvia had these marvellous black lace things, know what I mean? I suppose you couldn't...'

'No,' Anna said. 'I couldn't. Is that one of your ground rules?'

'No, no. Ground rules apply to serious things like place, time and fidelity,' he said. 'You are going to be faithful?'

'Are you?' Anna said.

'Course. You have to be very careful these days,' Owen said. 'But I mean can I trust you? It won't work otherwise. I can't afford to take risks, can I, with six children to feed?'

'I suppose not,' Anna said. She hadn't realised until now how much she liked the pretty packaging bit, how she depended on it, perhaps women did, but she liked Owen more. 'And I suppose there's also a risk we might fall in love?'

'No chance!' Owen snorted. 'No sense banging your head on a brick wall, baby, all you get is bruises. Maverick I may be but liar never. Falling in love is incompatible with the cyberspace age and besides it's the young who *really* turn me on. Man in my position has to think of the law,' he added cagily. 'Best ever was a girl of sixteen who looked thirteen.'

'Lolita!' Anna said, wondering if the girl concerned had been a student at Brandon Lodge. 'You don't think you're suffering from arrested development?'

'Who isn't?' Owen said.

'With men going for teenage nymphs,' Anna said reflectively, 'what's going to happen to the lonely middle-aged wives?'

'They can all live together in deserted convents and redundant schools and do good works,' Owen said. 'We're all trapped on the flywheel of history. Did we say Monday at your place definitely? Is that the *arrangement*?'

'Definitely but not indefinitely,' Anna said. 'Sorry. I mean...'

'Christ!' Owen said. 'Are we back to the chocs and flowers bit? Talk about blackmail!'

'It's not that,' Anna said. 'It's just I'm going to be very busy with the summer school all August... not to mention stressed out... and right now I've got to get it all together, haven't I? So can we leave it for a bit?'

'Backing out?' Owen said. 'Cold feet?'

'Not at all,' Anna said.

'You get sick of jerking off my age,' Owen muttered, flicking through the pages of his diary. 'Shall we make it first Monday in September then?'

In the evenings OldPlace was at least quiet now. Patsy wandered in the front garden under clear blue sky. Could it be more clear or blue in Hydra where Harriet and Patrick were currently staying according to the postcard, she wondered?

It was five years since she had had a holiday. Whose fault was that, Harriet had said when Patsy mentioned it. But *fault* didn't really come into it. For years and years she had cared for the children, ferried them everywhere they wanted to go. It was her turn now, at least it ought to be. Harriet could have taken her to the Greek islands perfectly well. She would have sat on the beach and been no trouble. Didn't she always do what Harriet told her? Hadn't she agreed to divorce Mark because Harriet told her?

Patsy circled the house, crossed the cobbled yard and climbed the gate into the orchard. It was something else she had not done for years but did every evening now. The remains of the trees had gone, uprooted by mechanical diggers, the dry grass scabbed by patches of brown earth. A white board announced in green letters 'GREEN ORCHARD ESTATE – Twenty-one luxury executive houses.'

'Green Orchard Estates is Mark,' she murmured to herself over and over as she paced up and down the five acres which had once been hers. There were pegs in the ground now joined by strings and the square-edged pits of foundations already started. But that was only the beginning. Eventually there would be twenty-one cars coming and going, babies screaming, washing hung out, hordes of children spinning about on bikes and scrumping her remaining apples. Would barbed wire keep them out or just lead to torn skin and litigation, Patsy wondered? What was trespass?

Late in the Day

Anna might know but she couldn't phone Anna, wouldn't give her the satisfaction after the cruel things she had said. She would have to wait till Harriet came home.

Harriet would know.

Chapter Sixteen

Term finished mid-July and the corridors of Brandon Lodge were quiet except for the secretarial staff and an occasional lecturer. As the English Language summer school approached, Anna, having accepted Mr Austin's suggestion that she should teach, asked him for a few days off. Perhaps he recognised in her shadowed eyes a fellow anxiety victim. He smiled gently and let her spend the rest of the week at home.

It was still hot and after two days poring over syllabus and text books Anna decided that perhaps staying at home was not the most sensible course. The indignant gaze of the tenants upstairs kept her out of the garden. Reading about it in the stuffy little sitting-room was one thing but faced with ten expectant faces staring in her direction was another. What was she going to say, Anna wondered? Even visualising the scene made her feel queasy. Francesca brought round a tutor's handbook. It explained that student concentration was limited to twenty minutes, thus it was essential for a teacher to provide three variations of activity during each hour. If she had six teaching hours a day with the same group, how could she possibly provide eighteen variations, Anna thought desperately. When Olly phoned he heard of her predicament.

'Sounds naff to me,' he said. 'Better get round to the doc, Mum. Get yourself tranked up, otherwise you'll be useless.'

'You think?' Anna said, breathless.

'I know,' Olly said. 'He'll give you beta blockers or something.'

'I suppose I might,' Anna said, wondering whether to say anything about his A-levels, venturing, 'Are you going to take your Maths again?' But Olly had already hung up.

Anna opened the window wider. How could she flourish, how

Late in the Day

could anybody flourish with nothing but bricks and macadam to look at? She had to dip her head even to see a strip of sky. How had Mother managed, she hadn't complained about the flat, and why, living at Bexley House, had she suddenly stopped using scarlet lipstick? Pink was actually a great improvement but had she been *got at* by Mrs Dewar? Surely Anna ought to say something? What about respect for her personal freedom?

Anna sighed. She needed fresh air, a vista, a garden of her own, everybody did though they didn't all achieve it. Could she get all that for say £70,000 and keep a bit in reserve, she wondered, turning to the estate agents pile and flicking through. It seemed she could, but Rupert had not contacted her since the lunch, and before the rift between them Patsy had insisted there was no For Sale notice on Rose Lodge, nothing in the Stratton agent's window either. Was Rupert ignoring her? Wouldn't be the first time. Was she going to have to pursue him through the courts? Did he think she wouldn't? Perhaps after all she ought to phone Patsy and make peace. People couldn't help being as they were.

'I need some beta blockers, please,' she said, presenting herself at Dr Wilding's surgery the next day.

'Indeed?' Dr Wilding said, suited appropriately for the hot weather in pale grey. 'Have you been prescribed them before?'

'No,' she said. 'But I'm teaching English as a Foreign Languge at a summer school in three days' time and I've never done that before either.'

'I should have thought you would have taken it in your stride, Mrs Bolt, a sophisticated lady such as yourself,' Dr Wilding said, smiling. He glanced at her notes. 'How's the rash by the way?'

'Bit better, thanks,' she said. The improvement was marginal but no sense offending him.

'I'll give you some beta blockers,' he said, typing it into his computer. 'But you had better give yourself a trial run first. They can have side effects.' He tore off the prescription and signed it with his usual flourish.

'Such as?' Anna said.

'If I disclosed that you'd be sure to get them. Good luck with the summer school. Don't forget your students will be twice as nervous as you.'

'Thanks,' Anna said. Did people wish you luck on your way to execution, she wondered?

Geraldine Kaye

* * *

Patsy walked slowly up through the house. With its steep-pitched roof and thick walls, the upstairs was deliciously cool even in hot summer and the attic was quieter than anywhere else since its dormer windows looked over the lane. Her hands slid into the familiar drawer and came out with the bundles of Mark's letters: green ribbon secured the ones written before Cambridge, red for the letters they had always exchanged on their wedding anniversaries, a tithe she had extracted with increasing difficulty. 'Why don't you burn the lot, Mother, make a fresh start?' Harriet had suggested a few weeks ago but what could someone of Harriet's age know about love?

Patsy heard the car, Mark's car, their car, the familiar engine of the black Citroën, how could she mistake it? It was coming slowly along the lane. At the gate of OldPlace it seemed to hover but then move on, turning into the track which led to the new development. The track was well rutted by the passage of lorries; beyond the hedge the black top bounced like a fretful horse. That Mark was visiting the site was natural enough, he *was* Green Orchard Estates. She had to remind herself every few minutes but she accepted it now.

There was nothing Mark could do which she couldn't accept. Get yourself a life, Anna said, but Patsy didn't want a life without Mark.

She ran downstairs and into the yard. She could see him in his green helmet strolling between foundations, hands in pockets, talking to the foreman, joking guardedly with the men.

At one moment he turned towards the house and gave it a lingering stare. Patsy raised her arm and waved. Mark saw her, hesitated, then raised his arm and waved back.

'Tea?' Patsy called loudly in what the children called her Harrods voice. 'Ready in a few minutes?' She ran back inside OldPlace: switching on the kettle, diving to the back of the cupboard for the dusty teapot, sweeping the faded flowers from the hall vase, grabbing the lavender-scented spray polish. She had let things go with Harriet away.

Mark would certainly despise the bright pink sundress bought at the shop in the village, run by Mrs Bond's cousin. She looked like an overstuffed armchair with her arms burned bright pink to match. She ran upstairs flinging it off, selecting the plain blue linen which Mark had always liked, dragging the comb through her thick hair and filling her eyes with tears.

His first visit was an occasion and she must seem adjusted to her role as ex-wife or he might never come again. Mustn't fuss, he hates fussing, Patsy thought. Quarter of an hour later she allowed herself to walk back to the orchard hedge. The Citroën had gone, somehow Mark had slid away down the track and turned into the lane without her seeing. The men sat round a scarlet thermos drinking tea.

'Fancy a cuppa, missus?' one of them said cheerily.

'Er . . . have you seen Mr Simpson?'

'Went off right away. Never stops anywhere long.'

'Don't dare give the flies a chance to settle.' A guffaw of laughter all round.

'Flies?' Patsy murmured. Black wings flickered at the edge of her vision.

'No flies on his nibs, no flies on Mr Green Orchard Estates, I can tell you that.'

'Just as well I looked in when I did,' Mrs Bond said to her husband that night. The debacles of Patsy's life had added an extra dimension to their own. 'When you think what could have happened . . . that grass was tinder.'

'Whole place could've gone up,' Frank remarked, wishing it had. Stratton needed a bit of excitement, scarlet fire engines dashing out from Weston, could have been on *Points West*.

'A premonition,' Mrs Bond said, respectful of her own well-authenticated powers. She had taken to going round to OldPlace before dusk every evening while Harriet was away. She had seen the fire from the lane.

'I'm burning all your letters, Mr Green Orchard Estates,' Patsy had shouted loud as she could.

Mark had no capital of his own, never had had. He had financed the Green Orchard development just as he had financed Simpson and Cape by salting away his salary into a private account all through the loving years. Her royalties and the dwindling income she had from her father's investments had always gone into their joint account to prove she trusted him. She had wondered why the joint account emptied so fast but never bothered to go through the statements. Finance was Mark's department. It was plain to see when she finally checked them.

'Mr Who?' Mrs Bond said, puzzled. Burning paper was blowing everywhere, dangerous with the old beams, though really she had better things to do than chase round after her ladies.

'I'm burning his letters,' Patsy shouted. Her face was all smuts and her dark eyes were wild. 'Every single bloody letter he ever wrote.' The flaming pile collapsed round her feet and just for a moment it looked as if she might throw herself on the fire. But Mrs Bond put out her arms and for a moment they stood locked together.

'Do you know how many times he said he loved me?' Patsy whispered.

'There there.' Mrs Bond rocked gently. 'None of 'em's worth it, my duck. All sweet talk and soft soap if you ask me.'

'Why did he have to keep saying it?' Patsy said.

'Don't trust one of 'em further than I could throw 'im,' Mrs Bond said. Fragments took off round them like black butterflies edged with crimson.

'Shall I get the books?'

'Go on then,' Mrs Bond said. But the cupboard in the study was locked. They couldn't get it open at first but then she remembered the rusty gaff lying there in the barn, running out to get it started the guinea pig chirruping. There were books in the cupboard all right, as she told Frank after, photographs of girls with no clothes, close-ups of girls doing things to theirselves, men and girls doing things to each other, things you never would have thought of in a hundred years.

They carried the books down and threw the whole lot on. For a moment the bonfire went dark and seemed to fizzle out but the blaze took hold as if it was angry, the photos crackling, the girls twisting like salamanders in the punishing flames.

'His precious books, he paid the earth...' Patsy said and suddenly began to sing. '"Double, double, toil and trouble; Fire burn and cauldron bubble."' She skipped round the fire and a moment later they were both skipping and singing round until the fire died down.

'That's what happens,' Patsy said, flopping breathless into a kitchen chair as Mrs Bond put the kettle on. 'They turn us into witches then they burn us.'

'Books like that are better off burned,' Mrs Bond said primly.

Late in the Day

Such wicked heathen books, she'd get to church on Sunday, make Frank come.

'You know what you want to do?' she said, sipping her tea. 'You want to sit down and write one of your lovey-dovey books.'

'I wonder if I could?' Patsy said thoughtfully. She had been younger and still believed in love as life's salvation in those days.

'Time you was in bed,' Mrs Bond said, washing up the cups. 'I'll be off then when I done this.'

'Could you wait till I'm in bed?' Patsy said in a small voice.

'Course I will,' Mrs Bond said. It was like the children all over again, she thought, as ten minutes later she went up and tucked her in. 'Good night, sleep tight.'

She let herself out of the front door and tramped round the black patch where the bonfire had been. Stamping to see it was all safe. Walking down the lane in the moonlight.

In front of the chattering telly Frank was fast asleep.

It was shady between the raspberry canes as Francesca searched for the last of the crop, each berry warm and soft like a little animal. Hadn't she watered them every night despite threats of drought from Wessex Water? The summer school students were arriving over the weekend, work started on Monday, surely she had already dealt with all possible last-minute headaches. Nothing more could go wrong.

She was temporarily estranged from Antonio who had been offended by her suggestion that he should stay on after the end of term and do the summer school course too. 'My English too good everybody say,' he had protested, pouting childishly. But he had stayed none the less and if he wanted to sulk for a few days she was glad of the respite. It amazed her that after a night with Antonio, eighteen now and inexhaustible, every time she glimpsed a tiny section of his bronzed body she experienced what she thought of as a *great leap* inside her. She had no intention of stopping her HRT pills now despite warnings in the Sunday papers. But she probably would if Freddy came back.

Not that she had grieved for Freddy but she did grieve for Jack metamorphosed into a belligerent stranger demanding angrily, 'Did you want something?' when she went to his workshop to ask for more keys to the summerhouse. Jack who had been so entranced by her response. Was it Anna said men were scared by the sexual passions of women and devised purdah and crinolines and clitoridectomy to both control their fear and obliterate the passion itself? Could that be right?

Fortunately Jack's anger had been before Antonio started sulking and Antonio had put a new lock on the summerhouse door and now she had lots of keys. He had a natural confidence in his abilities and was soon as competent with Freddy's Black & Decker drill as Freddy had ever been.

Francesca put the basket of raspberries and a handful of raspberry leaves on the car seat beside her. Lottie had looked tired the week before, huge and exhausted. The baby wasn't due for another two months but Hugo and Lottie were hopeless about dates. Was it because she had suggested an abortion that she longed to see this particular baby?

The front door was open, the house quiet. Lottie lay in the long grass of the back garden like a beached whale.

'Oh, it's you, Francesca.'

'I brought you some raspberries.'

'I'm afraid Hugo's not here,' Lottie said, putting raspberries in her mouth one by one, fingers precise and delicate as the pecking of a bird. 'He's taken the children up to City Farm.'

'It was you I wanted to see actually,' Francesca said. You could hardly call it *manipulative* when everything she did was for their sakes. 'You know I sold the rocking-horse?'

'Yes,' Lottie said, shaking raspberries into her palm. There was a special quality about Lottie, Francesca thought, a natural acquaintance with the heart of things.

'Raspberry leaf tea is good for pregnant women,' Francesca said.

'Tastes all right,' Lottie said, rolling the leaves into a small green sausage and biting with her front teeth.

'The rocking-horse attracted a lot of attention,' Francesca said. It had not seemed necessary to tell Hugo and Lottie it had actually been sold for two hundred and fifty pounds. 'Brandon Lodge isn't your run-of-the-mill adult education place, you know. We're always trying something new like this English Language summer school.'

'Mm,' Lottie said, munching.

'Way I see it the system is too hierarchical. But places like Brandon Lodge are able to experiment with community education, know what I mean?' Francesca went on, trying to dumb down

Hugo's point of view without actually quoting him. Grovelling in a good cause, she thought. Hadn't she grovelled for years to keep the marriage going for the boys?

'That's what Hugo says,' Lottie said. Just as well she wasn't too bright, Francesca thought, with a sharp glance. The sad droop of Lottie's eyes and her sombre expression made Francesca feel fussy and trivial.

'My friend Anna Bolt's working at Brandon Lodge too now, teaching at the summer school, and I've managed to convince them that we need a part-time art and craft teacher,' Francesca went on but the expression on Lottie's face suggested she wasn't listening. 'I haven't said anything to Hugo but what do you think, Lottie?'

Lottie's eyes had widened like dark ponds and seemed to fill her entire face. 'I think you'd better phone the hospital.'

The ambulance slid to the kerb and Lottie walked along the passage and across the pavement with an air of concentration.

'There's a good girl then,' the ambulance man said cheerily as he opened the back doors. Francesca followed with the plastic bag which served as a suitcase.

'Oh, where is Hugo?' she murmured, looking over her shoulder back along the road.

'Bit pressed for time, love,' the ambulance man said, nodding her into the ambulance where Lottie was bending forwards, her belly clutched in the circle of her arms. 'Can't hang about with number four, know what I mean?'

'Sorry.' Francesca clambered in. 'It's my son should be here. Hugo.'

'Oh!' Lottie grabbed Francesca's hand, twisting hard as the contraction rose through her body like a ring of fire.

'Easy does it, love,' said the ambulance man.

Going up in the hospital lift, Lottie still held Francesca's hand but she seemed scarcely aware of her surroundings. As if her eyes, as well as her consciousness, were turned into her body. The waters broke as they got to the labour ward.

'Do you want me to stay until Hugo comes?' Francesca said tentatively – Lottie must know about the abortion she had suggested, well recommended and offered to pay for privately; Hugo chronically unemployed; three skimpy little children reared on social was enough, surely. Perhaps Lottie would feel her presence was an ill-wishing one. Unlucky.

'I'd rather have you here anyway,' Lottie said, staring at the white mountain of her belly. Francesca was touched. Why was she so reluctant to be there, she wondered? Why had she felt so strongly about this baby anyway?

As a young woman her own fecundity had thwarted both her and Freddy's attempts to control it. Freddy had accepted the two boys with indifferent grace but he had refused absolutely to let her continue her three subsequent pregnancies. If she did, he said he would leave her. The doctor was no help under the old law. She had wandered down a mean back street with an address scribbled on a bit of paper but even that was more than they could afford. Francesca had got a book from the public library in the end. She was ignorant but had never been frightened by the intricacies of her own body.

'Oh!' said Lottie, twisting suddenly. 'Oh-oh-oh!' Her cries rose like a seagull's and died away.

'Shall I get someone?' Francesca said.

'Not yet,' said Lottie, closing her eyes. Limbo, Francesca thought, there was nothing to be done but wait.

Squatting on the bathroom floor all those years ago she had studied the diagrams and soaked her hands in Dettol. She had felt the tiny sac, pulled with her fingertips hard as she could. Nothing happened but two specks of bright blood on the bathmat. She had had to fetch Hugo from infant school at half past three. Spilt milk streamed across the supper table.

'I've had enough,' Freddy had said, picking up his chop and two vegetables and striding away to his study. 'We have both had quite enough. Too bloody much.'

'Another one coming,' Lottie panted, trying to smile. 'Did they ever give *you* raspberry leaf tea?'

'Won't be long now,' Sister said, burrowing briskly. 'You're fully dilated, Mrs Smith. We'll get you up to the delivery room in a jiffy.'

'Oh, where is Hugo?' Francesca said desperately. He should be here, a husband should be there. Freddy might have liked his children better if he had seen them born.

'Please stay, Francesca,' Lottie murmured. Her face looked grey against the white hospital gown. 'Please come with me.'

Late in the Day

'Only husbands and mothers in the delivery room,' Sister said, her eyes inquisitorial. She resented the invasion of what had once been her private domain. 'Are you Mrs Smith's mother?'

'Course she is,' Lottie said, tilting back her head as the trolley slid away down the corridor. 'Come on, Mum . . .'

'Coming,' Francesca said. Lottie needed her, needed Sister and the little pink-faced nurse too.

Francesca had needed someone that night. They had gone to the Odeon cinema which was a breakthrough. Having made his views of her pregnancy known, Freddy had not spoken to her for two weeks. In the middle of *Look Back in Anger* the pains had started, hot blood trickling against her thighs. She had had to run out to the Ladies, sat there in the urine-scented gloom, hearing the blood plop until she passed out on the floor. Freddy's name was flashed on the screen.

'For God's sake why didn't you tell me?' Freddy said.

'A deep breath, Mrs Smith, take a deep breath,' Sister said, pulling on her rubber gloves. Above, the mirror stared down like a round silver eye. 'Hang on a moment, dear.'

'Can't,' said Lottie huskily, but her voice was lost as her body took control. Francesca stared at the mirror hypnotised. Lottie's knees and the black patch of pubic hair. A long, low moan, a cow-like bellow. Too bloody much.

'Push, dear, *push*, Mrs Smith.' A round head shot out, yellow hair, flat against a palpitating scalp. Another loud bellow and the whole length of bloodstained child slid from between her legs, swinging in Sister's hands.

'There you are,' she said. 'A lovely little girl.'

'A girl,' Francesca breathed. What had that other child been, she wondered? The Odeon was a bingo hall now.

'Francesca,' Lottie said. 'We'll call her Francesca.'

Chapter Seventeen

Patsy woke to the usual intrusive clatter coming from the old orchard. Monday morning, but the old life had gone, incinerated with the letters and ribbons and books last night.

A new life. Was forty-six too late for a new life? How and where did one start?

Patsy stomped across to the window on the soft but solid pillars of her legs and stared down at the large black patch.

'I did that!' she whispered, not quite believing she could perpetrate such desecration. But Harriet was due back the day after tomorrow and what would she say about the damage to her precious lawn? One had to get out of a rut somehow, a butterfly has to get out of its chrysalis, and like the butterfly maybe what she needed were new clothes. She had an account at Dingles, no one would know she was broke. She could drive into Bristol this afternoon and go shopping, go to the cinema even.

Patsy dressed and made coffee, carried a cup to her study where the windows looked over the front. She could hardly hear the noise from the orchard with the door closed, 'sporting her oak' as she used to call it, controlling but not entirely preventing interruption by the children. Those days were gone but there were other days somewhere, *her* days if she could only find them.

Her eyes travelled slowly round. She had never allowed Mrs Bond or anyone else to tidy in here. The electric typewriter sat in the middle of the large desk, she ran a tentative finger across its cover furry with dust. Several typed pages lay scattered round. Large, slightly faded publisher's photographs of herself, yellowed pictures cut from newspapers headlined 'Patricia Simpson Addresses Romantic Novelists Association' and 'Patricia Simpson Opens Library Wing' decorated the walls. Whatever had she said on such occasions, Patsy wondered? All those words she had lost for ever. If only she had taped them.

She gathered the scattered papers into a pile. She would go through them later. There used to be a blue duster in the desk drawer. The blue duster was still there.

Monday morning Anna swallowed her beta blocker with orange juice and made herself coffee and toast. Sensible to eat an egg, she thought, but her fluttery stomach couldn't face it. Her hands however were steady as she gripped the steering wheel of the 2CV and drove with care to Brandon Lodge.

Half an hour later she faced the class, Group Three in Classroom Three, for the first time. Her eyes flicked from face to face of the seven students so far assembled. She felt perfectly calm but her body no longer seemed to belong to her. She felt faint too. Suppose she passed out in front of them, what would the poor things do, she wondered?

'Welcome and good morning, all of you!' She spoke loudly and clearly but her voice dipped and quavered. 'I am Anna Bolt, your teacher. I want you all to write your names on this paper large enough for me to read.' It had been Francesca's suggestion and involuntarily Anna delivered it in imitation of Francesca's vigorous tone. The voice lent her courage as she handed out paper and then demonstrated, writing her own name in large black felt-penned letters and propping it up on her desk. Several students nodded and smiled and suddenly a brilliant excitement rose and then grew inside Anna, mingling with and finally overwhelming her nervousness.

I can do it, she thought. I am doing it.

She smiled and behind their newly written labels the seven students smiled back with varying degrees of perplexity: Esau Etim, a middle-aged Nigerian student, in a flowing sky-blue robe with elaborate white embroidery round the neck, Mei Lin and Ah Lin, two Chinese girls from Singapore, Fabiola a pretty Italian girl, Hans and Wolfgang from Germany and Liv, a young woman from Sweden. Except for Esau Etim and Liv in a beige linen trouser suit, everybody wore jeans.

A few minutes later Anna had organised the class into pairs, partnering Esau Etim, the odd one out, herself, and instructing every student to talk to their partner for two minutes and then each introduce the other to the class. The more advanced grasped the procedure at once, others whispered for a while, heads close together, eyes darting nervously.

'Tell me about yourself and your family?' Anna suggested to Esau Etim.

'Good morning, Mrs Bolt,' Esau Etim began with a wide smile. 'I am coming from Lagos in Nigeria. I am being business man with taxi business, cocoa business, oil business and all sorts. I am having big family in Lagos and other places. I am learning English at school in boyhood and soon I am starting new business, private school in Lagos for learning very fine English Language.'

'Goodness, what sort of school?' Anna asked, intrigued. 'You mean for Nigerian children?'

'School for children and big persons too, plenty children, plenty parents, plenty grandparents. All come to English College, Lagos to make speaking of English tongue perfect.' A laugh rumbled inside his voluminous sky-blue robe. 'Teaching very good,' he insisted in his fluent if idiosyncratic English.

The rest of the class, younger and less endowed with self-confidence, stared at Esau Etim transfixed.

'Hot, isn't it? How's it going?' Francesca inquired at lunchtime. Snack lunches had been organised in the cafeteria for the staff and students of the summer school.

'All right, I think,' Anna said. 'But I'm completely exhausted already.'

'Teaching's always like that for two or three days, then you get a second wind.' Francesca's restless blue eyes swept round the tables searching for Antonio, found him in conversation with a pretty Italian girl and flicked away. 'How are you getting on with Mr Esau Etim?' she inquired.

'OK,' Anna said.

'He came round to my house yesterday evening,' Francesca said. 'Whisked out to Combe Dingle in a taxi. Said he wanted me to give him extra coaching in the evenings in English and French, know what I mean?'

'Not sure I do,' Anna said. 'How did he get your address?'

'Asked at the office, I suppose,' Francesca said, her eyes creeping back to Antonio's table.

'Are you going to do it?'

Late in the Day

'Certainly not,' Francesca said. 'Too much on my plate already, not to mention babysitting.'

'The baby's OK?'

'Seems to be,' Francesca said. When Lottie went home the baby's name had been modified to Frances which Lottie explained would avoid confusion. 'Honestly, I hope I never have to go through that hospital bit again.'

'I dare say Lottie shares your sentiments,' Anna said drily.

'I doubt it,' Francesca said. 'If only she was more practical. You know Antonio, last year's catering course and helped at the Snape memorial party, do you see the girl next to him?'

'Fabiola Travolta,' Ana said, pleased to have the names in her head already. 'Pretty, isn't she? In my class. Why?'

At half past five Anna negotiated the car into a parking space just outside the door of the Hotwells flat. Two bunches of pinks wrapped in fancy paper lay on the doorstep and she added them to the exercise books lumped under her arm and let herself in. She opened all the windows in the oven-hot rooms and made herself tea. The first and she supposed the worst teaching day was over, and she was exhausted; her back and head ached but she was radiantly happy too. She had had no idea beforehand that she would feel like this, find she could teach and actually enjoy doing it. Perhaps after all she had a future in her own hands, something she could develop, change, something she could do.

She put the pinks in a glass vase. The rooms away from the street were the coolest and presently she lay down on the kitchen floor. Why not? The occasion as well as her aching back seemed to deserve such a gesture, the world her oyster.

'I did it,' she announced to the fly monotonously circling the white glass lampshade. 'And I did it quite well. Thank God for beta blockers!'

Not that the day had been an unmitigated success. Two boys from Hong Kong, Bo Teng and Victor, had arrived and there had been incomprehension and irritated mutterings round the class at times and Wolfgang had been positively cheeky. But she had kept most of her students' attention most of the time, they had all joined in the conversational exercises, especially Esau Etim, and settled to their written work. Now all she had to do was correct it.

Francesca had been teaching French and English courses for years but for Anna it was breakthrough time.

She was high as a kite. She had not felt as good as this for years, not since... well not since the children were born and before that when she got the exhibition to Newnham. But then Miss Snape's pleasure had been so intense it diminished her own. She imagined visiting her mother and saying, 'Today I taught English to nine foreign students!' Surely her mother would want to reply to that? But of course in the real world she had organised Cathy to do weekday visits for the summer school fortnight.

How to celebrate, she wondered, champagne on your own was expensive and pathetic. She could phone Owen and ask him round. She wasn't going to reject him for confiding sexual kinks he couldn't help, but Owen was too egocentric for any celebration not his own. Besides she was too tired for Owen.

Breakthrough time. There was the house, Rose Lodge, of course. She could phone Rupert, ask what was happening about the sale. Did he have a Monday evening surgery, she wondered, pleased to discover she didn't remember. She made herself a large plate of salad and picked up the phone.

'Rupert? About Rose Lodge?'

'What about it?'

'Well, we talked about selling it, didn't we? Er... have you put it up for sale or what?' Anna said, conciliatory.

'What are you on about? I put a hundred thousand in your bank account last week. There may be a bit more when the bills are settled.'

'A hundred thousand pounds?' Anna whispered. 'Why didn't you tell me? Have you sold it privately or something?'

'Haven't sold it at all, didn't have to. Deirdre's parents bought her half. *Financial planning*, they call it, a way of not paying Inheritance Tax. We had to *do things properly*, go up to Peterborough, get the marriage blessed in church, the full works, marquee on the lawn. Didn't anybody tell you?'

'Congratulations!' Anna said, aware of a chill, a shadow descending on her hot skin. Did she mind more because Rupert was so pleased, why should she mind? 'Lucky old you!'

'Don't I know it. You OK?'

'Fine, thanks. And thanks. For the money, I mean.'

'You're welcome,' Rupert said.

Late in the Day

One hundred thousand pounds. Anna dropped on to the sitting-room settee and stretched a languorous arm towards the estate agents pile. Surely there was something here she wanted for less than a hundred thousand? A house with a vista and a garden and an upstairs. A house of her own. Rupert and Deirdre had married as soon as the divorce came through because of the practice. Her marriage to Rupert was over long ago. One hundred thousand pounds was the only significant change.

The phone rang. Rupert again, what now, Anna thought.

'Hello?'

'It's me,' Owen said. 'Did you get the pinks?' He sounded excited, breathless. 'Peace offering. I met this New Zealand girl aged twenty-six, Noleen, thought I ought to phone and let you know.'

'Let me know what?' Anna said flatly. 'Why?'

'Because of the arrangement. I mean she was crazy for me, we made it in the sack three times the first date.'

'Congratulations,' Anna said coldly.

'I thought you'd be furious,' he said after a pause. He sounded disappointed. 'Really bawl me out. I mean I did promise to be faithful but the arrangement doesn't really start till September, does it? Thought I ought to tell you though because I'm seeing her tonight.'

'Goodbye then,' Anna said and put down the phone. Her hands were shaking and her mouth was dry. Why did things like this always happen to her? Middle-aged sex should above all be seemly.

The front door bell rang sharply. Esau Etim resplendent in sky blue stood on the doorstep and mopped his shining face.

'I am needing extra evening coaching, Mrs Bolt,' he said. 'How much you charge for extra French and English teaching?'

Driving in and parking the Mini on Monday evening, Harriet, who had engaged all the way from Heathrow in a dismal post-mortem of the holiday with Patrick, was struck by the change at OldPlace. Pinkish-brown dust from the building site lay everywhere, dimming the bright green of the garden. The first Green Orchard Estate houses, grey walls of building blocks encased now in red brick, were already visible beyond the hedge.

'You gave me quite a turn,' Mrs Bond said, sitting at the kitchen table with a cup of tea. 'Your mum wasn't expecting you, not till day after tomorrow. Gone into Bristol, shopping, won't be back till late. Had a good holiday, did you?'

'Lovely, thanks,' Harriet said. How many times would she have to say it? Such lies were a matter of face. Not to enjoy your holiday was one thing but to *confess* to not enjoying it was terminal defeat and would embarrass people too. At least the holiday was over. She would never again sit on a balcony waiting for Patrick, never again walk through the warm darkness to find him sitting in the bar of the Cafe de Athena with his arm round a blonde girl.

'You'll find things a bit different here,' Mrs Bond said. 'Quiet now but ever such a racket from the building site all day, foreman forgets his mobile, comes in here to use the phone. Cheek of it! Puts his money in the box, mind, enjoys a chat if you ask me. Well this won't get Frank's tea in the oven.' Mrs Bond levered herself up on her plump elbows. 'And your mum's a lot better, clearing old stuff out the attic.' She gave Harriet a quick glance. 'Burnt it on the lawn.'

'Not before time,' Harriet said.

'Easy to talk your age.' Mrs Bond unhooked her jacket from the back door. 'She's stopped talking about Woodman, leastways she has to me. I fed your Monty for you. See you Thursday then.'

Harriet unpacked her bag straight into the washing machine, washing out for ever the salt of the Aegean mixed with her own tears. She carried the almost empty suitcase upstairs to her bedroom. OldPlace was so quiet after the constant chatter of garrulous Greeks and tourists. She opened the window and looked out. She was incapable of relating to any man, Patrick had said, tossing back the fears she had so unwisely confided in the early days of love. Perhaps Patrick was right.

A man in a torn plaid shirt and jeans, fair-haired and suntanned, came round the end of the barn with a mug in his hand, tiptoeing at first, glancing into the empty kitchen, then walking boldly across the cobbles but alert still. Like a fox, Harriet thought.

He filled his mug from the garden tap by the back door, gulped water noisily and moved towards the empty cottage. Harriet leaned forward. She could only see the top of his head now, brick-dust in his hair, the glint of two days' growth on his cheekbones as he pressed his face to the cottage window and then moved on round the corner. She imagined the sitting-room as he was seeing it, the chair and sofa with the cretonne loose covers, the bamboo coffee-table bought in a Habitat sale.

'Did you want something?' she called. He came back then, caught off guard and surly.

'Seems like you got this cottage empty?' he said, looking not at her but across the garden. 'Not right, place empty when there's people give their eye-teeth for somewhere to live.'

'Are you looking for a place?' Harriet said. 'My mother does let the cottage sometimes. If she can find the right person.'

'Been looking six months. Wife and child and another expected, all in the one room at her mum's place. What sort of life is that?' He paused, his anger and frustration seeming inappropriate for a warm summer evening. She wasn't bad-looking if she did herself up a bit, he thought.

'Must be awful for you. My mother's out for the day.' Why had she told him that, she wondered? 'But if you'd like to look round, I could get the key.'

'Might as well,' he said, laid-back. He knew how the world ticked, being keen would do him no good. 'Rick's the name, by the way. Rick Clapton.'

Harriet came downstairs, collected the key and walked across the yard. She was acutely aware of the swish of her cotton skirt, the rhythm of her sandalled feet, the bounce of her breasts. Like a slow motion film, she thought, like being under water... or jet lag maybe?

She unlocked the front door. Bills lay on the mat, a tortoiseshell butterfly dead on the window sill. How long had it fluttered there, trapped, dashing wings on the glass? 'Bit dusty I'm afraid,' she murmured as he followed her into the sitting-room.

'Bit of dust don't matter,' Rick said. 'Gas cooker. On the mains, is it?'

'Calor,' Harriet said. The word seemed to have a special resonance. 'Bathroom's in there.' The cottage stairs went straight up behind the front door. Harriet walked up slowly, conscious of his eyes upon her bottom, his bulk blocking her retreat.

'There's just two bedrooms,' she said as he crossed to the window and stood looking down. Heat came from his body as if he had accumulated the long hot summer in his reddened skin.

'Know what rent she's asking?' he said hoarsely.

'Not really,' Harriet said, not wanting to muddy the moment with the cash nexus. 'I think the last lot paid two hundred a month.'

'Two hundred, eh?' He gave no sign whether he considered this fair or outrageous. His eyes considered her shrewdly as they walked slowly back, the key swinging from her hand. 'Would she let me have it, I mean if you was to have a word?'

'I've been away, she might have got somebody. But I'll certainly recommend...' She faltered under the intensity of his gaze, aware of her hot pink face getting hotter and pinker. 'Like a cup of coffee, Rick?'

'Don't mind,' he said softly. 'Nice old house you got here,' he added with a determined lack of reverence. 'Must take a bit to keep it up-together.'

'Like to see round?' Harriet said, switching on the kettle. 'I mean if you're interested... it's the only moated farmhouse in Somerset still in domestic use.'

'Is that right?' Rick said. There was a swagger in his manner now, as he calculated his chances and his eyelids thickened. She moved up the stairs in front of him, footsteps soundless in the deep-piled carpet.

'This is my mother's bedroom,' she said, knees quivering as she went on down the landing. 'And this is mine.'

'Is that right?' Rick said. She could feel his breath against her neck but she didn't turn round. His arm came across her shoulders, his lips touched her skin. She turned then, already locked in the circle of his arms, and pressed her burning face to him.

Downstairs the kettle boiled for a minute, puffing out steam and misting the windows; the automatic mechanism had never been perfect. Finally it switched off.

Half an hour later Harriet came down. Rick had already pulled on his shirt and jeans. 'Look at the time, she'll have my guts for garters. Put in a word to your mum. Cheers then.' He had disappeared downstairs and round the barn.

Harriet sat dreamily at the kitchen table for a long time, testing her slightly bruised lip with her tongue, feeling her scraped cheeks. She wanted to extend the moment, keep something of him on her face and skin. Inside her head their bodies twisted in eternal dance while a song like the murmur of bees repeated, 'I'm not frigid. Whatever Patrick says, I am not frigid.'

PART FOUR
Into Autumn

Chapter Eighteen

At OldPlace Patsy had begun to find her study a refuge from the noise of the building site and the disappointments and despairs of the outside world. Had it always been like this, she wondered, had she neglected real life and escaped into the fantasy world she was weaving? Was that why Mark had resented her writing? Not that she thought about Mark much any more. She had spat him out, incinerated his image with his letters. She had grieved for long enough, too long.

She was married to OldPlace now.

Boring, Anna had said. How could anyone find the revealed and palpitating heart of their closest friend boring? She was never going to speak to Anna again, well not for a long time anyway.

So Patsy mused, making herself coffee. She needed her writing, recognition of her work and the money she hoped it would bring. Her typing had deteriorated and it took more effort to blow up the romantic balloon and keep it aloft but Patsy was determined and she needed the money. OldPlace was expensive to keep up.

The cottage being let was a help, even if the Claptons were not exactly the tenants she would have chosen. Harriet seemed to get on with them and they would probably leave when the Green Orchard Estate was finished. She wouldn't have chosen Harriet's job at the local pub, the King's Head, four evenings a week either but then she hadn't been asked. Harriet herself was uncommunicative; apparently the relationship with Patrick was over. But didn't Anna once say that if you worried about your children, they didn't have to which meant they didn't grow up. Perhaps Anna was right.

Patsy sighed and resumed her typing.

* * *

Waking in the room next door, Harriet turned over in bed. It couldn't be, could it, she thought? It was just the hot weather and breaking with Patrick had upset her body rhythms or something? After all they had been together for almost a year. But suppose . . . just suppose . . . it was . . .

The new term at Brandon Lodge did not start until early September so, the summer school over, Francesca and Anna had two weeks' holiday. Not that Francesca took it, two days was enough, after that she went in each morning. Mr Austin was away in the Seychelles and there was correspondence to be dealt with, not to mention inquiries from all over about whether there was going to be a summer school next year. Antonio had vanished without a word, almost as if he was ashamed of what they had done together. The house seemed particularly empty.

As usual when she was lonely she thought about Willy. That last evening in the summerhouse. Willy coming on to her, she responding, but suddenly Miss Snape was there, flinging back the doors like Sarah Bernhardt, shouting 'Francesca Alexander, how dare you?' How had she known they were there? It was true what they said, you never did quite get over your first love, especially a love cut short.

The long hot summer had produced a drought and a hose-pipe ban which Francesca continued to ignore. Her neighbours' gardens had turned the colour of string but hers continued to burgeon in wicked, incriminating green. How could she let the garden go when she had another Snape memorial fund luncheon planned, even if she hadn't fixed the date? Coming in from the garden she kicked off her shoes and helped herself to a chocolate mint from the box on the table. The students had been particularly generous this year. She was pleased to see Anna did almost as well in chocolates and roses as herself but it did suggest that the young were not too clever in estimating competence. Francesca took another chocolate mint.

For years Anna had told herself she needed change but during the late summer changes seemed to take over. Was it the money from Rose Lodge coming at last or the arrangement with Owen falling through or her teaching at the summer school which had set her going, she wondered? As a teacher she had not been marvellous, she realised a few days after the course finished, but she had been adequate and she had seen it through.

And now she had put in an offer for a house, subject to the surveyor's report. Precipitate yes but it was a good time to buy everybody said, and she didn't want to hang about. One change seemed to stimulate another and the following day Anna signed on for a six-week course at South Bristol College in Teaching English as a Foreign Language which started in October.

'What about your job?' Cathy was exasperated.

'Oh, I'll have to give it up, won't I?' Anna said casually. 'End of September.'

'So what will you live on?' Cathy said. 'Spend, spend, spend. You're in good nick, Mum, but you can't afford to run through all your capital at your age.'

'I suppose not,' Anna agreed meekly but making changes seemed to be compulsive once you started. Besides, Mr Etim was staying on in Bristol for a few weeks for *business reasons* so he said and still came for coaching. Perhaps she could get other students and once she had a house she could let a room to keep herself going. And it was high time she got herself properly qualified, Anna told herself. Maybe she should study for a degree with the Open University as Olivia Porter had suggested; the new academic year started in February. Making changes was heady stuff but were they actually the changes she wanted? Rupert always said she never knew what she wanted, only what she didn't want. Maybe Rupert was right.

On Friday afternoon she visited Bexley House. It was not her usual time and her mother was in the sitting-room with nine other old ladies, watching a film on television with the sound turned very low. They nodded and smiled as Anna arrived but soon their eyes slid back to the television.

'We could go to your room if you like,' Anna said but it occurred to her that her mother might behave better in the presence of the others. 'Or I could bring the cups in here?'

'Please yourself,' her mother muttered. 'You always do.' Saying anything was progress, Anna thought. Perhaps her mother's vow of silence would gradually melt away. She smiled as she carried the largest and most prestigious of Bunny's silver cups back to the sitting-room and settled herself in the vacant chair next to her mother.

'How are you, dear?' she asked rubbing at the cup's silvery cheek. It was what she usually said and she supposed the regularity might be comforting. 'You know I work at Brandon Lodge,' Anna went on, keeping her voice low. 'With Francesca Smith, you remember Francesca Smith, very pretty fair girl, we were both at Avon Towers... well anyway she's got a new little granddaughter called Frances, her son Hugo's baby. We've both been working at this summer school at Brandon Lodge for the last fortnight.' She tried to keep her voice natural. After all it wasn't so different from the days when she used to visit the flat and tell herself that her mother was entitled to be treated as a person and talk on and on about Cathy's doings and her own, tweaking truth to make the story more interesting.

'That's better,' Anna said, holding up the cup and then peering at the inscription. 'What did Bunny get this for?'

'Judas!' her mother said suddenly. Nine white heads swung round towards her like sunflowers to the sun.

'What did you say?' Anna said. 'Whatever do you mean?'

'You took my flat, didn't you?' Her eyes were bead-bright in their shadowed hollows and her voice was shrill.

'It wasn't like that,' Anna stammered.

'You wanted my flat, didn't you?' Her gaze swept round the others, a small patch of pink dotted each cheek. 'She put me in here so she could get my flat. My own daughter!' A long pause, the others glancing at Anna and away.

'My daughter's ever so good,' one of them remarked.

'That's not fair, Mum... I know it seems like that to you but...' Anna tried to keep her tone reasonable but she could feel the blood rising in her own cheeks now. 'I had my own flat when you came in here. And you couldn't manage any more, you know you couldn't. Your flat was already left empty, so I moved in.'

'Put me in here, so she could get my flat.' Her mother's voice rose to a shriek. A girl in a blue nylon overall looked in and quickly withdrew. 'Greedy, always was, grabbing things.'

'Anyway I'm moving out of the flat soon,' Anna said. 'I'm getting a house of my own.'

'Where's the money coming from I'd like to know?' Her mother waved her cane. 'You should have stopped at Rose Lodge like I said.'

'I can't do anything right for you, can I?' Anna stood up. 'And I never could. How unkind you were, beating me with that riding switch of yours when Daddy went out, do you remember? What a way to treat a little girl.'

'Lies, all lies. Never laid a finger on her,' her mother shrieked to the room. 'Jealous of my son, Bunny, always was. Her father's girl, apple of his eye . . .'

'Hush now, dear,' Mrs Dewar said, bustling in and assessing the situation with an experienced eye. 'We can't have you wearing yourself out like this, can we? What you need is a nice rest before tea and one of Dr Purdy's pills. Come along now.' Anna followed, hovered meekly at the door of her mother's room.

'I think I'd better just go,' she whispered as Mrs Dewar came out, closing the door behind her.

'Just as you like, Mrs Bolt. Don't worry, we're quite used to these little ups and downs. Leave her a week or two, I should. She's getting on quite well with the other ladies now and your daughter . . . er, Cathy is it, with the kiddies? Yes, they get on like a house on fire . . .'

In Bristol the rush hour had already started and as Anna drove away the traffic was gathering momentum.

'Shouldn't have got cross like that,' she murmured, negotiating the 2CV into the moving stream. 'We've all done things we regret, haven't we? If Mother's forgotten she should be left in peace and forgetfulness. '"Father forgive them they know not what they do,"' she added. Was she talking to God or to poor dear Daddy?

Anna shrugged her shoulders, shifting the tension in her neck. Getting cross with her mother was always a mistake; nothing came of it but spiky pain. Nowadays people recommended expressing yourself more fully, slamming doors and breaking vases in the interests of long-term tranquillity. Dr Wilding had even suggested she should buy herself a punchball to express and relieve repressed anger. She wasn't sure he had been joking.

But *Judas*, Judas was too much, curious how hate and ignominy still clung to the name. But it was ridiculous to let it upset her. As Miss Miles pointed out, it was years since her mother had been rational and a long time since she could conduct a sensible conversation.

Geraldine Kaye

Five o'clock would not be a good time to phone Cathy, thinking about the children's tea, but Anna phoned anyway.

'Mum?' Cathy's voice was high; a child, probably Edward, was crying in the background. 'Something wrong?'

'I've just been to see your grandmother,' Anna said. 'You told her I was living at her flat. I did ask you not to.'

'She asked me. Do you expect me to tell lies?' Cathy said.

'You could have *prevaricated*, surely,' Anna said. 'You know what she's like. She made a big scene.'

'I thought she wouldn't speak to you?'

'Well today she did. In front of half a dozen of the old things. Called me Judas,' Anna said. Cathy gave a muffled snort. 'It's not funny, not if you're a clergyman's daughter.'

'Sorry, Mum,' Cathy said as the crying behind her crescendoed. 'Must go.' She slammed down the phone.

'Is something wrong, Mrs Bolt?' Mr Etim said, arriving for his English coaching half an hour later. She had explained at the outset that she couldn't manage French.

'Well . . . it's just my mother,' Anna said, her eyes prickling.

'Your mother is ill?' Mr Etim said.

'Oh, she's quite well. It's just . . . she's angry with me,' Anna said and burst into tears.

'Angry? Your mother is angry,' Mr Etim said, putting his arm round her shoulders. 'That is not good . . . not good at all.' She could feel his deep voice vibrating against her, smell the coconut oil mingled with the flower-smell of his aftershave. 'Do you like to tell me why your mother is angry with her good-good, hard-working daughter?'

'It's a long story,' Anna said. 'She's quite old now and not quite . . . well, she lives in an old people's home and . . .'

'I am hearing of such things,' Mr Etim said. 'But in Africa old mothers stay in the village with their families.'

'But we couldn't do that here,' Anna said. 'I mean I go out to work each day, I really couldn't look after Mother. I mean she isn't quite right in the head . . .'

'You are respected professional teacher lady, what for you let very old mother be upsetting you?'

'I suppose it is a bit silly,' Anna said, breaking free and turning away to blow her nose. 'Excuse me a minute. Would you like some tea, Mr Etim?'

'Like very much,' he said as the front door bell rang.

Owen stood on the doorstep with a bunch of dahlias. He was smiling, eyes bright.

'Oh, it's you!' Anna said. 'I wasn't expecting . . .'

'What dahlias?' he said, sweeping past her into the passage. 'I suddenly thought I'd like to take you out to dinner tonight, nothing to do with the arrangement or anything, just a bit of a celebration. No strings. How about it?'

'You've got a nerve,' Anna said.

'But it's all over with Noleen . . . I mean that's what . . .'

'I don't think you've met Mr Etim?' Anna said. He was standing just inside the sitting-room, splendid in his sky-blue gown. 'He comes to me for coaching.'

There was a long pause.

'Coaching?' Owen said on a rising note. 'Coaching? That's a new one on me. I'm afraid I'm not fully conversant with today's trendy language.'

'Don't be ridiculous,' Anna said.

'You've had it now, you know that, don't you?' His voice rose as he moved unsteadily back to the front door. 'Finally and irrevocably had it, far as I'm concerned. Bloody women,' he shouted, slamming the door behind him.

Above the ceiling a chair leg scraped across the floor.

'Very angry fellow,' Mr Etim said, his smile complacent and perfectly calm. 'No respect for beautiful mature womans. No respect at all. I am not liking that behaviour.'

'Would you still like some tea, Mr Etim?' Anna said. Her hands were shaking and her whole body felt limp.

'Tea very good but please call me Esau,' he said.

Chapter Nineteen

The first day of term at Brandon Lodge was always chaotic. Students stood in clumps all along the corridors exchanging greetings, exam results and holiday conquests in loud, cheerful voices. Others gathered in front of the notice board or besieged the registry office, indignant or disappointed, sometimes accompanied by an indignant and disappointed parent.

Withdrawing from the mêlée Anna applied herself to her word processor. Francesca had put a pile of letters on her desk before she arrived. But she had to catch Mr Austin and Francesca, preferably together, as soon as possible and tell them about the changes in her life plans. It would be better to get it over, there was never going to be a *right* moment.

Why was she suddenly so determined to leave, she wondered, when she had a reasonably pleasant job for the first time in four years? Was it because of Owen? She had been upset by the rudeness and violence of his rejection on the entirely false pretext of her relationship with Esau. But the breakdown of the arrangement had come as a relief. In theory the idea was sensible but in practice she couldn't like it and she wasn't going to pretend. Did that mean she was beginning to take charge of her own life?

As soon as she heard Francesca go into Mr Austin's office Anna knocked on the door. A line of students sat outside.

'Come.'

'Can I have a quick word?' Anna said.

'Of course.' Mr Austin looked up from the timetable he was perusing with a pale smile. 'Er . . . I should tell you how pleased everybody has been with your performance during the summer school. Students couldn't praise you enough . . .'

'Does it have to be right now, Anna?' Francesca intercepted,

Late in the Day

brisk in her new blue trouser suit. 'We are *frantically* busy this morning . . . naturally.'

'I'm afraid it does,' Anna said. 'Won't take a minute. The thing is I've applied to do a course at South Bristol, six weeks this October going into November, Teaching English as a Foreign Language, for the Preliminary Certificate. I was wondering if I could have a six weeks' leave or something . . . like a sabbatical?'

For a moment they stared at her in silence.

'Of course not.' Francesca's eyes were wide. 'How can we give you leave after you've been here four months? People get sabbaticals after six years' hard work if at all.'

'Sometimes we stretch a point,' Mr Austin said with an ameliorating smile.

'But we don't stretch it five and a half years,' Francesca said sharply. Hadn't she done her very best for Anna?

'I'm sorry,' Anna said but she wasn't sorry, she realised, and she wasn't going to feel guilty, she was *not*. 'Because I do understand it was you two who gave me this job and then asked me to teach when somebody dropped out. But then I discovered I could do it, teach that is, and what's more I liked it, so I have to think of getting properly qualified, I mean it's what Brandon Lodge is all about, isn't it? GNVQs and B.Tecs and all that, people getting proper qualifications?'

'Qualifications are exceedingly important,' Mr Austin conceded. 'But your situation is rather different, Anna, as a lady from Newnham College, Cambridge. And I'm afraid the local authority wouldn't even consider . . . I mean there'd be absolutely no precedent. Perhaps if you could postpone . . . apply again in a year or two . . . give us more warning.'

'Well then . . .' Anna said firmly. It was her life, wasn't it, what was left of it? 'I shall have to give you a month's notice.' She had never given anybody notice before: not Kellys or Brewsters, not Rupert.

'But that's ridiculous,' Francesca said reasonably. 'I mean what are you going to live on?'

'Perhaps you should think this over,' Mr Austin said. 'We'll talk about it later, shall we?'

'If you like,' Anna said. 'But it won't make any difference.'

Half an hour later Francesca came to Anna's office.

'Why on earth didn't you come and see me first?' she said. 'Talk

Geraldine Kaye

about a slap in the face. You wouldn't have *got* the job here without me, you realise?'

'Course I realise,' Anna said. 'And I'm grateful, Fran, but things have changed. I've changed,' she added and hoped it was true. 'It isn't just the TEFL course. I told you I'd got half the money for Rose Lodge and I've put in an offer for a house like you said I should and the agent thinks they'll accept it and I've got to get it all together, know what I mean?'

'Well that's good news,' Francesca said. 'But how long is the money going to last? You won't be able to claim social if you give us notice. Not for weeks...'

'I know that,' Anna said. There was always a price-tag for changes. 'I'm sorry, Fran. But I just don't want to do secretarial work for the rest of my life. And now it seems maybe I don't have to. You've been really good to me, really helpful but I've got to stand on my own feet, make my own decisions, haven't I?'

'Well that's it then,' Francesca said. 'I wash my hands of it all.'

Owen knocked on her office door next day.

'I understand we're losing you,' he remarked with a wary smile. 'I hope it wasn't anything to do with me?'

'Nothing,' Anna said coolly. 'Things do sometimes happen without your assistance, Owen. The world keeps turning.'

'Touché.' Owen stepped closer. 'I'm sorry about the other day, flying off the handle like that. I hope I didn't upset you?'

'You did as a matter of fact,' Anna said.

'Mea culpa, mea culpa,' Owen said.

'Quite.'

'I wanted to tell you it's all over with Noleen. I found out she'd had her tubes tied, so she couldn't have kids. What sort of woman would do a thing like that?'

'A sensible woman if that's the way she feels,' Anna shrugged.

'Unnatural,' Owen said. 'That black chap, you must admit it did look as if...'

'Don't be ridiculous,' Anna said. 'Anyway it's none of your business.'

'I said I'm sorry. You're really something when you're angry. I suppose you wouldn't consider starting again... going right back to the beginning?'

'No,' Anna said.

* * *

Late in the Day

For the rest of that day Francesca was distant with Anna, even frosty, but she could never sustain the mode for long, it was too unrewarding. Anna had let her down, exploited her generosity, but Anna had to be forgiven. Francesca was used to forgiving. Hadn't she forgiven Miss Snape for her iniquities, Hereward and Freddy for theirs? Bearing a grudge, you tainted your own life.

Anna was entitled to do her own thing, chance her arm, perhaps fail. A postcard from Antonio had arrived by the late post and was lying on the mat when Francesca got home. One side a detail of the Sistine chapel, the other a scribbled message, 'Love and thanks. A.' and a kiss composed from lots of little kisses. She knew by instinct it was the last she would ever hear of Antonio, knew by *experience* she corrected herself, chastened. Freddy, the pedant, had frowned at her too-casual use of the word *instinct* but she knew what she meant.

Francesca carried her supper tray up through the warm evening garden to the summerhouse. How Antonio had loved the summerhouse, but relaxing on the daybed and gazing up at the curtain of clematis Montana she found herself thinking of Willy and the old summerhouse at Avon Towers. Everything would have been different if the summerhouse hadn't been so close to Miss Snape's drawing-room. But perhaps it was that dangerous closeness that had made it so exquisitely exciting?

When it was dark she took the tray inside and fetched the hosepipe, dragging the green snake of it behind her as she sprayed life-giving water.

Later she phoned Anna, spoke in her usual voice, sweet and enthusiastic, making over the situation to her advantage. She wanted to fix a date for the next Snape memorial lunch, and as she expected Anna, relieved to find Francesca no longer annoyed, agreed to the date in October without arguing. She even offered to address the envelopes and to cook a couple of quiches. Francesca accepted with good grace. Anna was only a so-so cook but her quiches could go at the back of the table.

Patsy got up at six o'clock. She liked to make a start early while OldPlace was still quiet and entirely hers, every blade of grass and ancient stone and mossy roof tile. She slipped into her dressing-gown and went downstairs, tiptoeing past Harriet's closed bedroom door. Was Harriet even there, she wondered, what time had she come in, that job at the pub was all very well.

She made herself some coffee, carried it up to her study and sat down at her typewriter. She read through the last lines she had written the previous day and began to type. She hardly seemed to think, she didn't have to. Once she was started the words dripped from the ends of her fingers in a spontaneous flow. It had been like that and now it was again.

Two hours later she made her way down to the kitchen for toast and further coffee. The noise of the building site had started up but at least the workers parked their cars the other side of the hedge now. She was surprised at the putter of a motorbike in the yard and, looking out of the window, saw Briony park and glance apprehensively at the house, tuck her helmet under her arm and approach the kitchen door.

'Hello, darling,' Patsy shouted, leaning down to undo the heavy farmhouse bolts. 'Dropped in for breakfast have you?'

'You could say,' Briony said.

'Ages since I've seen you. Toast OK? I've got some honey somewhere.' Patsy peered helplessly into the over-filled and untidy cupboard. Why did Briony always make her feel so useless, she wondered, aware of Briony's luminous dark gaze fixed upon her. My daughter is beautiful, she thought, a really beautiful girl. 'How are things? How was the grape-picking? I didn't even know you were back.'

'OK,' Briony said, fidgeting with the chinstrap of her helmet. 'It's just I wanted to see you about something.'

'See *me*?' Patsy said, surprised.

'Has Dad phoned?'

'Not recently,' Patsy said. 'Well, we don't ... I mean everything has to go through the solicitors at the moment ...'

'Oh!' Briony said. 'The thing is he's taken me on. I mean there's been nothing anywhere jobwise, nothing in the *Evening Post* even.'

'Who's taken you on?' Patsy said, staring as if through mist, her story still bright in her head.

'Dad. He's given me this job, sort of a trial.'

'Who?'

'Dad, for God's sake.'

'Job? But you read sociology.'

'Oh, Mum, the job market's flat as a pizza. Wrote to fifty-three

Late in the Day

places and only got one interview and then I didn't get it, most of them don't even reply and nobody's even heard of sociology. Like Jasper says it's not what you know it's who you know nowadays.'

'Who's Jasper?' Patsy said.

'Doesn't matter. Well I know Dad, don't I, so I went to see him and he offered me a job just like that.'

'What job?' Patsy dropped on to a kitchen chair.

'With Green Orchard Estates. Starting right at the bottom, making the tea, sweeping up, driving the digger, carrying hods up ladders. And I've got to do this evening course at the tech on bricklaying and stuff and take an A-level in technical drawing. Dad says I've got to learn all the different skills for two years and after that he *might* fork out for me to go back to university and do engineering or architecture and then I can work up to be a partner in Simpson and Cape.'

'I see,' Patsy said. Treachery, she thought. My daughter is beautiful but treacherous.

'So that's that,' Briony grinned, having imparted her information, got rid of the burden. 'That OK with you?'

'Suppose so. Well, he's your father, isn't he? Anyway who's Jasper?' Patsy said, trying to grasp the real world.

'Nobody. I mean just a bloke, he came to France with me grape-picking. Dad was going to ring you, he thought you might be a bit upset,' Briony said. 'But I don't see why, do you?'

'It's your life,' Patsy said. People came and went, grew up and went, stitched you up and went. But what you made yourself was always your own, the books and stories you wrote could not be there without you. 'Want some toast?'

'No thanks,' Briony said, jumping up. 'Bit of a rush.' She deposited a flying kiss on Patsy's cheek, first for years, Patsy thought.

'Next time you see me I'll be wearing a green helmet!' Briony said. 'Miss Green Orchard Estates!' She assumed a model's pose, grinned and disappeared towards the building site.

Patsy spread honey on a piece of toast and wondered how upset she was at Briony's defection and whether to phone Anna.

Upstairs Harriet's footsteps sounded in the passage, the bathroom door opened and closed. A retching followed by a splash, early morning sickness.

'Oh darling,' she whispered. 'Oh Harriet . . . oh help!'

'I am liking very much to take you for dinner to Brown's on Triangle, isn't it?' Esau Etim said at the end of his private lesson, eyes shining, dark as prunes.

'I *would like* very much . . .' Anna corrected. 'Well . . . that's kind of you, Esau, but I'm not quite sure . . .' She searched her handbag for her diary. 'I'm moving house next week and . . .'

Why was she hesitating, she wondered? She had never had a date with a black man but then, except for her visit to the Welsh National Opera with Owen, she had hardly had what was called a *date* with anybody except Rupert.

It was presumptuous to assume that a man who asked you out was *after* you, but men and women did often find themselves at cross purposes. He thinking he had to, she thinking she had to too. But it wasn't like that with Esau. She had been giving him private lessons for six weeks now. She knew he had three wives, one in the village he came from, two in Lagos, and nine children. They had discussed the details of his plan to start an English Language school in Lagos. His plan had at first been vague, even inconsequential for an experienced business man. Anna had persuaded him to define more carefully for whom the school was intended and what he wanted to achieve.

'I cannot say things very well but I am wishing to express much thanks and gratitude at Brown's restaurant on Triangle to fine-fine lady teacher who has given much help with many-many private lessons before I go back home to Nigeria. Perhaps we will talk of future?'

'You are going quite soon?' Anna said, aware of a hollowness inside. How quickly you got used to a pattern. Esau had been coming three evenings a week since early August. He did his homework exercises conscientiously but his progress had not been remarkable.

'Soon I must go home and see to family business in Lagos.' A laugh like thick honey bubbled deep inside his sky-blue gown. 'And family business up country too.'

'Yes, I see,' Anna said. Autumn made her nostalgic for Africa, swallows gathering on telegraph wires, flying south.

'So I wish to book table for two and dinner with you at

Late in the Day

Brown's on Saturday night before I leave,' he said. 'As we say in Nigeria, "Share meal with friend rich in fortune."'

'Thanks,' Anna smiled. 'I'll look forward to it, Esau.'

Chapter Twenty

Esau Etim was waiting on the steps as she approached the Venetian-style building that was Brown's, conspicuous as always in a newly washed and pressed sky-blue gown of which he evidently had a number. She would miss him, Anna thought, his cheerful and confident presence was comforting and his English, particularly his vocabulary, had improved. She wondered what they would find to talk about. She knew only the bare facts about his family and his life in Nigeria though he was so extrovert. His private lessons at her flat had made questions seem too personal, too vulgarly curious. She had left it to him to offer such intelligence as he wanted her to know.

'Am I late?' she said, passing a young beggar seated at the base of the steps. In recent years beggars had become invisible, she thought.

'Not late at all,' Esau said.

Anna followed him into the large room filled with bentwood tables and chairs, leafy green palms in pots and slowly revolving ceiling fans which lent an old-colonial air. A waitress with a blonde ponytail smiled charmingly as they ordered melon for starters, followed by seafood pasta and white wine.

'Have you noticed how young all the staff here are?' Anna whispered. 'Nobody over twenty-five.'

'Young people very good for business, make customer feel young also, like dancing girls,' Esau said, glancing round.

'No dancing girls I'm afraid. Have you booked your flight yet?' Anna asked.

'Not quite yet. Not for few days.' His eyes came back to her and seemed, she thought, speculative. 'Must go soon-soon.'

'Your family will be getting impatient, your wives?' Anna

looked away. In England polygamy was regarded as humorous. With the millennium approaching her life suddenly seemed narrow, circumscribed.

'Yes-yes,' he said. 'My wife, Ata, she is not liking this stay business. Every week I phone and she is impatient.'

'I'm not surprised,' Anna said.

'My wife, Ata, is chief wife where I am living in Lagos. Ata has plenty children, big house and household to take care of, very busy. She is looking after taxi business too.'

'I think you said you have nine children?'

'My wife, Ata, has seven,' Esau said. 'My wife in village, Laba, where I am born, has two. Grown up now, soon my son is making me grandfather, isn't it?' He chuckled. 'New wife, Dawn, none yet.'

'You must be a Muslim then, Esau?' Anna said, twisting pasta round her fork.

'Christian now,' Esau said. 'Roman Catholic, drink wine.'

'And they let you have three wives?'

'You thinking it is more Christian to send away two wives and their children? Where they are going? Eh-eh, you want we have people begging on streets like you?' He laughed uproariously at this proposition. 'In Nigeria we understand better such things. My new wife, Dawn, she is living at my house now. She is very young woman. Ata my big wife care for her, how you say "keep eye on her" while I am away. Lagos not good place for very young woman, plenty bad boys, veranda boys, plenty AIDS in West Africa.'

'And Ata . . .' Anna paused as the starter plates were removed. 'She doesn't mind Dawn being with her?'

'Why mind?' Esau said with his deep-belly laugh. 'Dawn help with work. Ata big wife for home and seven children, Dawn small wife for play. In Africa we have such things "above board" as you say in England. This seafood dish very good, like Lagos stew but eat better with "fufu", Ata is making very good fufu.'

Anna smiled and allowed him to change the subject, wondering whether women in Africa really accepted co-wives with such easy equanimity. Was it perhaps that they had no choice?

'So now you want to go back to Nigeria and start your language school?' Anna said.

'I am telling you what I am wanting,' Esau said expansively.

'Building I have already, old house I get from my father, very-very big house, but now I am wanting principal. Where do I find very good excellent principal for First Class English College, Lagos?' He sighed gustily and again the gleam of his black eyes was speculative. 'Now I am needing your help.'

'What kind of help?' Anna said uneasily.

'I am wishing Missus Anna Bolt to be principal to start up First Class English College, Lagos.'

'Me?' Anna said, astonished. 'Esau, I couldn't possibly. I'm not at all practical or organised. I wouldn't know how to start organising in Nigeria and I'm not qualified . . .'

'You live in Gambia long time and you like. You work in office long time so you are knowing office work, you go to Cambridge University and you teach at English Language summer school and just now you do course in teaching. What for you say *not qualified*? This excellent qualified for First Class English College, Lagos.'

'But Esau, I'm in the middle of buying myself a house,' Anna said breathlessly. 'And what about my old and confused mother and my children?' How could she tell him she was only just beginning to take charge of her own life when he had such an overblown view of her capabilities?

'Old mother come too, Ata take good-good care of old mother. House can wait for you, children grown up . . .' he said, dismissing all problems with a graceful wave of his hand. '"To lose elephant for a wren is foolish."'

'But you can't just bundle up old people like bits of furniture,' Anna protested. 'I live here where I feel safe. I've never even been to Nigeria but it's not a democracy. I mean there's trouble about the Ogoni people and Ken Saro-Wiwa being killed and lots of others. I couldn't live in a place like that.' How could she tell him she was only just beginning to feel her own life belonged to her?

Esau shrugged. 'Ogoni people make trouble but we are far from there. Nice apartment for you at top of First Class English College,' Esau went on, used to getting his own way. 'Ata fix all that. First Class English College is needing first-class English lady. Already I have some teachers, my sister's sons and daughters. And you will get more teachers, young like waiters in this restaurant, short-term contracts, very good pay. I am busy with taxi business and oil business.'

'But Esau, what about work permits? I mean you can't just go and work in another country nowadays, especially not in Nigeria where unemployment's high. And the government expelled thousands of Ghanaians a few years back. It was all over the papers.'

'Eh-eh, work permits no big trouble for me, I know plenty people in government. Soon fix paper stuff for you. You are not poor unskilled woman wanting to be prostitute like those Ghanaian women. You beautiful English lady with excellent education. You come and look first? I pay fare, Anna, you see big house for First Class English College. You like... you principal.'

'But...'

'I am good friend, I wait.' He shrugged. 'Expatriate allowance for you and air fare for mother. What you want?'

'You don't understand, Esau. I mean I like teaching but my life is here in England and I want to study some more...'

'Sweets?' The waitress with the ponytail whipped the plates away and held out the menu.

'Just coffee for me,' Anna said, exhausted.

'Double ice cream, kiwi and mango flavour,' Esau said, certain he would get what he wanted. Did he think he could change her mind even now?

How could he? How could she? Could she?

'But darling, what are you going to do?' Patsy said.

'Nothing,' Harriet said, sitting at the kitchen table with Monty in her lap. 'What did you expect me to do?'

'Well, I...' Patsy was for once lost for words. 'Where will you go?'

'I shall stay here of course. Babies get born every day of the week, don't they? It's no big deal.'

'But it's my grandchild,' Patsy said. 'If you hadn't been so keen to take the Claptons, you could have had the cottage, you and the baby.'

'Yes, Mother,' Harriet said.

In late September Anna moved into her own house.

'That's about it then,' she said, piling plastic bags on top of the dustbin at the Hotwells flat like a clutch of fat black eggs. Was she developing her mother's need to accumulate, she wondered?

Esau had continued his private lessons and now and then repeated his offer.

It was Saturday and Anna still had another week's notice to work out at Brandon Lodge. Jasper and Briony had already loaded the settee and bed from Sofa, her mother's bureau and other items, the last of the vicarage, into the van.

'Ready for the off then?' Jasper said.

'Think so,' Anna said. 'Better have a last look round.'

'Know something, I could build up my own business doing this,' Jasper said, getting in the cabin. 'Get the enterprise allowance, why not?'

'Yeah?' said Briony, slamming the van door. 'Go for it.'

Anna glanced into the small abandoned rooms. Leaving was always sad. The flat, her sanctuary for months, reverted now to being her mother's old flat.

Anna slammed and double-locked the front door.

'I'd better lead, hadn't I?' she said.

'Excellent,' said Jasper.

The back of the 2CV was piled so high with boxes of saucepans, crockery and clothes, she couldn't see out. But the car started at once and she waved as it rattled its way cheerfully down to the Hotwell Road and then up towards Bishopston. Would Esau find his way up here, she wondered? She smiled as she reached the house, parking possessively in front of it and then moving forwards to give Jasper best access.

It was an ordinary enough mid-nineteenth-century terrace house with a minute cobbled garden in front and a long rectangle of wilderness at the back. She had had it carpeted right through in a light tobacco colour the week before and pieces of furniture from Rose Lodge, her own bureau, a table and four chairs, and the furniture from Olly's old bedroom now filled the front room.

Yesterday evening she had hung the William Morris strawberry thief curtains; apparently Deirdre had never liked them. The fit wasn't perfect but for the moment they would have to do, Anna thought, depositing a box of crockery on the kitchen table. The room at the back had French windows to the garden, perhaps she would have the two rooms knocked into one.

'Nice pad,' Briony said as she and Jasper dispersed the Rose Lodge furniture under Anna's instruction and then began to bring in the contents of the van.

Late in the Day

'Thanks, you've been absolutely wonderful,' Anna said, making coffee with her new electric kettle. 'How much do I owe you?'

'On the house,' Jasper said.

'I'm a wage-earner now, you know,' Briony said. 'Working for Dad, dogsbody on the Green Orchard site. Could be worse.'

'What does Patsy say?' Anna said.

'She's all for it, matter of fact,' Briony said. 'Sees me in my green helmet every day, usually waves.'

After they had left Anna began to wash the cups but the water was cold. She switched on the immersion heater and wandered from room to room.

'My own house,' she whispered, testing the words. But they did not stimulate the excitement she had anticipated. It was a sort of equation: the years running Rose Lodge for husband and children being equal, in the opinion of society, to a house of her own.

Pity it had no garage; such houses didn't unless they were end of terrace with extra space. Fortunately the road was quiet and parking easy. Yet the house still didn't please her. Had she made a wrong choice? She had had so little practice. Rupert's career had conditioned decisions in their early years. Ever since she had stayed in boring jobs and inconvenient flats to avoid the burden of choice. Now suddenly she had closed her eyes and jumped – jobwise, careerwise, the future, whatever. Had Esau sensed her uncertainty, was that why he had stayed?

Anna made herself a lettuce and peanut butter sandwich and wandered through the house. Cathy and the children were coming that afternoon and now she began to look with Cathy's critical eyes. The cream walls and light brown carpet would show every mark and the garden would take months to get into order and the house fronted on to quite a busy road and . . .

'Fitted carpet, going it a bit, aren't we?' Cathy said standing on the bit of path holding Edward's hand with Gilbert on her hip. 'This carpet'll show every mark, you realise?'

'Whose house is this?' Katie inquired in a babyish voice.

'Granny's new house as you know perfectly well and mind Granny's precious new carpet,' Cathy said as the children stepped high over the threshold. 'Want their shoes off, Mum?'

'Course not,' Anna said as the children moved warily along the passage. 'Hello, darling, hello Edward.'

'Why does Granny need such a big garden?' Katie inquired, using her mother's tone. 'It's much bigger than our garden.'

'I don't exactly *need* it,' Anna said. 'But I am very fond of plants.'

'So am I,' Katie said. 'My best friend Chelsea's got three Barbie dolls of her own but I haven't even got one.'

'I'm going upstairs,' Edward said.

'Don't touch anything,' Cathy called a moment later as feet pounded across the floor above.

'Hello, little Gilbert,' Anna said, reaching to take him from Cathy's hip, but he twisted away in alarm.

'It's Granny, silly,' Cathy said, putting him down on his feet. 'Show Granny how you can walk, Gilbert.'

'Clever boy,' Anna said as he ran down the passage and then collapsed. 'Whoops.' He rolled on his back and lay staring at the ceiling sucking his thumb.

'Like some tea?' Anna said. 'I bought a new kettle.'

'Aren't we well organised?' Cathy said, following Anna into the kitchen. 'It's all very nice, Mum, but honestly I don't see why you didn't get yourself a modern flat. I mean a house and garden, it's such a hassle.'

'I shan't let it be,' Anna said. 'And I hate flats.'

'Some people are hard to please,' Cathy said.

'There's a black man knocking at the front door,' Katie called out loudly.

'Oh, ask him in,' Anna called, walking to meet him. 'Hello, Esau. I wasn't expecting you until next Monday.' His figure, triangular in a cream-coloured gown embroidered with white, filled the narrow hall. Was the change significant, she wondered? 'This is my daughter, Cathy, this is Esau Etim from Nigeria. He was on the English Language summer school course.'

'Very pleased to meet daughter of Missus Bolt, my teacher and alma mater, isn't it?' Esau said, shaking Cathy's hand. His accent seemed to regress as if he was playing a part. 'Your mother is best teacher in summer school, every person saying this.' He patted Edward's head. 'Eh-eh, so many pickin is like African family, mother of three fine-fine pickin is lucky woman, Missus Cathy.'

'Thank you,' Cathy said.

'Gilbert's going upstairs,' Katie announced.

'Why don't you children go and explore Granny's garden?' Cathy said.

Late in the Day

'Eh-eh, I am not coming for lesson today,' Esau said. 'I am just ascertaining location of new house for peace of my mind, isn't it? And bringing small good-luck gift for house warming.' He took two pottery mugs from the voluminous folds of his gown. 'To show my appreciation.'

'Thank you. How very kind,' Anna said, blushing. 'Really you shouldn't...'

'See you next Monday for lesson, er... Anna?' he said, retreating to the front door.

'Honestly, Mum, whatever next?' Cathy teased as it closed behind him. 'The moment my back is turned!'

'I told you I was giving private English lessons,' Anna said steadily. 'He's starting a language school in Lagos.'

'Well watch it! There was a distinct brightness in his eye when he looked at you and you are alone in the house, Mum.'

'He has asked me to be the principal of his new school,' Anna said. Cathy stared.

'Is he off his trolley? I mean surely you have to be qualified for something like that?' Cathy said.

'I'll have my certificate by the end of next month, God and the Royal Society of Arts willing,' Anna said. 'Lots of EFL teachers don't even have that.'

'You're thinking of going?' Cathy's eyes widened. 'How many wives has he got?'

'Three,' Anna said. 'But what's that got to do with it?'

'Three wives at the same time? He's Muslim, I presume?'

'He's Christian now.'

'With three wives?'

'Would it be more Christian to discard two of them?' Anna said. 'And their children?'

'But you can't be thinking of marrying him?' Cathy said, her colour rising.

'No,' Anna said and wondered for the first time if she was. 'But I am thinking of being principal of First Class English College, Lagos.'

Chapter Twenty-one

By the end of November Anna had finished her course and got her certificate, she had learnt a lot and the supervised teaching practice helped stabilise her self-confidence. The house in Bishopston was beginning to be as she wanted. Esau still came for his private lessons but as it got colder he grew less cheerful. He was losing weight and his skin looked greyish, his bulky figure muffled in pullovers.

'Today lessons finish, tomorrow I fly from Heathrow,' he announced one evening.

Anna, both relieved and disappointed, drove him and a quantity of luggage to Temple Meads station the following day.

'Plenty presents,' he explained, excited and happy again now he was going home. 'Everybody in family waiting for presents. This big custom in our country.'

He stowed his luggage and returned to the carriage door, entirely filling the open window.

'I shall miss you, Esau,' Anna said, realising she hadn't noticed how wintry it was, how bleak, until this moment.

'I too will miss,' Esau said. 'Maybe we get married?' he said and laughed uproariously. 'What your family are saying if you go marry black man?'

'Never mind my family,' Anna smiled, not sure he was serious. 'Anyway we're not like that, we've had black mayors in Bristol, you know? But you've got three wives already.'

'Three wives not married in Christian church,' he said. 'You and me first Christian wedding, plenty white lace isn't it?'

'And what would Ata say?'

'Ata good wife, Ata is always chief wife, she understand English wife very good for First Class English College, Lagos.'

Late in the Day

He laughed and she realised how subdued he had been in recent weeks. Now he was happy to be going home.

'I am thinking Anna Bolt make good wife for me,' he said as his laughter subsided. 'Very good first-class wife.'

'I'm not much good at marriage, Esau,' she said. Was he teasing, did he take anything that seriously? Perhaps Africa had suffered too much to grieve over personal dilemmas.

'I am excellent at marriage, that enough good for both of us, plenty practice, three times with three wives,' Esau said, pushing his hand into the folds of his gown. 'I give you amulet.' He held out a small pouch on a leather thong. 'Wear round neck, keep you safe and bring you to Nigeria.'

'Thank you.' She stretched on tiptoe to kiss his cheek.

'All my wives very happy. Eh-eh, I tell you I am not paying money for lessons when we are married.' He laughed again.

'You'd better ask somebody else,' Anna said as the train began to move. 'But I shall miss you, Esau.'

'I wait. Know what they say?' he shouted. '"Go to Africa to cure a sick heart." I wait. I know you come.' His sky-blue arm was still waving as the train slid out of sight.

'For God's sake, Mother, are you ready or aren't you?' Harriet said, summoned to help Patsy select the dress for Francesca's lunch-party. 'You look fine. Honestly.'

'You don't think the green . . .'

'No,' Harriet said. 'Get going or you'll be late.'

'All right, all right,' Patsy said. She walked downstairs, glanced in the hall mirror and drove off, spattering gravel. She was fed up with the way her children treated her. It was high time she asserted herself, went out more. But going out was hazardous. Like that man trying to give her his pup, putting its string in her hand. 'Christmas present, missus.'

Harriet stood on the drive. Her eyes searched for Briony's green helmet, she wanted to tell her about the baby. The near estate houses had their roofs on already and the furthest were equipped with foundations.

Rosie Clapton came out of the cottage and pegged nappies on the line. She and the new baby had only been home from hospital two days. The toddler pottered beside her.

'You OK?' Harriet said.

'I'll do,' Rosie said, glancing round.

'Terry towelling?' Harriet said. 'I thought everybody used disposables these days. Course they are expensive.'

'It's Rick,' Rosie said as Harriet lingered. 'Into the environment.' Her eyes on Harriet's stomach. 'Expecting?'

Harriet blushed. 'Didn't know it showed.'

'Fancy a cup of tea?' Rosie said.

Had she come to Francesca's lunch on the wrong day, Patsy wondered uneasily? She was already late and on the previous occasion cars had been parked all along the road, the front door wide open with people kissing and calling out. 'You haven't changed a bit.' 'I'd have known you anywhere!'

Now the front door was shut and Francesca's grey Volvo parked on the drive was the only car in sight. Patsy's energy drained away. 'A lady is equal to any occasion,' Lady Violet always said but away from OldPlace Patsy was liable to panic attacks. She considered turning round, going home, but Francesca came running out.

'Lovely to see you, Patsy, darling,' she said, helping her out of the car in what Patsy considered an offensively proprietorial way. 'And looking so well!'

'I'm not an invalid,' Patsy said.

'Course not, darling.' Francesca modified her tone. 'Like the hair. Très chic.' Actually she considered Patsy's hair, cut very short now and grey as a brillo pad, a big mistake. But she looked well enough in her blue wool dress with the single string of small real pearls.

'Where is everybody?' Patsy said, reaching the sitting-room. Her face had lost its blankness but her smile seemed experimental, as if she had only just learned how to do it. Francesca's long table was laden as before with dishes of cold ham and turkey, two quiches, salads and a meringue pavlova.

'I wish I knew,' Francesca said. 'Last time they all seemed so keen about a memorial for Miss Snape. I sent out over fifty invitations ... anyway let me get you a drink?'

'Just an apple juice, please,' Patsy said.

'Oh ... there's somebody else at last,' Francesca said as the doorbell rang.

'Sorry, we're a bit late,' Anna said. 'Hello, Patsy!' Her smile was conciliatory. 'Good to see you.' She and Elfrida Bantock had arrived at the same moment.

'Isn't anybody else coming?' Elfrida said, wondering why she had come herself. She liked to do what *everybody* was doing and avoided poorly attended ventures like this.

'That's just what I was saying,' Patsy said. 'You're sure you sent the invitations off, didn't shove them in a drawer, like I'm always doing?' she added with an exaggerated laugh.

'Some RSVP'd and some didn't,' Francesca said, flicking back her long blonde hair. In her candy-striped dungarees she looked slim, but strained. Hardly surprising with so much food prepared. 'But you can't rely on that nowadays ... I hoped they'd just come.'

'Voting with their feet?' Elfrida said, pleased to know the expression.

'Looks like being just the four of us,' Francesca said. 'Just like old times.'

'Well ... I've got something to tell you!' Patsy said and waited until all three pairs of eyes had swivelled towards her. 'I'm writing again and I've just sold a story.'

'Oh, wonderful, Patsy,' Anna said. 'Congratulations.'

'Isn't it amazing after all this time?' Patsy said. 'And listen, I've started a new romantic novel.' Her full hips undulated nervously under their concerted gaze, as if she half expected her success to arouse resentment.

'Double congratulations,' Anna said. 'Which magazine bought the story?'

'A small one. Well, it's really too downmarket to mention.'

'Don't be so snobbish,' Francesca said.

'But I am a snob. It's the way I was brought up,' Patsy said, gathering confidence. 'And it's all coming back, you know ... right ways of behaving, where you've come from ...'

'What makes you say that?' Anna said doubtfully.

'Aren't you fed up with the welfare state, people living on benefit for three generations, living off the taxpayer which is you and me ... and so much crime ...?' Patsy paused. It was a long time since she had said as much as this.

'Just aren't enough jobs, are there?' Elfrida said vaguely. 'Not for unskilled people.'

'Maybe we'll end up like Huxley's *Brave New World*?' Anna said.

'People specially designed to *like* doing unskilled jobs with bribes of sex and that drug, soma.'

'There you are then,' Patsy said, triumphant. 'Only now we've ecstasy and speed to keep the unemployables happy.'

'Or dead?' Anna murmured.

'Writers are today's prophets ... seeing the future.' Patsy's voice rose with excitement.

'Do you remember your first story? You arrived in my kitchen with champagne under one arm and Harriet under the other,' Anna said. She and Patsy had been close then.

'No champagne today,' Francesca said. 'Anyway here's to Patsy.' They clinked glasses and smiled. Friendship was friendship. Francesca put her arm round Patsy's shoulders. 'Us four, The Three Graces... and Elfrida of course. Do you remember that time you stayed with us all summer, Patsy?'

'I think Mother just forgot me. And your father spoilt us dreadfully, all those lovely tins of sweets he brought.' Patsy's smile slid a little, beset by less comfortable memories. How they had loved her dramatic imitation of Mr Alexander in the dormitory the following term. *Yes, Lady Violet, no, Lady Violet, three bags full, your ladyship*, delivered in tones of oily obsequiousness. It had always been hard to forgive Fran's generosity.

'I'm rather disappointed,' Francesca said, releasing them. 'Penelope Tabili absolutely *promised* she would come.'

'What do you think Miss Snape would have thought about one of her girls writing magazine stories?' Elfrida asked.

'She always admired achievement,' Anna said, restless with her own possibilities. What if she did go to Nigeria? She might have mentioned it but today was Patsy's occasion. What would they have made of Esau's proposal and his three wives?

'Are you going to write a *romantic* novel again?' Elfrida was inquiring. 'After your husband ... I wonder you have the heart.'

'Romantic fiction is booming,' Patsy said. 'Booming more than ever with the recession and Britain going downhill and everything getting so, well ... ugly. Romantic novels are really about *power*.' Patsy's eyes were bright with her newly recovered fluency. She had forgotten how much she liked being the centre of attention. 'The only time in a woman's life she has power is when a powerful man wants her and she can strike a bargain. That's what makes the romantic novel work.'

Late in the Day

Was Esau offering a bargain, Anna wondered? He thought so.

'Margaret Mead said men are afraid women will learn to manage without them,' she said.

'It's half past one,' Francesca said. 'Do start eating.'

'I believe you have a new grandchild, Fran?' Patsy said, helping herself to quiche and cold turkey.

'Yes, Hugo's fourth, little Frances. You wait till you have grandchildren, Patsy!'

'Is Hugo a Catholic?' Patsy said. 'I may turn Catholic myself, I like to think at least God is worrying about me.'

'But Catholics don't hold with divorce,' Elfrida said.

'Neither do I,' Patsy said. For a moment the smile slipped from her face but was quickly replaced. 'Harriet's pregnant.' She hadn't meant to say it. 'My Harriet.'

'Good,' Anna said. 'Least I hope it is?'

'Of course divorce is easier for the working classes,' Elfrida observed. 'My help goes off to bingo every night.'

'I must be going,' Patsy said abruptly. Suddenly she was very tired. She put down her plate and hugged Anna which was usual and then Francesca and Elfrida which was not.

'See you,' she called, crossing the front lawn to the car. It was only her second outing by herself and she didn't like to be away from OldPlace for long. Besides she had to get on with her book. A book was a long hard haul from start to finish, Patsy knew that. Life was a long hard haul, she knew that too. But it had its moments, gold beads in a long string of greys. She wasn't sorry for herself now she was writing again and there was a baby to think of, Harriet's baby and Patrick's she supposed, though Patrick had been out of the picture quite a time. Babies were the best part of life.

'So that's that then,' Francesca murmured, waving as Elfrida departed soon after Patsy. 'Looks like I'm the only person in the world wants a Snape memorial.'

'Sorry, Fran,' Anna said. 'I should forget it.'

'I can't. Penelope sent me a hundred pounds.'

'Send it back,' Anna said. 'Was she that Penelope Aston who played the violin rather well? Freckles and red hair?'

'No,' Francesca said. 'I think she was blonde.'

'Is a hundred pounds enough for a small plaque somewhere?' Anna said. Francesca looked forlorn, Fran who had looked after her, made a job for her. 'I could let you have something.'

187

Geraldine Kaye

'We'll see,' Francesca said.

After Anna had gone she packed the food into plastic boxes. She would take it over to Hugo and Lottie tomorrow. She needed something else, but what? Francesca sighed and wondered.

The chilly afternoon was descending to a chilly dusk when the doorbell rang. The Celt was standing there, the hood of his anorak shadowing his face.

'Your kitchen,' he said, aggrieved. 'Magnolia, was it?'

PART FIVE
Flying

Chapter Twenty-two

'Olly, darling!' Anna said, startled to find him waiting on the doorstep on a darkening Friday evening. She hugged him, kissed his cheek. A stale smell of drink came off his skin and his chin was prickly. 'I've been out shopping. Before the last mad rush. Why didn't you let me know you were coming?'

'Your phone was switched off,' Olly said, smiling down at her under the street lamp. His tall dark figure had seemed menacing for a moment but now his expression was reproachful. She had forgotten how tall he was, how like Rupert. He didn't need to explain that his writing a letter was out of the question, they both knew that.

'Hang on, I'll let you in,' she said, leaning into the back of the 2CV to retrieve shopping, fumbling in her handbag for the front door key. The porch was already stacked with Olly's luggage.

'Wait for it!' Anna said, opening the door with a flourish. 'My house! What do you think?'

'OK,' Olly said, gathering up his large battered case, rucksack and a bundle of books tied with string and following her inside. 'It's OK. Nice, Mum.'

'How did you get here with all that luggage?' Anna said.

'Hitched,' Olly said. 'People get quite decent round about Christmas, stop for you even if you have got loads of stuff. Like all my worldly goods.'

He walked along the passage with the case bumping one side, the rucksack dragging against the other and marking the wall. He deposited both just inside the sitting-room and flung himself down on the sofa.

'Your prodigal son has come home, Mum. Could do with a fatted calf right now. Haven't eaten since yesterday.'

'Come *home*?' Anna said. Was Olly entitled to use such a word about a house he had never even seen, her house? He was twenty-three after all. Did he intend to stay indefinitely?

'It is *my home*, isn't it?' Olly said, stretching out long legs like two chopsticks. 'Like you're still my mother?' Thoughts flew back and forth between them like silent birds.

'I suppose so,' Anna said. 'But you did say Bristol was naff and London was the only place to be, didn't you?'

'I was younger then,' Olly grinned. 'Streets weren't paved with gold. Sorry, Mumsy, I've come home.'

'That's all very well,' Anna said. There had to be an end to mothering for everybody's sake. 'What about your job?'

'Lost it, didn't I?' Olly said. 'Anyway did you think I was going to be a van-driver for the rest of my puff?'

'No, but . . .' She wanted to stop worrying about Olly and out of sight had been more or less out of mind, but already the familiar anxieties about his competence came rushing back.

'Anyway I've applied to University of West of England for next October. I expect I'll get a place but I might not.'

'Oh well I'd better get something to eat, hadn't I?' Anna said, going through to the kitchen. The casserole she had made yesterday and expected to last until Monday at least should be enough for both of them, eked out with a tin of beans. She had just bought new potatoes and mangetout. But Olly was such a gannet.

'Nothing like home-cooking,' he said quarter of an hour later, swallowing beef and bean casserole in gulps. His legs were too long to go under the kitchen table and he sat sideways tucking them obligingly round his chair. 'All right this stew. I suppose we've got to go to Cathy's for Christmas Day?'

Francesca parked the Volvo on the drive. Curtains were not yet drawn and squares of yellow light shone from the houses either side. There were lights in her house too; she had left the Celt painting the kitchen. Christmas was always special for Francesca who loved good food and abundance and giving. This year it would be extra special with Hugo and family coming for Christmas dinner which in previous years they had never agreed to do. And besides there was the baby, Frances. The Christmas tree was the biggest she could find. Papa had always bought the best. She could remember the needly green top pushing right up between the banisters, almost touching her bedroom door. The man at the garden centre had carried her tree out to the car for her. It had scratched at her neck all the way home.

'Declan?' she called from the front door. 'Can you help me a minute, please?'

'Where do you want to put it then?' Declan said as he carried the tree inside. A certain amount of magnolia had been added to the spatters of paint which covered his overalls. An illustrated diary of his working life, Francesca thought. He had filled out since she had started on the kitchen, looked less haunted.

'In the hall, I think, don't you?' Francesca said. 'So they see it right away as they come in?'

'Lovely old tree,' he said, depositing it by the window and tenderly smoothing the disturbed needles. Lovely green pussy cat, he thought.

'Leave it there then,' Francesca said. 'You can help me put the bits and bobs on later if you like?' The boys had always loved doing that, Hereward and Hugo, her little boys. She had bought Hugo a new shirt for Christmas; he had to look halfway respectable for the interview at Brandon Lodge. Mr Austin had promised to give his application full support. She had bought a similar shirt for Declan who was, now she looked more closely, rather larger in the neck. Declan seemed dispirited.

'Let's have a look at that kitchen, shall we? My goodness, you've nearly finished,' she said, making her eyes wide with surprise. 'Talk about a fast worker!'

He gave her a look. 'Not finished yet.'

'Finish it then,' she said. 'I was just going to get the dinner. Like to stay for something to eat?'

'Don't mind,' he said, returning to the stepladder.

Francesca carried the basket in from the car and began to put things away. The kitchen wasn't magnolia, she thought, nothing like. It was yellow, margarine yellow, but she wasn't going to say anything, not just before Christmas with Declan so moody. Sometimes you couldn't get a smile out of him.

'How are you fixed for Christmas Day?' she asked. 'You can come to us if you like but there's the three children and the baby.'

'Don't mind,' Declan said but he looked a bit brighter. 'Just finish the kitchen, shall I? Thanks very much.'

* * *

Geraldine Kaye

Anna woke on Christmas morning and looked out at the garden, the clump of leafless black-twigged trees at the end, the grass, crisp and white with frost. What time had Olly come in from the pub last night, she wondered? He had settled himself into the bedroom with the furniture from his bedroom at Rose Lodge. No point in looking for a job until after Christmas, he said. He spent most of his time winkling out friends from schooldays and meeting them in pubs. Anna sighed and her thoughts switched to Esau warm in the arms of Nigeria and three wives. What was it like to be Ata or Dawn or the other one?

At least Cathy was cooking the turkey this year. A plastic bag full of wrapped presents rested on the chest of drawers. Christmas dinner with the children would be fun, if they didn't get too excited. Cathy was a dedicated mother, thank God, but liable to lose her cool. More casual might be better but you couldn't be casual unless you were basically placid, and neither she nor Cathy could lay claim to 'placid'. Katie's cough was probably asthma the doctor said, possibly stress-related. But asthma was caused by the droppings of house mites, according to Anna's *Good Health Guide*. Soft toys should be hot-washed and then left overnight in the freezer. She must remember to tell Cathy, but not on Christmas Day.

Anna made herself an early morning cup of tea, carried it back to bed and listened to the phone calls to what was left of the Commonwealth on Radio Four, a tedious but comforting ritual. Cathy had talked of having Grandma out for the day but Grandma had opted for the festivities at Bexley House, thank you very much. Did they celebrate Christmas in Nigeria? In Gambia they had seemed to celebrate every Muslim, Christian and African festival in the calendar.

A wintry sun came out mid-morning as Anna and Olly got into the 2CV with the plastic bag of presents.

'Here we go,' Anna whispered and as the car started first time she added, 'Merry Christmas, little car.'

'Really, Mum, you're pathetic!' Olly said grumpily.

'You got a hangover?' Anna asked. They drove to Cathy's in silence and parked in a convenient gap in front of the house next door.

'Granny, Granny, Granny.' Katie, bright in pink-patterned leggings and pink and blue jersey, came running out, flinging her arms round Anna's waist and then more gingerly round Olly's long legs.

'Where's my present?' Edward said, following.

'You mustn't ask, it's rude,' Katie said, skipping round and round the bag on the pavement. 'Granny won't give you your present if you keep on asking, will you, Granny? She'll give it to a poor little boy in India who *didn't* ask, won't you, Granny?'

'I think that would be rather too difficult,' Anna said, wondering where Katie got her ideas from. Did she go to Sunday school?

'Turkey's in the oven, all's right with the world,' Dennis said, appearing at the front door. 'Cathy's upstairs with Gil.'

'Gilbert's done a great big ginormous smelly poo,' Edward said. 'For Christmas.'

'That's rude,' Katie said. 'You shouldn't say rude things on Christmas Day, should you, Granny?'

'What a beautiful Christmas tree!' Anna said, going into the sitting-room. Her eyes saw first the new baubles, shining silver and green, and then the old familiar ones, the battered feathery bird of peace, the red wax Father Christmas, the pair of golden angels which had hung on the Christmas tree all the years at Rose Lodge.

'You got to put all your presents under the tree,' Katie said, pointing to the accumulated pile. 'Presents are after dinner.'

'Looks to me like some people have opened theirs already,' Anna said. The sitting-room floor was littered with scarlet paper.

'Only our stockings,' Katie said. 'Father Christmas filled our stockings upstairs and we put a mince pie out for him, didn't we, Edward?'

'I don't like mince pies!' Edward said.

'Can I whisper, Granny?' Anna bent down. 'I have to pretend about you-know-who, so as not to spoil things for Edward,' she confided sibilantly.

'So what's new, Olly?' Dennis said, squaring his shoulders.

'Not a lot,' Olly said.

'Have a sherry?'

'Have you got Guinness?' Olly said.

'Guinness it is,' Dennis said.

'I'm collecting up all this red paper and making it nice again,' Katie said, smoothing it with her hands. 'Because of the trees.'

'Good for you,' Anna said. 'What did you get in your stocking?'

'Father Christmas gave me a satsuma and a lollipop,' Katie said, walking across to Anna on her knees. 'And a packet of nuts and two hair bands, same as the ones in Boots, so I know where Father Christmas got them but I have to pretend about you-know-what because of you-know-who.'

'Merry Christmas, darling,' Anna called as Cathy came down the stairs with Gilbert. 'Do you want some help?'

Cathy looked pale and harassed, as well she might. Anna got up and followed her out to the kitchen.

'Merry Christms, little Gil!' Gilbert smiled and put his thumb in his mouth.

'Teething,' Cathy said. 'Poor Gil.'

Anna sniffed the air. 'Smells lovely. Can I peel some potatoes for you or something?'

'All done, Mum. I got up at the crack of . . . before the kids woke and got everything ready, more or less. We're having presents after dinner.'

'Yes. Katie told me. New dress?'

'Had it before Gil but I didn't get the chance to wear it,' Cathy said. 'Bits stick to it rather!' She picked at the top and then swept at the skirt with her hands.

'Suits you anyway,' Anna said.

'Everything all right with you?' Cathy said. 'What about Olly?'

'He's applied to the University of West of England, the old poly. Says he's going to look for a job after Christmas.'

'Let him sort himself out, Mum. And don't run round after him. He's a big boy now. What about your Mr . . .'

'Esau Etim,' Anna said. 'He's gone back to Nigeria.'

'Not before time,' Cathy said, taking a packet of frozen peas back from Gilbert and cutting off the top.

'I miss him a bit,' Anna said. She could feel the amulet under her jersey. The pouch had proved to contain two tiny red stones, garnets or rubies perhaps. What did they signify? 'Well I miss him quite a lot, actually.'

'Hold Gilbert, will you?' Cathy said, seizing a thick cloth and opening the oven door. A waft of turkey and loud sizzling.

'That's the lovely turkey,' Anna said, carrying Gilbert to the window. 'And there's a lovely blackbird.'

'All right now,' Cathy said, slamming the oven door.

Late in the Day

'Did you go to Rupert's blessing thing in Peterborough?' Anna asked, wanting to know.

'You got to be joking.' Cathy stood up, pink-faced. 'Right up to Peterborough with the kids! Anyway he didn't even ask Olly.'

'Oh well ... Happy Christmas, darling.'

'And you, Mum. Did I upset you about that other bloke? Don't remember what I said but ...'

'Doesn't matter,' Anna said. 'Neither do I. Pax, eh?'

Katie and Edward ran into the kitchen. 'Daddy says how long till dinner? Daddy says do you want the high chair for Gil?'

'Of course I do,' Cathy said, exasperated. 'Tell him dinner in ten minutes.' She reached to the top of the cupboard and popped a white pill into her mouth.

'What was that?'

'Only Valium,' Cathy said. 'Helps me be nicer to the kids.'

'But you shouldn't take things ... I mean suppose you are pregnant ...'

'Have to be an immaculate conception,' Cathy said sourly.

'Would you like a sherry, darling?' Dennis shouted.

'Not when I'm doing the gravy, thanks,' Cathy shouted back. 'Expect Mum would.'

'Coming up, Mother-in-law!'

'You do sound snappish,' Anna murmured. 'It is Christmas.'

'I feel snappish, if it's all the same to you. That's why I take Valium. Merry Christmas everybody.'

Gilbert fell asleep over his sieved turkey breast and Dennis carried him upstairs. After dinner and presents Dennis and Olly took Katie and Edward for a run in the park. Anna and Cathy tidied the sitting-room, collecting up paper and string.

'Thanks for the talc, Mum,' Cathy said, studying the label. 'Let's hope Dennis finds me irresistible with Coty's L'aimant behind my ears.'

'Doesn't he always?'

'You'd be surprised,' Cathy said.

'Perhaps you should be more flexible, try something new.'

'What? Silicone boobs and a scarlet nightie? You're talking to your daughter, Mum.'

'I didn't mean that exactly.'

'What did you mean *exactly*?'

'Well I sometimes think we expect too much of men, insist they

197

have to be sensible, dependable, reliable . . . all that.'

'Tell me about it,' Cathy shrugged. 'All I know is it takes something I haven't got to get him going nowadays.'

'Better not tell me about it,' Anna said quickly. 'I mean personal things . . . better not.'

'I've got to tell somebody. What are mothers for?'

'Well, but I may get confused when I get old . . . say things which would . . . upset Dennis and be very awkward.'

'It's awkward already,' Cathy said.

'Most marriages go through bad bits,' Anna said.

'If you're the big expert when do the good bits come then?'

'I can tell you breaking up is the worst of the bad bits,' Anna said suddenly but had it been that bad, wasn't it also a relief?

'Oh, it won't come to that,' Cathy said.

'Well, don't let it,' Anna said as the children ran back to the front door and rang the bell on and on. 'You don't seem to talk to each other much, you and Dennis. Talking is important.' Upstairs Gilbert woke and began to cry.

'Like now you mean?' Cathy said, running up the stairs in a chorus of ringing and screaming. 'When do we get the chance?'

Dennis opened the door with his key. 'Anoraks on pegs, please,' he shouted as the children erupted into the hall and Olly followed.

'Tea and Christmas cake?' Anna said.

'I don't like Christmas cake,' Katie said. 'Can I have a chocolate biscuit?'

'Can I have loads of chocolate biscuits?' Edward said.

'What did you see in the park?' Anna asked. 'Any ducks?'

'No ducks,' Katie said. 'I think somebody ate them.'

'Father Christmas ate them,' Olly said, sending Katie into peals of laughter.

'Getting dark already,' Dennis said, drawing the curtains.

'Don't let them get chocolate all over themselves,' Cathy said, coming down with Gilbert. 'He's had a very long sleep. God knows when we'll get him down tonight.'

'Why didn't you give me a Christmas present?' Edward stood in front of Olly.

'Sorry, haven't got any money,' Olly said, pulling his jeans pocket inside out to illustrate.

'There's ten p in there,' Edward said.

Late in the Day

'That a five p, silly,' Katie said.

'That won't get you very far,' Dennis said.

'Will you give us presents next year?' Edward said. 'So I don't get disappointed.'

'Hope so,' Olly said.

'Lovely Christmas cake,' Dennis said.

'Mum made it,' Cathy said. 'She's a wiz at Christmas cake.'

'Congratulations, Mother-in-law,' Dennis said. 'Another cup of tea?'

'No thanks. Time we were going home. You ready, Olly?'

Outside it was quite dark now and the 2CV wasn't there. Wasn't outside the house next door either.

'My car's gone,' Anna stammered.

'Can't have gone,' Olly said.

'It's been stolen!' Anna said. 'Was it here when you got back from the park?'

'Didn't look,' Olly said.

Dennis dialled 999.

Chapter Twenty-three

On Boxing Day the police phoned. They had found what remained of the 2CV. In the afternoon Dennis drove Anna and Olly to Novers Hill in Knowle. It was cold, the sky solid and steel grey. They walked across a flat square of rough grass at the top of the hill. The 2CV would not have been identifiable except for a bit of emerald green on the rim of one wing. The wheels had gone, the registration been ripped away and found in an adjacent street, the chassis burnt out.

'My car . . . my poor little car,' Anna said and her eyes pricked. She turned away to stare over the valley below. In the lavender dusk, street lights ran like strings of pearls along the straight grey road which led back to the city centre.

'Who could have done this?'

'Kids. Joyriders,' Olly shrugged. 'Come on, Mum, it's only an old car. What the hell! You'll get the insurance. You can get another 2CV or a Mini, whatever.'

'I don't want another car,' Anna said, quavery. 'I shall never want another car. I want *my* car.'

'Bad luck, Mother-in-law,' Dennis said, kicking through the scorched grass. 'I know just how you feel. Enough's enough.'

Quarter of an hour later he drove them over to Bexley House. In Park Street the lighted Christmas mobiles flashed on and off, a candle flame flicking left and then right, the face of Father Christmas winking one eye.

'Costs the council thousands, you know,' Dennis said cheerily. 'They do the rounds, these sets of lights, this year Birmingham, next year Ipswich.' A few subdued window-shoppers perused the signs for coming January sales.

'No homeless for once?' Olly remarked.

Late in the Day

'All gone down to "Caring at Christmas",' Anna said, damp with grief for her car destroyed. It was only a car and an old car at that, she told herself again and again, but it felt like a bereavement she would never get over. 'That deconsecrated church in Victoria Street, St Thomas's I think.'

Inside Bexley House the lights were already switched on, excluding the cold afternoon. A large silvery bell hung in the centre of each window backed up by row upon row of scarlet paper chains. A Christmas tree with coloured lights stood in the hall.

'They certainly do their best here,' Dennis said. 'I'll say a quick hello to Grandma and then get off home.'

'And me,' Olly said as they walked upstairs. In the sitting-room more paper chains ranged across the walls and the ten old ladies sat in their armchairs staring at the television. Today the sound was audible.

'Hello, Grandmother.' Dennis stretched his hand and leaned forward to peck her cheek.

'David,' she said, flushed and flustered. 'Isn't it?'

'*Dennis*,' said Dennis. Her nails as well as her lipstick were now a discreet pink. Had the scarlet lacquer been confiscated, Anna wondered?

'Happy Christmas, Mother,' she said but her mother stared a moment and then ignored her. 'Happy Christmas, everybody.'

'And to you, Happy Christmas,' Mrs Green sitting next to her mother said and the other old ladies turned from the television smiling and nodding. 'Merry Christmas.'

'And Oliver, my grandson, Oliver,' her mother said loudly, keeping hold of his hand for their benefit. 'And what are you doing down here, Oliver?'

'Staying with Mum at the new house.'

'What new house? What's happened to my flat?'

'Haven't you told Grandma about the house?' Olly said, going pink.

'The Hotwells flat belongs to the church, Mother,' Anna said. 'They'll be putting another tenant in now.'

'How are you, Oliver?' her mother said, fidgeting forward so she could turn her back to Anna.

'Fine, Grandma, don't get up,' Olly said anxiously.

'Such a long time since I've seen you. How are you ... er, getting on at school?'

'I've left school,' Olly said, glancing round like a trapped animal. 'Ages ago.'

'She never told me,' she said and her voice rose. 'She never tells me anything.'

'What about the rest of you?' Dennis smiled round the circle. 'Had a good Christmas? Looked after you, did they?'

'They do us very well here,' Mrs Green said from the next chair. 'Nothing's too much trouble.'

'Nothing's too much trouble,' several others echoed in chorus. Was it a kind of touching wood, Anna wondered?

'This is my grandson, Oliver, and this is my, er . . .'

'Dennis, your grandson-in-law, and your daughter, Anna.' Dennis smiled round. 'Happy Christmas, everybody.'

'Anna?' Her mother blinked in Anna's direction. 'My daughter's got her own cap and gown.' Did her two terms at Newnham entitle her to such a description, Anna wondered?

'Happy Christmas, Mother,' she said.

'They don't get on,' Mrs Green confided to the room in a loud whisper. 'Mrs Jennings and her daughter, like cat and dog, the two of them.'

'How are the children, dear?' her mother said vaguely, her smile a creditable imitation of the one she had offered the bishop in the days of her matronhood.

'Katie and Edward and Gilbert are fine, Grandma,' Dennis said, enunciating carefully. 'Excited, of course. Bit over the top. Mince pies to sustain Father Christmas all round the place. Isn't as if we had a chimney even.'

'Mince pies for tea tonight,' Mrs Green said. 'Always cold supper Boxing night. Bit of ham, it's out on the sideboard already, saw it when I went to the you-know-what.'

'Girls got to have their time off,' another old lady remarked. 'Can't keep your staff nowadays if you don't give them plenty of time off. Mrs Dewar was telling me.'

'They're very good here. Nothing's too much trouble,' Mrs Green said and heads nodded all round.

'Glad to hear it,' Dennis said. 'But well I think I'd better be getting back now. Cathy's all alone with the children. Happy New Year to you.' He planted a kiss on Grandma's cheek. 'In case I don't see you again before that.'

Late in the Day

'I'm off too, Grandma,' Olly said, dropping his salute three inches above her head. 'See you.'

'Happy New Year, everybody,' Dennis said, waving from the door.

'I know what you two naughty boys are up to,' Grandma cackled merrily. 'Got some pretty girl waiting for you, shouldn't wonder?'

'I wish,' Dennis said from the passage. 'Bye, everybody.'

'You'll be all right getting yourself home, Mum?' Olly said.

'Course,' Anna said. She picked up a hard chair from the edge of the room and pushed it towards the space beside her mother. Mrs Green moved obligingly.

'How are you, dear?' Anna spoke quietly, not wanting to be the centre of attention. Why was her approach always so conventional, she wondered? Was her mother's silence just a protest against boredom? 'I want to talk to you, Mother. I've just bought a house in Bishopston,' she began.

'That's nice,' Mrs Green said and raised her voice so the others could hear. 'She's just bought a house in Bishopston.'

Heads nodded. 'Nice out that way. Plenty of shops.'

'Bishopston?' her mother said, surprised out of silence.

'Yes. And this teaching course I did in the autumn, I've got my certificate.' Her mother's gaze had gone back to the television.

'Congratulations! She's got her certificate,' Mrs Green said loudly. 'Your daughter's got her certificate. Aren't you going to congratulate her?' A pause. 'She never says much, does she?' Mrs Green added, accustomed to pouring oil on troubled waters.

'School certificate?' one of the others said. 'I never did my school certificate. Didn't have the chance.'

'I'm thinking of going abroad,' Anna said. Her mother's puzzled eyes turned back to her and then brightened.

'Australia?' she whispered hoarsely. 'To see Bunny?'

'Not Australia. Nigeria. In Africa. I shan't stay long.'

'What about the children?' her mother said.

'Olly and Cathy are grown up, dear.'

'Nobody comes to see me. Not even Christmas Day.'

'Cathy did ask you for Christmas lunch, Mother,' Anna said.

'Lovely turkey, we had,' her mother said and the pink lips smiled. 'Treat us like queens here.'

'Good girls, all of them,' Mrs Green said. 'And Mrs Dewar too of course. Nothing's too much trouble.'

'You don't mind if I go to Nigeria then?' Anna said.

'Please yourself,' her mother said, turning towards the television. 'Be quiet now. I'm watching this.'

'Time I was going anyway. It's quite a walk back to Bishopston,' Anna murmured.

Outside it was quite dark. At OldPlace Patsy cracked a walnut and threw the bits of shell on to the fire which flared and crackled, gleaming on the crimson-berried holly cut from the garden and tucked behind picture frames, fighting with Christmas cards for space on the mantelpiece. A log fire, she thought, a log fire was one of the best things in the world as well as being free. At first Harriet collected wood from the orchard and hedge in front but now she went for a long walk each afternoon and came back dragging ragged branches which she sawed up and stacked to dry off in the barn.

'Have a walnut?' Patsy said. Her fingers scuffled in the debris in the wooden bowl at her feet.

'No thanks,' Harriet said. 'Anyway you've eaten them all.'

The room was warm for once and she got up, Monty in her hand, to close the curtains. The apple trees in front of the house were years old, centuries even, and full of mistletoe. Harriet, reluctant to bring an emblem so emotive into the house, had sold three bunches to the landlord of the King's Head where she worked. Just in time as that night the rest had been stripped. Still, three bunches had paid for the chicken.

'You won't want to bring that Monty in here once the baby comes,' Patsy remarked.

'Why ever not?' Harriet said irritably.

'Germs,' Patsy said. 'You mustn't worry about anything, darling. A baby is the best thing in the world. You know that, don't you?'

'I know you keep telling me,' Harriet said.

'I'll be there for you, I'll be your partner. Lots of mothers and daughters bring up children together nowadays. I mean it's better than being a single mother.'

'Mm.' Harriet shifted resentfully.

'That chicken was very delicious,' Patsy said. 'We used to keep chickens when we were first married. Would you be interested in keeping chickens?'

Two days away from her book was obligatory for Harriet's sake. And after all Christmas was the festival of babies but tomorrow she would get back to work again.

'I suppose I might,' Harriet said without enthusiasm. She craned her neck. 'What's that?' A motorbike was puttering up the drive. 'Briony and somebody, Jasper looks like.'

'Put the kettle on,' Patsy said.

Jasper, riding pillion, dismounted and pulled off his helmet. Light was coming from the kitchen window but he followed Briony the other way to a bit of garden at the side where winter daphne, sweetly scented, flowered each year.

'Here,' she said, picking off the tough little twigs. 'Gorgeous, isn't it?'

'Gorgeous,' Jasper agreed, sniffing and looking at Briony. This could be the most important moment in his whole life, he thought, but he only said, 'Frigging cold out here.'

'Mister Softee,' Briony said, cradling her helmet and moving round to the back door.

'Hello,' she said. 'Hello, Mum, this is my friend, Jasper.'

'How do you do?' Patsy said. Quite a good-looking boy, she thought, but nothing compared with Briony, not in the same league. Still, handsome is as handsome does.

'We thought we ought to come as it's Christmas, well I mean Boxing Day, as we spent Christmas Day at Dad's.'

'Let's have some tea, shall we?' Patsy said and wondered why Briony always had to spoil things.

It was not yet dark when Anna left Bexley House. It was a long walk back to Bishopston but still she liked walking and knew the district well enough to leave the wider streets for short cuts towards the watershed of Whiteladies Road. Besides, she liked residential streets, curtains not yet drawn on warm front rooms, Christmas cards on strings, paper chains, trees hung with red and green baubles.

A drunk tottered towards her, spread wide arms to bar her way, behind him a rickety Alsatian pup dragged on its string.

'Present for you, darling?' he said, trying to put the string into her hand.

'No thanks,' Anna said, stepping round them into the road and walking on. She felt her heartbeat rise as the man yelled something and stumbled on. Poor starving pup, she thought, poor man.

At least Mother had spoken to her today but that didn't mean the silent days were over. How did you talk to your mother in her eighties when communication between you had never been easy and was now meaningless? Mother was no reason for staying and no reason for going either.

But it's my time now, Anna thought, turning into Park Street and walking slowly up the steep hill. She thought of the 2CV chugging bravely up, how she had depended on it. As Olly said she would get the insurance money but it wouldn't be much on a fifteen-year-old car. Bristol had more cars per head of population than any other city in Britain. Was it right to add to this polluting statistic?

People stole and vandalised cars all over the western world. Why? In defiance against a present or perhaps absent and unknown father, a situation exacerbated by a scattered greater family who no longer knew or cared? Or was it resentment by those who didn't have cars towards those who did, aggravated by the decline of religious belief? Or just a blow against the impersonal contemporary world where a handful of highly paid technocrats were all that was needed?

HOMELESS written on cardboard, a young person crouched in a shop doorway, head bent forward. Anna paused and dropped a coin from the small change in the bottom of her pocket into his tin. He raised a pale narrow face with red-rimmed eyes and stared at her but didn't speak. Anna walked on.

The year rolled round from Christmas to Christmas, each different and the same. So what was wrong with *this* Christmas, she wondered? Last year, when Gilbert was new, she had stayed two nights at Cathy's and cooked the turkey. She had a job at Brewsters then and Dennis had fetched Mother for Christmas lunch and different flashing lights had hung above Park Street. Since then she had pushed her life forward and bought her own house but had she made anything actually better?

The streets were empty now. But as she walked towards Dingles, whisperings and stirrings came from under the portico in front, 'This one's mine.' Anna hesitated, stepped sideways but hands were grabbing her, grabbing her handbag, four or five girls dragging her off the pavement into the shadows.

'Help! she shouted. 'Stop.'

'Shut your cake-hole!'

A girl was tipping the contents of her handbag out on the ground. The smash of glass, the tinkle of coins, the flutter of notes as hands rifled her purse and wallet.

'Leave my keys,' she muttered but the girls were already running on whooping wildly.

Red 'Sale' signs and winter-coated models stared and smiled impassive as Anna dropped to her knees. A glass splinter pricked and blood oozed through her tights as she swept the scattered contents into her bag, got to her feet and leaned a moment against the plate-glass window. At least they hadn't found the amulet, the amulet that was meant to keep her safe.

Anna walked slowly on. Past a terrace of Edwardian houses, past the sand-coloured neo-classical façade of the renovated BBC building which had an air of calm tranquillity. Tactful, they said; the harsh concrete of modern construction was threatening and increased the risk of vandalism.

The house was in darkness as she approached and the telephone was ringing. Olly, she thought, burrowing for keys in her violated bag, something's happened. She unlocked the front door and dived in.

'Anna? It's me,' said Owen's voice. 'Compliments of the season and all that. Something to tell you . . . but anyway how are you?'

'I've just been mugged,' Anna said, breathless.

'Christ! Are you all right? Shall I call an ambulance?'

'Just shaken, that's all. I've only just this minute got in. What did you want to tell me?'

'Well I had this postcard from Noleen . . .' Owen said.

'Who?'

'Noleen from Dunedin. That girl I had the hots for. I thought you'd like to know she's just got married.'

'What?' Anna said. 'Why? Why should I like to know?'

'Well . . . she broke us up, didn't she, broke up the arrangement. We could have another crack, maybe we should talk about

Geraldine Kaye

it. I could come round right now. Make you a cup of tea, fix supper for you . . . anything . . .'

'Please don't,' Anna said and put the phone down.

Chapter Twenty-four

'Goodbye then. Good luck. Keep in touch,' Francesca said to Declan on her doorstep. It was what she always said and usually meant. But she didn't want to see Declan ever again. Her invitation to stay on Christmas night had resulted in his staying until the New Year by which time she was well aware he was not her sort. Besides, suppose Freddy had called on some pretext, something he was quite likely to do? Fortunately Freddy hadn't. Declan, on his way now to a contract job in Leeds, seemed to have no presentiment of his dwindling status in her affections. Another time, Francesca promised herself, she would be more circumspect.

'I will that,' Declan said.

Francesca looked at the sky. There was something up there, a silver plane in the wintry blue, perhaps it was Anna flying off? She ought to get away herself, she deserved a holiday.

'I'll be back down here in six to seven weeks,' Declan was saying with a smile. 'So I'll be in touch?'

'I shall be away then,' Francesca said, deciding on the instant to visit Washington and the Vietnam memorial.

Why shouldn't she, surely *she* was entitled to a sabbatical, she worked hard enough. Mr Austin wouldn't like it and he had been really good, going all out in support of Hugo's appointment despite his scruffy appearance and disagreable manner. Why couldn't he have worn the new shirt she gave him for Christmas? Anyway she wouldn't be away long, just long enough to see the name, *William S. Greenland*. Would it be written in gold or engraved in the stone, she wondered? What was the S for?

Willy had been her first and best love and had changed her for life, not that she would have thought of actually marrying a boy of such limited prospects. But the abruptness of its ending, Miss Snape erupting into the summerhouse with vengeful shouts, had marked her so she could never forget him. Couldn't remember him either until Antonio, also seventeen, had reminded her. Now the search was over. Perhaps the trip would settle her. She had to go before Freddy came back because Freddy considered flying abroad anywhere an unnecessary extravagance. Perhaps she could visit Hereward and Carmel too. How far was Bogota from Washington?

'Taxi for Temple Meads is on its way, Olly,' Anna said, depositing two cases just inside the front door. 'It's all happening. Don't forget to visit Grandma. Take her a couple of tubes of fruit pastilles.'

'I wish I knew how long you were going for,' Olly said, tightening his dressing-gown round him. He wanted her to go but resented it, tripping round the world in search of the real you was, he considered, the prerogative of the young. 'I mean it's just a visit, isn't it?'

'Don't know exactly,' Anna said. He ought to be more worried for her, more concerned. She admitted the thought, sighed and dismissed it. 'Depends on the set-up ... I mean it's difficult to tell from this distance. I might be back next week but I might stay much longer.'

Freedom, she thought. Was it the money from Rose Lodge and paradoxically the new house that had set her free? Or was she like the swallows flying south, responding to some inner compulsion like the need for sunshine, the need to be needed, the need for love?

'Are you serious?' Olly said.

'Course I am. I told you Esau Etim wants me to be principal of this college of his and, well, I must see the place before I decide. I mean I'm not sure he knows what he's about himself.'

'Brilliant,' Olly said.

'It does sound a bit ... well, unlikely, but I can't be reliable all the time. I mean losing my car and everything and then getting mugged ...'

'Don't they steal cars in Nigeria?' Olly said.

'I expect so but it's not only that,' Anna said. 'I mean now you and Cathy are both grown up, I'm free to do what I like for the first time in years. Did I tell you somebody offered me a half-starved Alsatian pup the other day?'

'A freeby?' Olly said. 'Why didn't you go for it? I could have fed it up. I really like Alsatians.'

'Anyway take care of the house, please, love. The council tax and mortgage are on standing order but you'll have to pay the electricity bills etcetera . . . if I don't come back . . .'

'Yeah-yeah. Just hope you know what you're doing, Mum.'

'Well I shall find out, shan't I?' Anna said jauntily. 'And don't sit about here for six months, get yourself a job.'

'It's my life, Mum,' Olly said.

'Yes, well . . . make the most of it,' Anna said as a taxi drew up at the door. 'You've only got the one, far as we know. Bye, darling, don't forget to visit Grandma.' She hugged him quickly. 'Take care of yourself.'

Olly stood at the window as the taxi drew away, sighed and went back to bed.

'Mum?' Cathy came charging along the station platform. 'Thank God I caught you.'

'Where are the children?' Anna said, flustered.

'Waiting in the car with Dennis,' Cathy stammered, out of breath. 'I wanted to say goodbye again. Had to. You going off like this all of a sudden . . .' Her voice quavered.

'Isn't all that sudden,' Anna said. 'Just I couldn't make up my mind.'

'You never can,' Cathy said. Her eyes were wet, shiny-bright.

'Well now I have . . . and after years and years of indecision I dare say it's a bit of a shock,' Anna said.

'And if you like it there you might stay?' Cathy said.

'Well that depends on all sort of things . . .'

'Like Esau Etim and his three wives?' Cathy said.

'Well yes but . . . not the way you mean. It depends on the climate and whether I can cope and the building and my flat and whether I can get a work permit and whether I want to stay.'

'But what about the violence, the killings? I mean it's not exactly a safe place. And what about malaria and AIDS? Have you got your pills and condoms?'

'OK on both counts, thank you,' Anna said.

'Seems crazy to me when you've just got your own house,'

Cathy protested as the InterCity train slid into the station. 'It's not too late to change your mind.'

'And waste my ticket, you've got to be joking,' Anna said, climbing on to the train. She deposited her cases and came back to the window. 'You'll be all right, love.' She tried to sound reassuring. 'You've got Dennis and the children. Dennis is a gem, you know. You could try being nicer to him.'

'What's he been saying?' Cathy said.

'Nothing,' Anna said as the train began to move. 'Nothing at all. But he's so steady and patient and good with the children and everything.'

'What do you mean *everything*?' Cathy shouted, walking beside the carriage. 'It's just he's so ... I mean I know he's good, but he's just not ... not ...'

'Nobody ever is, sweetheart, nobody ...' Anna shouted above the clunk of the wheels.

'What?' Cathy was trotting now.

'Nobody ever is ...'

'Is what?' Cathy shouted.

'Perfect. Bye, darling.' Anna waved and drew back from the window and said to herself, 'Poor Dennis.'

Why was she going to Nigeria, she wondered, settling herself in her seat. Because people had wrecked her car and the police had been irritatingly laconic about it? Or was she really going to escape her children and Mother, to do a job and prove she could, to feel the sun on her skin and the warmth of the people, to get away from England, no longer a safe place itself, where the homeless begged and young girls mugged you and stole fifteen pounds, to get closer to Esau? What?

The same bright morning Patsy stretched one arm into the air and flicked back the curtain. A plane had disturbed her and now she could see it, a tiny silver plane, a fly on the ceiling of the world. Could it be Anna up there, deserting her?

Patsy let the curtain go, switched on the tea-maker and thought about the book. Once she got started she worked fast, never bothered with corrections. What were editors for? She wanted to get it finished before Harriet's child was born. Baby-time starting all over again. Children were entitled to their mother's care for three years at least, as she kept telling Harriet, a privilege Patsy herself had been denied. Harriet and the baby would stay on at OldPlace for three years and Patsy would write to support them. This baby should have the best of everything, was their achievement, hers and Harriet's.

She hardly thought of Mark now, had just stopped, she didn't know why. It was like a soldier who holds on against all odds and then suddenly deserts. There was no going back. Besides, her head was entirely filled with Dominic, the hero of the new book, but she did sometimes think about Patrick, wondered about the colour of his hair and eyes for instance, about which Harriet was not forthcoming. Suppose the baby was nothing to do with Patrick? Harriet had lived in St Pauls. Suppose... just suppose... the baby wasn't *absolutely* white?

That afternoon Francesca pushed the pram along the path of the cathedral garden and stopped by the seat with a small brass plate. It had transpired they no longer put plaques in the cathedral itself. 'In Affectionate Memory of Miss Arabella Snape, Headmistress of Avon Towers School, Bristol, 1956 to 1977.'

'This lady was headteacher at my school. Let's sit here a minute,' Francesca said, dropping on to the bench and letting her fingertips touch the bright surface. Baby Frances slept peacefully.

'I don't want to sit down,' Carrie said, pushing out her lower lip and shrugging her small shoulders.

'You run and play then,' Francesca said. It was almost warm in the patch of afternoon sunlight but the flowers had gone, replaced by wallflowers under-planted with bulbs just pushing through for the coming spring.

Her pleasure in having Frances for the afternoon was somewhat diminished when Carrie insisted on coming too. Francesca tried to be fond of the child, conceal her preference for the baby. Could love be wrong because it was partial, imperfect? No doubt Hugo thought so, Hugo had reason. She had loved Hereward too much, smothered him, according to Freddy. But it was all such a long time ago.

Frances slept and Francesca closed her eyes, escaping to the past, Miss Snape whose implacable disdain had revealed a side of human nature previously unknown to the indulged child, reared by her loving papa and selected au pairs. In expelling her from school Miss Snape might have crushed a weaker spirit but she had *tempered* Francesca, rendered her resilient as steel for the difficulties of life to follow. Wasn't that why parents beggared themselves sending their children to public schools, because they wanted them toughened to cope with life? She would like to put Frances down for Benenden or Badminton, paying the fees herself of course, but would Hugo and Lottie agree?

'It's raining,' Carrie shouted and Francesca opened her eyes. Fat wet coins were splattering the hood of the pram. Frances woke and began to cry.

'Quick,' Francesca cried, fastening Carrie's plastic cape under her chin. 'Run to the car.'

It was raining heavily as they ran along the pavement, people scattering and scurrying in all directions.

'Where is it?' Francesca wailed, peering through a straggle of wet fair hair. 'I left it on this corner, I know I did.'

'Over there,' Carrie said, pointing to the Volvo which was suddenly peacock blue. Francesca blinked and remembered. Sam, newly arrived at Brandon Lodge to run the motor mechanics' course, had sprayed the Volvo a few days before on his own premises, just for the cost of the paint wholesale. The panic of the rain had wiped it right out of her head.

'Yes, of course, silly Granny,' Francesca said, inserting the key into the lock with a shaking hand. Carrie scrambled into the back.

'Silly Granny, silly Granny,' she chanted as they drove back to Combe Dingle.

Francesca made toast and tea and hot Ribena and was briskly towelling Carrie's hair when the doorbell rang.

'I want to open it,' Carrie cried.

'Go on then.' Francesca heard the door opened. 'Who is it, Carrie?'

'Grandad,' Carrie said. 'And two big huge cases.'

'Oh, Freddy?' Francesca said.

'What's going on?' Freddy said, eyeing his granddaughter unenthusiastically.

'Come in. We're just having tea. You can see Frances.'

'I saw her in the hospital, thanks. I'll just put these cases upstairs.' Freddy raised his eyebrows. 'All right with you?'

'Quite all right,' Francesca said, smiling, but wishing she had already booked her flight to Washington. She might never get there now. She remembered how pernickety he was about his food, everything just so, still she seemed to need him and it would be restful... Freddy had never been much in bed...

Getting up at midday Olly made himself a fry-up and wandered through the house clicking his fingers to an imaginary Alsatian pup. He had the place to himself and could do what he liked. He peered into Anna's bureau; a package labelled Open University lay there. Olly looked inside. A letter offered a place to Anna Bolt, classes starting in mid-February.

Suppose she didn't come back, O. Bolt or A. Bolt, same difference, how could they know? Anyway he could easily change his name to Adrian or Athol by deed poll. He quite fancied Open University, he wouldn't get a grant of course but he could buy a few more beds and let rooms to students...

Anna addressed the aeroplane postcard to Edward and then stared out at the bright blue sky. January was a good month for a holiday in West Africa anyway. Taking off for Nigeria was impulsive, inconsequential, but taking thought had so often failed her. Perhaps she needed to embrace the inconsequential to grow. Olivia Porter talked a lot about *growing*, growing was PC. Could she actually be principal of Esau's First Class English College for a few years, supposing they succeeded in establishing it? She had booked herself in to stay four nights at the Worldwide Hotel in Lagos which the travel agency had recommended. After that it would all depend.

Would Esau be at the airport to meet her? All the Africans she had known made a big thing of greetings. It would be good to see him again. Did he live in a modern house or a compound full of huts? He had chuckled evasively when she asked.

Was there really a need for an English Language college in Lagos at all and could it be made to prosper? Would people flock to the door when they heard the principal came from Newnham College, Cambridge as Esau promised? Oh well... you could drive yourself barking mad working out all possible eventualities. In the end you just had to jump.

How serious had Esau been about marriage and a Christian wedding? She would take a rain check on the white ribbons but what about being a fourth wife? There was something very attractive about Esau, his self-confidence, his laughter, his warmth. Was the amulet round her neck drawing her there with its magic or his?

How could she marry Esau and look Ata in the eye? But perhaps the absence of fidelity wouldn't be so destructive if it was part of the contract, part of the expectation? Still, her life was her own and she liked it that way and was fairly sure she didn't want to marry anybody. Suppose she and Esau became lovers, would that make it more or less difficult to look Ata in the eye?

Anna closed her own eyes, flying into the dangerous sun like Icarus, a dream she had had a year or more ago. And here she was dropping out of the future she had worked out for herself all over again at forty-five and only marginally better qualified. Was the amulet round her neck drawing her on or was she like the swallows under some biological compulsion?

Still it was her life wasn't it and your life was the only thing you had in the end.

'New things lie in front of moving feet.'